3(

A Caverns and Creatures Mini-Adventure Collection

By Robert Bevan

This is a collection of the third six Caverns and Creatures Mini-Adventures. It includes:

Acknowledgements:

First, I'd like to thank Joan Reginaldo for her invaluable criticism. It's tough to find a good beta-reader. I went through a few before I met Joan. I can't stress enough how important it is to find someone who understands your vision and is able to help you achieve it. There's so much more involved than pointing out misplaced commas (though she did a lot of that, too). Go take a look at <u>Joan's blog</u> if you have a chance. She's got some good tips on writing. Leave a comment. She likes comments.

Next, I'd like to thank my beautiful wife, No Young Sook, for her constant support, and for getting up to get the kids ready for school every morning because I left early to go to the office to write some books.

Next in line to be thanked is my brother-in-law, No Hyun Jun. Every cover of mine you see is the end product of a communication struggle, his English being about on par with my Korean. But the guy can work some Photoshop magic. And he also helps out with the kids quite a bit. Thanks, Hyun Jun.

Finally, I'd like to give a huge thank you to all of my fans out there. You're the reason I keep on writing.

House of Madness

(Original Publication Date: September 18, 2014)

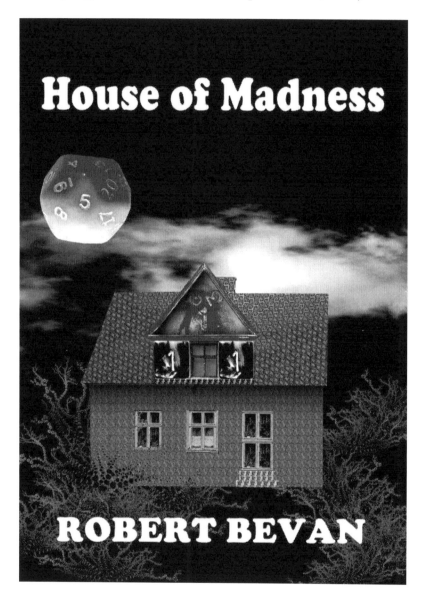

Julian and his friends were scheduled for shopping detail. Being an elf and therefore not requiring the sleep his companions did, Julian had grown bored in the stale, farty air of the Whore's Head Inn, and decided it might be a good idea to get a jump on the day.

Dave had been easy to convince, seeing the wisdom of arriving before the crowds. He had a Wisdom score of 17, after all.

Tim had taken a little more convincing, so Julian appealed to reason. The sooner they finished the day's obligations, the sooner he'd be able to start drinking. That was enough for Tim to scrape himself up off the floor.

Cooper, being neither wise nor reasonable, had required a more direct approach. A Ray of Frost under the loincloth had him wide awake, on his feet, and in a karate stance in an instant.

The effort proved worthwhile, as the marketplace was nearly empty, except for vendors opening up their carts, stalls, booths, and tents to hawk their days' wares. This made it extra startling when Tony the Elf suddenly stepped into their path from behind a vegetable cart.

"Just the fellas I was looking for."

"What did we do?" said Tim, glaring up at Cooper.

Cooper quickly removed his finger from his nostril. "What? I ain't done shit."

"Ha ha!" Tony the Elf said to Tim. "Good one!" After a few seconds of Tim not sharing in his mirth, he continued. "I'm not here to bring trouble." He took a knee to face Tim eye-to-eye. "I've got a lead on something you boys might be interested in."

Tim folded his arms and cocked his head to one side.

"What made you think we'd be in the market?" asked Julian, sharing Tim's skepticism. Tony the Elf wasn't normally one for a chipper good morning, especially to Julian and his friends. Dave said he'd even threatened to stab them in the face once, just for talking.

"Yeah," said Dave through a yawn. "Especially at this time of day."

Tony the Elf stood up. "I didn't. Just a matter of happenstance, that was. I was headed back to the Whore's Head to look for you."

"So what exactly is this great opportunity you've got for us?" asked Tim.

"Frank hooked me up with a lead on a haunted house. Hildegarde Manor, just south of town."

"Uh uh," said Tim flatly. "No thanks. We'll pass."

"Oh come on, Tim," said Cooper. "Please don't tell me you believe in ghosts."

"Of course I don't fucking believe in ghosts," snapped Tim. "I don't believe in half-orcs either, but take a look in a goddamn mirror."

"I'm with Tim," said Dave. "This is the Caverns and Creatures world. If there are ghosts in the Monster Manual, you can bet your beard that they're real."

"Can we fight ghosts?" asked Julian.

"We can't even touch them without magical weapons," said Tim. "But they can do some nasty shit to us. Frank's off his tits if he thinks we're going to go anywhere near a haunted house, not at the levels we're at."

"See now, that's the thing," said Tony the Elf. "I don't think the place is really haunted."

"And what makes you think that?"

"Frank and I got the scoop from Gorgonzola, who was inquiring about another matter."

"Using his Gather Information skill?" asked Julian. He'd seen Gorgonzola use the skill before, and it was remarkable how much information that little gnome had picked up in such a short amount of time.

"Yeah, right," said Tony the Elf. "He was out gathering information, and he heard tell of a man who barely made it out of that house with his life, after having watched all of his traveling companions murder each other."

Tim frowned. "You're not really selling this as well as you might think."

Tony the Elf looked left, then right, before whispering

conspiratorially. "But this guy didn't say anything about seeing a ghost. It sounds less like a haunting to me, and more like a curse."

Tim put his palms out to Tony the Elf. "Okay okay. I think I see where we're miscommunicating here. The ultimate thing I want to avoid isn't necessarily *ghosts*, per se." He stressed the word *ghosts* with finger quotes. "It's more like… um, how do I put this? Oh yeah, *being dead*." Again with the finger quotes.

"Are you being sarcastic?"

"No, I'm being condescending."

"Listen," said Tony the Elf. "Just hear me out, will ya?"

"I'm listening," said Julian. Tim gave him a quick glare, but he pretended not to see it.

"Curses can be avoided if you take the right precautions." Tony the Elf looked left and right again before reaching into his shirt's inside pocket. He pulled out a bunch of leather cords, each one adorned with a circular silver charm about the size of a half dollar.

Julian reached for one tentatively. Tony the Elf handed him one of the cords. On the silver charm, Julian recognized the nine-pointed star, the magical symbol for protection.

"What are these?"

"Talismans," said Tony the Elf. "I bought them off the old lady in the mystic tent."

"The blind one?" asked Tim.

"That's her."

"How do you know she's for real?"

"Oh she's for real, all right," said Cooper. "I wagged my dick at her a couple weeks ago. Bitch didn't even flinch."

"That's reprehensible," said Dave. "Mocking blind people? That's a new low, Cooper, even for you."

"Well I didn't fucking know she was blind until then, now did I?"

When Cooper got defensive, he got loud. Passersby were beginning to take notice of their little congregation.

"Let's talk somewhere else," said Tony the Elf. "There's a pub across the street. I'm buying." He gave Tim a take-it-or-leave-it look and started walking.

"What do you think?" asked Tim.

"I don't know," said Julian. "It's kind of early in the morning to be getting hammered, and Frank sent us out to buy supplies. He'll be pissed if we turn up empty handed and shitfaced."

"Again," Dave added.

"Frank greenlit this mission," said Tim. The promise of free booze had obviously opened his mind. "And we can always pin the blame on Tony the Elf."

"I don't think it's wise," said Dave, "to make decisions about taking on potentially life-threatening undertakings while under the influence of alcohol."

"I've got to agree," said Julian. "This whole situation feels wrong." He looked at the talisman in his hand. "Still, I'd better return this before we go."

They crossed the wide, cobblestone street and walked into the pub through the open doorway. Dave's boots echoed noisily on the dark, mahogany floor. This place was a world apart from the Whore's Head Inn. It smelled of pine and cloves, with maybe a hint of grandfatherly tobacco. There wasn't a whiff of urine or vomit in the place. Cooper would no doubt rectify that in the next couple of minutes. Julian laughed to himself. *Cooper. Rectify.*

Tony the Elf was the lone patron in the establishment, sitting by himself at a large polished table with four glistening mugs of beer and a bottle of stonepiss.

Dave licked his lips. "We could listen to what he has to say."

"It'd be rude not to," said Cooper.

"One drink's not going to hurt," said Tim.

Julian shook his head and stepped back outside. He whistled at the sky. Ravenus descended from about a quarter of a mile away, where there were still a bunch of normal ravens circling.

"Shopping all finished, sir?" said Ravenus as he landed atop Julian's quarterstaff.

Julian rolled his eyes. "We haven't even started yet. What's going on over there?" He nodded up at the black birds circling in the sky. "You making some friends?"

"Nah," said Ravenus. "Conversations with other birds just don't cut it for me no more. Not since I become all smart like. We're all just hanging around watching two cats fight. I reckon we might get lucky. They both appear to be in pretty bad shape."

"Just try to keep out of trouble for a bit," said Julian. "We'll be in here if you need anything."

Ravenus bobbed his head. "Getting an early start then, are you sir?"

"Hey now. None of your beak. Go on and enjoy your cat."

"Very good, sir."

Ravenus flapped away, and Julian stepped back into the pub.

Cooper's glass was already empty.

"Jesus, Cooper," said Julian. "I haven't been outside more than a minute."

"I have a different metabolism than you," said Cooper. He turned around on his stool. "Bartender. One more please."

"Right away, sir," said the proprietor, an older man. Human. Smartly dressed in a crisp linen shirt, clean brown doublet, and a stain-free apron. Pubs tended to be a little classier as they got nearer the market area.

Tim rapped his knuckles on the table as he chugged down the last quarter of his own beer.

"Make it two," said Cooper.

"Why would Frank sign off for you to buy magical talismans for a one-shot gig?" Dave asked Tony the Elf. They were the only two who appeared to remember what they were in there for. Still, Dave threw back a shot of stonepiss, then wiped his mouth on the leopard fur of his forearm.

"Imagine it," said Tony the Elf. "How many lost travelers has this old house lured in over the years. Decades? Centuries maybe? There's bound to be piles of dead bodies in there."

"So far this only sounds appealing for Ravenus," said Julian.

"Now imagine what these people might have had on them when they met their dismal fate. Money? Probably. Weapons? Almost certainly. Who knows? Even if they were all just carrying standard traveling money, that adds up."

Julian sipped his beer and smiled on the inside. Though it was warm, it was a much higher quality brew than what they served at the Whore's Head.

"We're not even necessarily talking about peasants here," said Tim, slamming his mug down a little too hard on the table.

"I'll have to ask you to handle the glassware more delicately, sir," said the owner, replacing Tim and Cooper's empty mugs with fresh beers.

"Sorry," said Tim sheepishly. He waited for the barman to leave before continuing. "Imagine if a group of mid-level adventurers ducked in there, rolled some unlucky saving throws, started going apeshit on each other. Think of what kind of loot they might have left behind." Tim was a walking billboard on the dangers of alcohol.

Several drinks and a large plate of breakfast sausages later, Tony the Elf stood up. "I've got to hit the can. Settle the bill while I'm gone?" He tossed a small leather sack to Tim. Coins clinked together as the bag hit Tim's face and fell into his lap.

Tim shook his head like he was just coming out of a dream. "Yeah, sure thing."

When Tony the Elf disappeared through the front door and the barman had gone into the kitchen, Dave leaned in. "So, what do you think?"

Julian was relieved that someone else was prone to suggest thinking at all. "I don't like it. We get into enough trouble as it is without actively seeking it out."

"Thinking like that gets you nowhere in this game," said Tim. "To get ahead, you've got to jump on opportunities like this when they –" *hiccup* "present themselves."

"You're drunk," said Julian. "And this isn't a game."

"Technically, it is," said Tim. "It's Caverns and Creatures."

"You know what I mean."

"You're both right," said Dave. "We're in some kind of alternate reality, but it's still the game. And the situation we're in right now feels very game like. Think about it. We're in a tavern, and we've just been presented with a quest of sorts."

"Whoa," said Tim. "You *are* wise."

"What's even better," Dave continued. "We've got inside information. If Tony the Elf's information all checks out, these talismans might just let us bypass the one trick that house has up its sleeve. Our only challenge might be the logistics of hauling out all of that treasure."

Cooper cracked his knuckles and belched up the Ghost of Sausages Past. "I'm up for that challenge."

"Come on," said Julian. "You call that wise? Haven't you heard *If it's too good to be true, it's probably...* I forget how it goes, but you know what I'm saying."

"Pfft," said Tim. "We can swap empty proverbs all day. Haven't *you* heard *When opportunity's knockin', don't come a-rockin'?*"

Julian narrowed his eyes at Tim. "I can honestly say I've never heard that before in my life."

"Dang! Blast it!" the tavern owner shouted as he stomped out of the kitchen. He was clutching his left wrist with his right hand. Blood seeped through his fingers and dripped on the floor.

"Sir?" said Julian. "Are you okay?"

The barman winced as he poured a trickle of stonepiss over his bleeding arm. "I done sliced myself open with a gosh darn breadknife."

"Damn," said Dave. "That looks pretty bad."

Julian slapped Dave in the back of the head. "You're a cleric, idiot. Go help him!"

"Oh yeah." Dave stumble-waddled to the bar. "Give me your hand."

The barman stretched his injured arm over the bar.

"I heal thee," said Dave, touching his hand.

The barman's eyelids fluttered as Dave's healing magic coursed up through his arm. The wound sealed itself.

"There you go," said Dave, looking rather pleased with himself. "Good as new."

The barman opened and closed his hand, stretching the newly-healed muscles in his forearm. "I can't thank you enough. Praise be to the good gods."

Dave waved his hand dismissively. "Don't even mention it. I'm happy to help. The food was delicious."

"You serve a fine sausage, sir," said Cooper.

The barman grinned. "So says the missus."

11

"What do we owe you?" asked Tim, holding the money pouch Tony the Elf had given him.

"Put that away!" said the barman. "Your money's no good here!"

"Fuck," said Cooper. "How are we supposed to pay?"

"You see?" said Tim, tucking Tony the Elf's money into his inner vest pocket. "When opportunity's knockin' –"

"Yeah yeah," said Julian. "Don't come a-knockin'. Let's get out of here before he changes his mind."

"And you, sir," the barman said to Dave. He produced two blue glass bottles from under the bar. They were about a liter each. "Please take these."

"What are they?" asked Dave.

"Stonepiss," said the barman. "Special blend. My son made these. He's a court recognized distiller, my boy."

Dave's eyes were fixated on those bottles like they were a pair of glass breasts. "That's really too much. It was just a simple healing spell."

"Not a word of it. That was a nasty cut I gave myself. If not for you, I might not have lived to see my son again, nor serve another drink. I insist."

"You're much too kind, sir." Dave shifted the contents of his bag around to make room for the two bottles. "You can be sure we'll visit here again real soon."

The barman flexed his left arm. He had some muscle on him for an old man. "I'll be looking forward to it."

Dave finished up his goodbyes and the four of them were soon out on the street again.

"What's keeping Tony the Elf?" asked Tim.

Dave frowned. "Maybe he didn't handle that sausage so well."

"Or maybe that's exactly what he's doing," said Cooper.

"What's that?" asked Julian.

"*Handling* his *sausage*." Cooper winked. "He's probably thinking about Tim."

They hung out in front of the tavern for another minute or two – just enough time for Julian to call Ravenus back – when Tony the Elf finally sauntered out from around the side of the building, straightening up his pants.

"You fellas ready to roll?"

"What?" said Tim. "You want to go today?"

"Now?" added Cooper.

"That survivor's still out there telling his story. Frank wants us to hit this place before someone else comes up with the same idea that we did."

"You wouldn't rather wait until we're sober?" asked Dave.

"You'll have plenty of time to sober up on the way."

"I don't want to sober up on the way," said Tim. "I only just started drinking."

As Tony the Elf led the way north, Julian noticed Tim sneaking shots from his hip flask every now and again. He might not be stone cold sober when they reached their destination, but hopefully he would be less shitfaced than he was now.

The western bank of the Bluerun River on the north side of Cardinia was like a distorted reflection of the south. Here, too, were large, two story homes built from brick or stone, luxurious by this world's standards, but most of them looked abandoned, in varying stages of ruin. Tree roots had cracked foundations. Toppled statues were thick with moss. Wild vines ran up walls and into cracked windows.

"What happened here?" asked Julian.

"War happened," said Tony the Elf like it was the most obvious thing in the world. "Ever hear of a little thing called The Wars of the Fractured Kingdom?"

"I think I remember hearing something about it in passing."

Tony the Elf stopped in his tracks and turned around to look at Julian. His grey eyes bored deep into him. It almost felt invasive.

"What?" Julian finally said.

"Hmph," said Tony the Elf. He turned around and continued walking.

"We almost there?" said Cooper. "I gotta drop the kids off at the pool."

Tony the Elf stopped again. He seldom had patience for Cooper. "I beg your pardon?"

"I gotta take a shit."

"Can't you hold it? We're nearly there."

"Maybe it'd be better for him to do that out here," said Dave. "The house is likely to smell bad enough as it is."

Tony the Elf looked quizzically at Dave. "Why would you say that?"

Dave shrugged. "Because of all the rotting corpses?"

Tony the Elf smiled. "Oh yes, of course. Now that you mention it, I wish I had thought to bring some mint leaves or something."

Cooper stomped off what was left of the old dirt road and disappeared into the tall grass. Tim swigged down some stonepiss, not even bothering to hide it anymore, while he urinated on the side of the road.

At least ten minutes passed. Julian was happy he had gone easy on the breakfast.

"What was in those sausages?" asked Dave.

Tim screwed the cap onto his flask and put it in his vest pocket. "That's a question you almost never want the answer to."

"I guess I'm lucky to have that +2 Save versus Poison."

"You have what?" asked Tony the Elf.

"Because I'm a dwarf."

Tony the Elf looked at him doubtfully. "Oh right."

"I don't like this," said Dave. "Something's wrong."

"You worry every time Cooper goes for a shit?" asked Tim. "You're going to have a heart attack before you're forty."

"Yeah, he shits a lot. But he's usually quick about it. He never takes this long."

"Relax," said Tony the Elf. "You said yourself it's probably just the sausages. You watch. He'll be back here any second now."

"Sorry for the holdup!" When Cooper jogged back into view, something was off about him. He looked cleaner somehow. Slimmer too, maybe.

From the look on Tim's face, he must have shared Julian's assessment. "How big a shit did you take?"

Cooper stopped jogging and frowned. "I, umm… I don't know how to answer that. Considerably?"

"So glad to see you again!" said Tony the Elf. If it was meant to sound sarcastic, he failed his Diplomacy check. "Look sharp, gentlemen. The next house up the road is our target."

"Shouldn't we get our talismans ready?" asked Julian.

"Oh right!" said Tony the Elf. "Good thinking!" He handed out talismans to each member of the party who, in turn, looped the chords over their heads and around their necks.

"What about Ravenus?" asked Julian. "Do you think he needs a talisman?"

Tony the Elf frowned. "I shouldn't think so. He's your familiar, right? Surely, your talisman will provide protection for the both of you."

"You don't sound very sure of yourself, and I don't want to take any chances." Julian whistled for Ravenus.

"Anything amiss, sir?" asked Ravenus, flapping down to perch atop Julian's quarterstaff.

"Why don't you sit this one out. We shouldn't be in there too long. Go see if you can't scrounge up a dead rat or something."

"As you wish, sir," said Ravenus. He pushed off from the quarterstaff and took flight.

Tony the Elf led the way up the footpath. Cooper walked at his side, trailing slightly behind. A few minutes later they stood before an ancient wrought iron gateway thickly overgrown with sickly, brownish-green vines. They wrapped around the bars like old people's fingers. The gate itself had been removed from the hinges, leaving just a curtain of vines for them to pass through. At the top of the gateway, the iron had been bent to form letters. *Hildegarde Manor*.

"Well," said Cooper. "This is the place, all right." He stepped through the vine curtain. Tony the Elf held the vines aside to allow everyone else to pass through, and he took the rear.

The house was much the same as the others they had passed. Two stories, brick and mortar, crawling with vines. Broken windows seemed to stare at Julian like dead eyes. It was everything a haunted house should be. Julian knew that his imagination was largely to blame, but this place truly gave him the willies.

"I don't like this," said Dave, digging in his bag. He had obviously caught a similar case of the willies. He pulled out one of the expensive bottles of stonepiss, uncorked it, and took a generous swig. A look of calm came over him. "That barman wasn't kidding. This is some good stuff."

Tim held his open flask to Dave. "Fill me up, would you?" Dave poured. Stonepiss spilled onto the ground, because both of their hands were trembling slightly.

"Come on, man," Julian said to Tim. "Don't you think you've had enough?"

"Liquid courage," said Tim. "I'll need a bit more before stepping into that creepy ass house." He took a small sip from his flask. "Hot damn, that *is* good!"

"You know," said Julian. "We don't actually have to go through with this. We can turn back right now."

"You guys are letting your imaginations get carried away," said Tony the Elf. "There's absolutely nothing to be afraid of." He grasped the talisman hanging from his neck. "We've got these, remember?"

Julian frowned. "Of course. What could be safer than walking into a cursed and/or haunted house with some trinkets you bought off a blind stranger?"

Tony the Elf grinned. "That's the spirit! Now come on." He and Cooper confidently strolled up to the door. Tony the Elf reached for the handle.

"Stop!" cried Tim, running up behind them.

Tony the Elf jerked his hand away from the door like he'd just noticed it was crawling with angry bees. "What?"

Tim shoved him aside. "What's the point of bringing me along if you're not going to let me use my rogue abilities?"

"What?" Tony the Elf repeated.

"Let me check the door for traps," said Tim. "Fucking noob."

"Noob?"

Tim pulled out his dagger, stood clear of the doorway, and tentatively poked at the handle. Nothing happened. He leaned in closer, running the dagger blade up the narrow gap between door and

16

frame.

Tim stood back and nodded. "It looks clear to me. Cooper, kick it down."

"Are you daft?" said Tony the Elf. "Why wouldn't you just try –"

"Stay back, Tony the Elf," said Tim. "This is how you gain the element of surprise. Kick that bitch down, Cooper."

"Umm… Okay," said Cooper. He paused for a moment, looking doubtfully at the door. Finally, he lifted his right leg. "Ya-ha!"

Ya-ha? Julian mouthed to Dave. Dave shrugged."

Cooper slammed his heel into the door, knocking himself on his ass. The door didn't budge.

"What kind of pussy kick was that?" asked Tim. "I could have hit the door harder with my little dick."

"Don't let me stop you," said Cooper. "That door's solid oak."

"Use your Barbarian Rage," suggested Dave.

Cooper sat on the front porch looking puzzled. "Barbarian…" He placed the tips of his index fingers on his temples.

"Coop?" said Julian. "You okay?"

"Barbarian Rage," Cooper said to himself. "I can use it once per day."

"That's right," said Tim. "So let's get it on. Get *angry*, my man!"

Cooper removed his fingers from his temples, looked at Tim, and shrugged "I just remembered. I already used it today."

"What are you talking about?" Tim demanded. It almost sounded accusatory. "We've been with you all morning."

"I used it when I was relieving myself," said Cooper. "I was having a little trouble *getting it out*, if you take my meaning. I needed a little extra push."

"You did *what*?"

"Those fucking sausages," said Dave, shaking his head. "Dammit, Cooper! Barbarian Rage isn't supposed to be used as a laxative! I can't believe you'd go and waste your one talent like –"

"This is stupid," said Tony the Elf, pushing his way past Tim. "It's a wonder how you four idiots make it through each day without drowning in your own drool." He pulled the handle. The door opened with ease. "See?" He stepped across the threshold.

17

Cooper stepped in after him. Tim took a nice, long swig of stonepiss and followed them in.

Dave and Julian stood just outside the open door.

"Are the talismans working?" asked Julian. "How do you feel?"

Tim smiled. "I've got a nice buzz going."

Tony the Elf looked down at him. "Do you feel like you want to stab me?"

"Kinda."

Dave rolled his eyes. "I guess they're working." He stepped into the house.

Fighting every fiber of common sense and self-preservation instinct, Julian stepped across the threshold. He was happy to note that, once inside, he felt no change. No murderous urges or thirsts for blood. The inside of the house, full of dust and cobwebs, was no less creepy than the outside. Dust motes swirled and danced like undead fairies in the few beams of sunlight which managed to penetrate through the cracks in the windows. This wasn't the sort of place Julian would ever want to visit at night, but the fact that he and his friends weren't all hacking away at each other was strangely comforting.

"Where are all the dead bodies?" asked Dave.

The air was thick with mildew and water rot, but Julian wasn't picking up the scent of any decaying bodies. Still, someone had been here. The dusty floor was littered with footprints of varying shapes and sizes.

Tim moved a wooden stool over to a desk next to the wall of what Julian guessed once served as a sort of living room. He climbed onto the stool, then opened the top drawer of the desk.

"Sweet! Candles!" He pulled out two handfuls of long, thin white candles. "Let's light these bitches up." He hopped down from the stool and handed everyone a few candles.

Julian, with his Low Light Vision, was able to see just fine with the meager amount of sunlight flowing in through the windows, but he had no objections to adding some more light, if only just to keep the creepiness at bay.

"I can only find this one candle holder," he said. "What are we supposed to do with the rest of the candles?"

"Think outside the box," said Tim. He pulled a small pouch out of his bag.

"What's that?" asked Julian.

"Caltrops," said Tim. "They have four sharp prongs on them, so be careful not to step on them. They're actually made to slow down pursuers. But if you poke one prong into the bottom of a candle, the other three prongs should keep it upright." He demonstrated, and set the shoddily-mounted candle on the floor. "Voila! Instant candle holder."

"That definitely looks like a fire hazard," said Dave.

"Explain to me why I'd give a fuck," said Tim. "All of you assholes can see in the dark. I can't see shit."

Before long, the whole room was awash in a warm, cozy glow. Candles stood on every available chair, shelf, and tabletop.

Tim climbed back up onto his stool, and from there onto the table. He wiped a layer of dust off a painting hanging on the wall, revealing the face of an elderly bearded man. Julian guessed he was probably the patriarch of the Hildegardes.

"Hey, Cooper," said Tim. "What's this picture of your mom doing here?"

"I'm pretty sure that's a man," said Cooper.

Tim pursed his lips and nodded slowly. "Hey, would you mind grabbing me that book up on the top shelf?" he asked, pointing to a nearby bookcase.

Cooper turned around and looked up at the shelf. "Which one?"

"The Dawn of the Third Age."

When Cooper reached up to grab the book, Tim pulled a length of rope out of his bag, jumped onto his back, and looped the rope around his neck. Cooper dropped to his knees, his eyes wide as he struggled to breathe. Tim pulled the ends of the rope ends tighter.

Julian gripped his quarterstaff with both hands, not quite sure of what he intended to do with it. "What the fuck are you doing?"

"Who are you?" Tim shouted into Cooper's ear.

"Oh my god!" cried Dave. "The talismans aren't working! We have to get out of here!" He ran for the door, but it slammed shut against his face. He fell to the floor, covering his face with his hands. "Ow! My fucking nose!"

Tony the Elf drew the twin machetes he carried on his back. "Let him go, Tim!" He took a step toward Tim and Cooper.

"Stop!" said Julian. Tony the Elf stopped, but he didn't look like he'd hold for very long. "Just give me a minute. I've got Diplomacy. Tim, what's going on, man? Why are you strangling Cooper?"

"This isn't Cooper!" said Tim.

"He's… crazy…" Cooper gasped.

"Come on, Tim," pleaded Julian. "You've had a lot to drink today."

"This is the place, all right," said Tim. Cooper's face was turning from grey to blue.

"What?"

"That's what he said when he read the sign outside," said Tim. "He *read* the fucking sign!"

Illiteracy was a barbarian class feature, but Julian hardly thought it was evidence enough to murder a guy. "He might have been just talking out of his ass."

"He read the spine of that book," said Tim, jerking his head up toward the top shelf of the bookcase. "He didn't have the strength to kick open a simple wooden door."

"Can't… breathe…" said Cooper.

"So he made a low roll," said Julian.

"He didn't get a 'your mother' joke!"

"I'll admit, that is compelling evidence. But to be fair, it was a piss poor effort at a joke. Just let him go. We'll talk this through."

Cooper's face was now a deep purple.

"Look at this big fucker," said Tim. "I'm what, like thirty five pounds soaking wet? He should be able to shake me off whenever he wants. I'm telling you man, this isn't –"

"I'M REALLY ANGRY!" It was Cooper's voice, but it wasn't coming from the half-orc Tim was strangling. It sounded like it was coming from outside.

Dave sat up. "What the –"

The door smashed in, flying off the hinges and into Dave's face.

Cooper stood in the open doorway, completely naked and bulging with muscles. Broken lengths of rope hung from his wrists and ankles. His giant, scabby half-orc dick stood erect like a +5 Staff of Leprosy. "WHERE THE FUCK ARE MY CLOTHES?" He pointed at the Cooper that Tim was still strangling. "YOU!"

"Shit," gasped Tim's Cooper. He shrank so quickly that he slipped right through Tim's rope.

Tim landed on his feet, length of rope still in hand, seething at a mirror image of himself. Only the mirror image was naked and standing on top of Cooper's loincloth.

"What the fuck is going on here?" asked Cooper. Confusion had overtaken his rage, and he was back to his normal, filthy, naked self.

"Doppelganger," said Tim.

Naked Tim kicked real Tim in the nuts. Tim crumpled to the floor like a poorly executed piece of origami, and Naked Tim bolted out of the room.

Tim groaned in a puddle of his own urine. "Don't just stand there. Go after him." He opened his eyes and found himself staring at Cooper's limp dick, hanging like the trunk of a diseased elephant. "Jesus, dude. Put your loincloth on."

"I heal me," said Dave, having shoved the door off of himself. His beard was slick with nose blood, but he looked like he'd survive. He was sitting in a puddle bigger than Tim's.

"Check it out," said Cooper. "Dave pissed himself too."

"What?" said Dave. "I didn't –" He looked down. "Oh no!"

"Dude, take it easy. I do it like five times a day."

Dave rummaged through his bag. "Oh no! Oh no! Oh no!" He pulled out a fragment of broken glass. "Goddammit, Cooper! You broke my booze."

"Oh shit. Sorry about that."

Dave got to his feet. "Let's go get that little bastard."

"Wait!" said Tony the Elf. "We can't just go charging in without a plan. What if there are more of them?"

"What if, indeed?" Julian whispered to himself. Tony the Elf should have been able to hear him. Being an elf, Julian knew what Tony's ears were capable of.

"Now Cooper," said Tony the Elf. "You're the strongest, but

you're very noisy…"

"Hey Tony," whispered Julian. "There's a spider on your shoulder."

"Julian," said Tony the Elf. "You and I are pretty good at stealth, but you've got the added benefit of –"

"Magic Missile!"

"Well yes, among other spells." With his eyes so focused on the hallway his partner had gone down, this Tony the Elf imposter didn't even see the glowing bolt of energy headed across the room toward him. "I was thinking just magic in gen—Aaaauuuugggghhh!" The scream sounded less like an elf and more like a giant robotic insect.

Tony the Elf instantly morphed into what Julian assumed must be the creature's true form, because it sure as shit wasn't any of theirs. It looked more like a Roswell alien. Tall, bald, grey, and gangly, with huge, shiny black eyes. Tony the Elf's clothes still hung awkwardly on it. The machetes it carried were still very real.

"Very clever, elf," said the creature, though it didn't have a mouth that Julian could see. Its voice didn't sound exactly like Darth Vader's, but more like James Earl Jones sucking down a helium balloon and talking through an electric fan. "You've discovered us for what we are. I suggest you leave this place at once, or you shall never leave at all." It took off in the direction its partner had gone in.

Julian sighed with relief. "They're letting us go."

"Good," said Dave. "Let's get the hell out of here."

"Fuck that," said Tim. He took a swig of stonepiss from his flask. "They just want to get rid of us because they know they're outnumbered. I came here to loot some treasure and see some dead bodies. I'll be damned if I'm not going to do one of the two." He grabbed a candle off the floor and stumbled off after the doppelgangers.

"Come on, Tim!" Julian called after him. "Let it go!"

Tim belched loudly from down the hall. It was about as reasonable a response as Julian had expected.

"We can't let him go up there alone," said Cooper. He followed Tim.

"Shit," said Julian. He followed Cooper, and Dave waddled along behind him.

The hallway led to a stairwell. Cooper convinced Tim to let him take the lead, since he had the most Hit Points. The stairs were wet and rotten. They felt like they could give way with each step. The mildew smell on the second floor was nigh unbearable. There were two closed doors at the top of the stairs. One of them had some frantic shuffling noises going on behind it.

Tim gestured to use the handle. Cooper nodded reluctantly. Tim held up his fingers. One. Two. Three.

Cooper opened the door and the four of them burst in. A false Julian stood next to a closet on the other side of the room, frantically trying to put on his robe. It was a lost cause. He'd be dead before he could hope to put on his serape.

"Damn!" said False Julian.

"Ah!" said Tim. Julian turned around. Two Tims, identically dressed, locked elbows and danced around in a circle. "But how will you know who is the real Tim?"

One of the Tims stopped the dance abruptly. "I pissed myself when you kicked me in the nuts."

Sure enough, the true Tim was identifiable by his wet pants.

False Tim closed his eyes tight and balled his fists. He grunted until a small trickle of urine ran down his pant leg. It wasn't nearly enough to be convincing.

"This is just embarrassing," said Cooper.

"Enough of this foolishness!" boomed a voice from the other side of the room. A white, translucent image of the man from the painting downstairs appeared in a wall mirror. "You have failed me!"

Both doppelgangers dropped to their knees and bowed on the floor.

"We're sorry!" wailed False Julian. It grated at Julian's ears, like listening to a recording of his own voice.

"Do I really sound like that?"

Dave shrugged and nodded.

"Please forgive us!" said False Tim. The pee stains on his pants grew more convincing.

"Okay now," said the ghostly image in the mirror. "That's enough of that. Stand up and take your true forms."

The doppelgangers got to their feet. The one dressed like Julian

23

looked as normal as an alien was likely to, but the one dressed like Tim looked ridiculous. Gangly as he was, he stretched his Tim costume to the limit. What were full-length pants now came up past the knees, soaking wet and squeezing his thighs. The tiny shirt and vest stretched around its ribcage, revealing his entire abdomen. Cooper started to giggle.

"SILENCE!" boomed the apparition in the mirror.

Thankfully, Cooper got his laughter under control.

"Now," said the ghost. "Who can tell me where you went wrong?"

The doppelganger in Tim's clothes hung his head. "I didn't stick to the plan. I saw an opportunity to take the half-orc out early, and I took it."

"Wrong!" said the ghost. "No matter how meticulously you think you've planned something, it will never play out exactly how you think. Improvisation and adaptability are vital. You showed initiative in taking out their strongest fighter early on."

"We didn't stake them out long enough?" said the doppelganger in Julian's clothes."

"Wrong again! Three weeks is more than enough time to learn to mimic their speech patterns and mannerisms. You're bloody doppelgangers, by the gods!"

Julian cleared his throat. "They shouldn't have left Cooper alive."

"Precisely," said the ghost.

"Dude!" said Cooper. "Whose side are you on?"

"I couldn't kill him," said the doppelganger. "I needed him alive so I could continue to read his mind."

"Then three weeks was not enough?"

"These people speak in strange ways. They speak of Hit Points and Saving Throws. It's some kind of code I have yet to crack. The half-orc uses over twenty different euphemisms to talk about his penis."

"Then just don't talk about your penis."

"That would compromise my cover severely. It's mostly all he talks about. Anyway, I tied him up really well. He shouldn't have been able to break out of those ropes."

The ghost raised its wispy, ethereal eyebrows at Cooper. "And yet here he stands." As he appeared to be waiting for some sort of explanation, everyone else in the room looked to Cooper as well.

Cooper mumbled something under his breath that Julian was quite pleased to hear, but was certain no one else in the room would be able to understand.

"I'm sorry, Cooper," said Julian. "Could you say that a little louder?"

Cooper growled in annoyance. "Ravenus clawed through the ropes."

"I beg your pardon?" said the ghost. "What's a ravenus?"

The doppelganger in Julian's clothes slapped himself on the forehead. "The elf's familiar!"

The ghost frowned. "This is most unsatisfactory. If you can't successfully infiltrate this band of drunken delinquents, how do you expect to avenge my death? I should destroy you both right now."

The doppelgangers dropped to the floor, bowing and groveling. The one in Tim's clothes pushed the limits of his pants. They ripped apart down the ass crack.

Both Cooper and Tim began giggling.

"Please, Lord Hildegarde! Don't kill us!"

"We want to have a family!"

"A FAMILY!" shouted the angry ghost. The house started rumbling as white fire burst out of the mirror. Cooper and Tim stopped giggling, in spite of the green shit splattering out of the newly-ripped pants. "Do you think *I* never wanted a family?"

Julian was terrified, but knew he stood a better chance of easing the tension in the room than anyone. Diplomacy or death. He gulped.

"Excuse me, my lord."

The white fire in the mirror intensified briefly as the ghost glared at Julian with wide, pupil-less eyes.

Julian stood his ground, unsure as to whether it was the house that was shaking more violently, or just his legs. He did his best to maintain the appearance of calm, innocent curiosity, pretending his asshole wasn't clenched tight enough to cut a steel rod in half.

The flames settled down and the house downshifted from shake to gentle rumble. "Yes? What is it?"

"I – I –" *Come on, Julian. Keep your cool.* "I couldn't help noticing you bear a striking resemblance to the handsome gentleman in the portrait downstairs." *Too much? Does he think I'm coming on to him?*

"You mean the one that resembles the half-orc's mother?"

Tim whimpered. "Sorry about that. It was just –"

"Aye, that was me," said the old ghost wistfully. The house stopped shaking altogether. "That painting was commissioned just before the Great War. I believe you young fellows have a fancier name for it now. With the northern hordes advancing, and the city walls too far from completion, the king decided to abandon this region. Cut his losses, if you will."

"Is that right?" said Julian, forcing himself to maintain eye contact with the ghost in the mirror. In his periphery, he noticed Tim sneaking a peek into the closet the two doppelgangers had been using.

"Aye, that's right! Now, that decision made us a prime target for thieves and looters. One such opportunist was named Zachary Figg. He broke into my house in the middle of the night and murdered me in my sleep."

"You don't say!" Julian made a concerted effort to pretend to be interested in this old man's life story. The fact that this lonely ghost was so starved for conversation was likely the reason they were all still alive.

"Robbed me blind, he did. And to make matters worse, this Figg went on to get caught up in the war. He rose through the ranks, and was eventually granted a lordship for valor. *Valor!* Can you believe such a thing?"

"How did you come to find out about all of this, what with being dead and all?"

"I still get my fair share of looters and squatters, much like yourselves and these two." He nodded down to the two trembling doppelgangers still prostrated on the floor. "I get what news I can out of them before I decide whether to use them or kill them."

"Or send them on their way?" Julian added hopefully.

The old ghost raised his eyebrows and grinned. "Not a chance."

The bedroom door slammed shut. A deadbolt slid into place.

Julian resisted his urge to start crying and groveling. There was still Diplomacy to be done. He might still be able to be reasoned with.

"You were murdered quite some time ago, weren't you?"

"Aye," said the ghost. "It's been nearly four hundred years, by my reckoning."

"Surely this Zachary Figg is long dead by now."

"Aye?" said the ghost, as if urging Julian to get to the point.

"How can you take vengeance on someone who's already dead?"

"He ended my line. I seek to end his."

Simple as that, eh? "You mean you want to kill his descendants?"

"My spirit will not rest until every last Figg – man, woman, and child – is slaughtered like the sons and daughters of the cowardly butcher they are."

"Dude," said Cooper. "That's kind of fucked up."

Julian glared at Cooper, but shared the sentiment. This old ghost's sanity was as dead as his body. There would be no reasoning with him. It was time to start working on a Plan B. In the meantime, he needed to keep talking.

"So that's what the doppelgangers are for? To infiltrate House Figg?"

"Aye," said the ghost. "But as you can see, they'll require a lot more training."

The doppelganger dressed in Julian's clothes raised his head. "So you don't aim to kill us, then?"

"No, of course I'm not going to kill you. Worthless as you are, you have skills uniquely suited to my needs. Who knows when I'll get another group of doppelgangers to sneak in here?"

Both doppelgangers stood up. "Oh thank you, sir. Thank you."

"Yes, yes," said the ghost. "Enough of that. But you need to learn ..."

Julian retreated to where Cooper and Dave were standing while the ghost conversed with his two minions. Tim was placing something into his vest pocket with a very satisfied grin on his face. Julian gestured for him to come join the rest of them.

Julian had an idea brewing. It wasn't a good one, but it was better than trying to have Cooper bust the door down. They'd all be ghosted to death before he made it to the door. Julian's plan involved confusion. It involved surprise. And like any of his other poorly thought out plans, it involved horses.

"Stay close together," Julian whispered when Tim joined the group. Taking the lead, Julian took a small step toward the center of the room.

"Where are we going?" asked Dave. "I thought you were trying to get us out of here. The door's over there."

"We're not going through the door," said Julian, taking another step. "Just stay close."

"... not enough to merely memorize patterns of speech and peculiar mannerisms," the ghost continued lecturing the doppelgangers. "You must *become* your characters, know their desires, their motivations, their fears. Only then will you be able to exploit this information to convince them to kill one another."

"Horse," said Julian once they had reached the center of the room. A spotted, brown draft horse appeared next to him.

Dave buried his face in his hands. "I should've known. This is so fucking stupid."

The horse whinnied and brayed at the sight of the ghost, but Julian had been expecting that. He stroked the horse's white mane. "Be calm, friend."

"What is the meaning of this?" demanded the ghost. "This is my bed chamber, not a stable!"

"Horse!" Julian said a second time, with an added bit of false confidence. A slightly smaller black horse appeared, and promptly started losing its shit.

"Get rid of these creatures at once!" roared the ghost. His face contorted with rage, and white flames engulfed the frame of the mirror.

"Um, Julian," said Cooper. "If you're trying to give this old dude a stroke, I've got some bad news for you."

The house shook violently. Julian had to hold on to Dave just to stay on his feet. The two doppelgangers stumbled toward the closet.

The posts of the old, mildewed bed came loose and crashed onto the floor. The mirror exploded into a billion shards.

Julian closed his eyes to protect them from the glass.

"Shit!" cried Tim. "He's here!"

Julian opened his eyes. Hovering before, and slightly above them, the ghost pointed a white, translucent finger down at Julian. "You dare defy me? In my own home!"

"Don't let him touch you!" shouted Tim as the ghost floated toward them, never taking his eyes off Julian.

Dave grabbed Julian by the serape. "If there's a Phase 2 to this plan, now is the time!"

"HORSE!" Julian shouted a third time.

"Jesus Christ, dude!" shouted Dave. "You can't solve all of your problems with goddamn hors—"

A grey mare appeared right in front of them, facing away from the ghost. Julian patted it on its long face. "I'm really sorry, buddy."

The horse let out an ungodly howling noise that no horse had any business making when the spectral finger penetrated its flesh. It fell to the floor, finally prompting the collapse Julian had been hopefully anticipating.

What Julian had not been anticipating, as the second floor smashed into the first, was for the entire place to be engulfed in flames. The combination of Tim's homemade candle holders, Dave's broken booze, and Mr. Hildegarde's rage-quakes had set the old house ablaze.

Julian immediately started hacking as his lungs filled with smoke and dust. He shut his eyes to keep out the flying specks of ash. A cacophony of sound whirled around him as he tried to hold on to consciousness. The roar of flame. The cries of horses. Dave shouting.

"Water!"

A second later, Julian felt his body be picked up roughly and thrown through the air into a softer light and a cooler breeze. He landed on soft, cool grass. He forced his eyes open. He was outside. He was alive. He was – "Shit!"

Tim flew out of the open doorway and smashed into Julian like they were long-parted lovers.

"Move your fat fucking ass!" Cooper shouted from inside the burning house.

"I'm going as fast as I can!" said Dave, waddling out of the house. His beard was black with soot.

Cooper ran out behind him. Once they were safely in the grass, he tackled Dave. With Dave pinned on his back underneath him, Cooper grabbed him by the shoulders and repeatedly smashed his back into the ground.

"What... the... fuck... are... you... doing?" asked Dave as the back of his head kept slamming into the ground.

Cooper stood up. "Sorry, dude. Your bag was still on fire." It made sense. It must have still been soaked through with top shelf stonepiss.

Julian wiped the tears out of his eyes. "What do you suppose happens to a ghost when you destroy the place it haunts?"

"No idea," said Tim, taking a swig from his flask.

"Let's not stick around and find out," said Dave, waddling quickly toward the front gate of Hildegarde Manor.

The rest of the group followed him. From within the second floor of the house, Julian heard the tortured screams of a man who had just lost everything he'd known for the past four hundred years, as well as the tortured screams of two doppelgangers who were most likely on fire. He quickened his pace.

"And by the way," Dave said to Tim. "That's *my* stonepiss you're drinking."

Tim grinned. "Don't worry, Dave. There's plenty more where that came from."

"What do you mean?"

Tim pulled a green silk pouch out from his vest pocket and shook it. It sounded heavy with coins. "I found this in the bedroom closet. Second time today I've robbed those doppelfucks. I say we hit up that fancy tavern on the way back to the Whore's Head Inn. Have ourselves some classy drinks, in loving memory of our dearly departing friends."

Julian wasn't sure if he liked the idea of celebrating the deaths of two people who were currently burning to death, but he was more than ready for a drink.

"How much is in there?" asked Cooper.

"Dunno," said Tim. "I haven't had time to count it. But it might even be enough for us to deck ourselves out with some shiny new weapons."

"Or we could use it responsibly," said Dave. "Put it toward magical research? Try to figure out a way back home?"

"We can talk about it," said Tim. "Let's just get to that tavern, settle into a round of drinks, and see how much gold we're talking about first, huh?"

"Agreed," everyone said simultaneously.

Julian shouted skyward, "Ravenus!"

*

As they approached Cardinia's city walls, the sinking sun underlit orange clouds against a lavender sky. With just a little bit of searching, they were able to locate the tavern they had drunk at that morning. It was much busier now, with only a couple empty tables left. Many of the patrons were uniformed city watchmen, and there were even a few Kingsguard.

Dave led the way inside, strutting up to the bar like he was a soldier returning home after personally punching Hitler in the dick. "Why hello there, good sir. We have returned!"

The barman turned around, gawking down at Dave with an expression of shock and bemusement. He rang a loud bell which hung above the bar. "It's them!" he said once he had the establishment's undivided attention. "These are the folks I was telling you all about!"

Several city watchmen stood up from their tables, forming a perimeter around the group. Two Kingsguard stood at attention in the doorway, covering their only hope at an exit. Something was definitely not right.

Dave waved a hand dismissively. "Oh please. You're really making too big a deal out of this."

"Too big a deal?" shouted the barman. "One of your lot clubbed me over the head, tied me up, stole my clothes, and then bled all over my bar! When I come to, I find two bottles of my finest liquor has been stolen, not to mention you didn't pay your tab! Now which part of that do you find I'm making too big a deal of?"

Dave looked like he'd just been stabbed in the soul. He reached his left arm back. "Tim! Money!"

"How much do you –"

"NOW!"

Tim grudgingly handed over the whole bag of coins.

Dave walked up to the bar, carefully placing the bag between himself and the barman. "Are you absolutely certain we're the men you're looking for?"

The barman opened the bag. Looking inside, his eyes went as wide as golf balls. "Sweet succubus!"

"Would you like us to escort you to the courthouse now," said one of the city watchmen, "so that you can press formal charges? Or shall we just throw them in a holding cell until you're ready."

"I'm terribly sorry, gentlemen," said the barman. "'Twas a false alarm."

"Are you quite sure, sir? They match your descriptions perfectly, right down to the curious band of leopard fur growing on the dwarf's forearm."

"I swear by the gods I've never seen these gentlemen before. Sorry for your troubles." He tossed the city watchman a coin from the bag. At first glance, it appeared silver, but shinier.

The watchman held the coin up to the light, then stared at the barman. "That's right generous of you, sir. Thank you very much!"

When all of the guards and soldiers took their seats, the barman addressed Dave. "I knew you was good lads! Now what'll you have to drink?"

Dave hung his head. "Three beers and a bottle of your cheapest stonepiss."

The End.

Naga Please

(Original Publication Date: October 3, 2014)

Dave leaned back against his tree and basked in sunlight and contentment. This was what life was about. Being outside with your friends, drinking and fishing. Sure, they hadn't caught so much as a single fish in the four hours they'd been out here, but that wasn't the point. The pine-scented breeze was alive with the chatter of squirrels and the distant rush of the waterfall which fed this elevated lake. Camaraderie and nature. Here or in the real world, these were the things Dave valued most.

"This fucking sucks," said Tim. "What's wrong with these stupid fish?"

"Maybe fish in this world aren't partial to worms?" suggested Julian.

"We bought them at a goddamn bait shop." Tim reeled in his line. The rods and reels Gorgonzola had put together at the Whore's Head were bigger and clunkier than their real world counterparts, but they worked surprisingly well. When Tim's hook broke the surface, it was empty.

Cooper snorted. "Maybe the fish are smarter than you give them credit for."

"They're fucking fish," said Tim. "They have an Intelligence score of 1. That's dumber than you."

"Hey," said Cooper. "If you're so hungry, why don't you eat my ass?"

"Fishing takes patience," said Dave. "If you didn't reel your line in every five minutes you just might –" Feeling a tug on his line, he sat bolt upright. "See? See what I told you? This is it!"

Tim folded his little arms. "Ten bucks says it's another boot."

Dave let go of the reel. Whatever was on the other end of his line gave it a good tug. "I'll take that action. You ever see a boot do that?" He grabbed the reel and started winding up the line.

The rod stayed bent as Dave frantically reeled, ignoring the bead of sweat that tickled the tip of his nose. He supposed Tim was right to be skeptical. They had hooked a conspicuous amount of junk from the lake floor. Three boots, none of which matched, two rusted helmets, a canteen, and even a broken short sword. But whatever he had this time was alive and fighting for its life. A late breakfast was mere minutes away.

"There it is!" cried Tim, licking his lips and pointing at the spot where Dave's line broke the surface of the water.

Dave had never seen anyone so eager to part with ten dollars he didn't have. His stomach grumbled as he found what Tim had spotted. Sure enough, it was shiny and scaly.

Cooper balled up his fists. "Reel, Dave! Reel like a motherfucker!"

Dave reeled as fast as his thick, stubby arms would allow. He yanked his prize out of the water. It swung toward him. He closed his eyes as it slapped him in the face. The feeling was suspiciously metallic.

"Well shit," said Julian.

Dave opened his eyes. Before him, water drained out of the fingers of a scale mail gloved gauntlet. His stomach voiced its disappointment.

Tim, his arms still folded, looked smugly at Dave. For Tim, apparently, spiteful satisfaction was more nourishing than food.

"It's not a boot," said Dave. "You still owe me ten bucks."

"Well done," said Ravenus, flapping down from a branch of a nearby pine tree. "There's not, by any chance, still a hand in there, is there?"

Dave unhooked the gauntlet and turned it over. Nothing but water spilled out. He tossed it onto the pile of junk they'd caught. "I could have sworn I felt a tug."

Julian skipped a rock on the surface of the lake. "That was just drag. It was a glove full of water. It was bound to feel heavier than it was."

"It just doesn't make sense," said Dave. "Cooper caught a sword. How is that even possible? I could put a sword into a bucket of water and try all day to pull it up with a hook, and I'd come up empty."

About fifty yards away, a fish jumped out of the water.

Cooper picked up a baseball-sized rock and hurled it into the lake. "Fuck you, you scaly bastard!"

"I'm done," said Tim. "I say we pack up our shit and chalk it up to another day of failure."

"Come on," said Dave. "There's still plenty of daylight, and we've still got half a box of worms left."

Tim stomped up to Dave and poked him in the breastplate. "If we don't get moving in the next five minutes, I'm going to eat those fucking worms."

Julian rested his slender hand on Dave's right pauldron. "We did our best. It's time to call it a day."

In a rare moment of bleak desperation, Dave turned beseechingly to Cooper. Cooper farted.

Dave considered threatening to stay behind and keep fishing alone, but they'd almost certainly call his bluff.

"Fine," he said, extra glumly. "Let's go."

Tim led the way back down along the stream that they had followed to get up to the lake. Sure-footed, nimble, and eager to get back to the Whore's Head Inn, he even managed to outpace Cooper's natural Base 40 Movement Speed.

Julian lagged behind with Dave, tossing what worms were left in the box up to Ravenus, who caught them in the air, while Cooper and Tim disappeared into the forest ahead of them.

"Do you think we'll ever get back home?" asked Dave.

"Sure," said Julian. "Like you said, there's plenty of daylight left, and it's always quicker going down than it is going up."

"I meant real home. In our real bodies."

"Oh." Julian frowned. "I don't know. I try not to think about it." He faked a cheerful grin. "Besides, being an elf's not so bad."

Dave kicked a rock into the stream. "Being a dwarf kind of sucks."

"Come on, " said Julian. "Let's catch up to Cooper and Tim before they get themselves –"

"There they are!" said Cooper, only his voice didn't sound like it was coming from the right direction. It sounded more like it was coming from –

"Dave! Julian!" Tim called out. "Up here!" He and Cooper were suspended upside-down, fifty feet in the air.

Julian stepped off the path, looking up at them. "How the hell did you get up –"

"Julian!" cried Tim. "No!"

Pop. Snap. Thwang. Swoosh.

Julian's left foot rocketed into the air, followed by the rest of him. "Shiiiiiiit!"

"Sir!" cried Ravenus as Julian flew past him.

"Fuck," said Cooper. "Our lives are in *Dave's* hands."

"Dave!" said Tim. "Don't move!"

Dave was already way ahead of him in that regard. He had no intention of taking a single step in any direction. "What should I do?"

Tim looked at the nearest trees surrounding him. Then he looked up at the rope he was suspended from. "I think we're all hanging from the same tree," he called down to Dave. "Our best option is probably for you to chop it down."

"With what?" asked Dave. "I use a mace. What am I supposed to do? Bludgeon a goddamn tree until it – JESUS CHRIST!" He jumped out of the way a split second before Cooper's greataxe could chop him in half.

"My bad!" Cooper called down. "Hurry up and chop us down. I gotta take a piss, and I don't want it running up in my face."

"Watch where you step!" said Tim.

Tim was the rogue. If he hadn't spotted the snares, Dave didn't stand a chance. The ground between him and the ground was covered in sticks and dead leaves, but appeared to be clear of ropes. He took a cautious step toward the axe.

Crack.

The axe disappeared. Dave jerked his head to the right to discover the blade of the axe embedded in a tree trunk. He looked back to where the axe had been to see what had flung it away. What he saw was whip-like, but much thicker, and covered in shiny, black scales. His eyes followed it around the back of a tree, then up the tree trunk.

"Hello," said a bald, human-ish head atop a snake's body. The skin of its face was as jet-black as the scales on its body. When it smiled at Dave, its forked tongue darted out between white, needle-like teeth.

Dave felt whatever courage he might have had run down his inner thigh. As he took a step backward, the snake-like monster slithered out from behind the tree. Its chest was broad where human pectoral muscles would be, but it had no arms. In their place was a great flattened hood, like a cobra's.

"Sami!" hissed a female serpentine voice.

The creature facing Dave blinked, translucent lids sliding sideways across its eyes. It stopped smiling. "Over here."

A second creature slithered out from behind some underbrush. This one was female, Dave guessed by its voice and smooth, nipple-less black breasts and full lips. She reminded Dave of Angelina Jolie, if Angelina Jolie was a black, bald, half-reptilian vampire.

"Shit," said Cooper from above. "Nagas."

"Don't call them that!" said Julian. "We're in enough trouble as it is!"

"Ow! What the fuck did you hit me for?"

Dave and the two creatures looked up. Cooper and Julian were swinging from their ropes, Cooper trying to punch Julian, and Julian trying to hit Cooper again with his quarterstaff.

"What did you go and set the snares again for, Sami?" asked the female creature. "We haven't even finished the group we caught last week."

"I grow tired of dwarf," said Sami. He looked at Dave. "No offenssse."

Dave swallowed. "None taken."

Sami looked up at his captives. "This is quite the diverssse group."

"Oh stop with the hissing," said the female. "Can't you see you're scaring this poor dwarf half to death?" She slithered over to the tree Dave was meant to chop down and reached her tail up over her head, into its lower branches. Cooper, Julian, and Tim began to descend slowly on their ropes.

"My wife, Trista," Sami said to Dave. "Motherhood has softened her heart."

"Congratulations?" said Dave.

"Dude," said Cooper as he, Julian, and Tim were being lowered to the ground. "You're not getting this. It's not *their word*. They're actually called nagas. They're based on ancient Hindu mythology or some shit."

Trista looked curiously at Julian, but addressed Cooper. "What does your elf friend have against nagas?"

"I've got nothing against… your kind," said Julian. Touching ground, he loosened his rope and stepped out of it. "I'm just not comfortable using that word. It sounds too much like… Can't I just call you Scary Snake Monster Lady or something?"

"Why certainly," said Trista.

Julian sighed and smiled. "Okay then."

"If you want those to be the last words you ever say."

"Oh."

"Why don't you just call me Trista?"

Julian laughed nervously. "Trista it is."

"And this is my mate, Sami."

Sami grinned at Julian. "You can call me Scary Snake Monster if you want."

Trista brushed aside some strategically placed greenery with her tail to reveal a small cave entrance. "Come on inside and see the naglets."

Julian frowned. "You really call them that?"

If Trista heard him, she ignored him. She slithered toward her cave.

"Dude," Tim whispered to Julian. "If you're going to turn off your Diplomacy skill, maybe you should just shut the fuck up."

Dave caught Tim scanning the scene for an escape route and Cooper sizing up Sami. Sami's grin grew wider, as if he knew exactly what the both of them were thinking and was hoping one of them would try something.

Dave tried hard to remember everything he knew about nagas from playing Caverns and Creatures at home. They didn't use them that often in the game, though, because their characters seldom survived to a high enough level to face one. Come to think of it, that was probably all of the information he needed.

"Let's go, Coop," said Dave.

Cooper broke his gaze from Sami. "Huh?"

"Let's go see the naglets." He spoke with innuendo heavy in his tone.

"Yeah, alright."

Tim nodded and reluctantly followed.

"I'd offer you something to eat," said Trista when they approached

the entrance to the cave. "But I'm afraid all we have is dwarf."
Sounds of gnawing and sucking echoed out from the darkness
behind her.

"Is it cooked?" asked Tim.

Dave glared at him. "Tim!"

"I'm fucking starving," said Tim. "And it's only technically
cannibalism for you."

"You are too good for my mate's hospitality?" Sami asked Dave.
Dave knew his tone well. He was a bully, just looking for any excuse.
The only hope any of them had was Julian's Diplomacy skill, and he
was off to a piss poor start with that.

"Sami!" Trista snapped. "They have a different culture than ours."
She picked up a pebble with the end of her tail and held it to her lips
and whispered the word, "Light." The pebble glowed with soft,
white luminescence.

They're spellcasters, Dave thought to himself. A more specific
reason not to fuck with them.

"I'm sorry, little halfling," said Trista. "We nagas eat our meat raw."
She laid the pebble on the ground and slithered to the left, revealing
six tiny nagas – each about a foot and a half long – gnawing and
tearing the flesh off a short, thick leg.

Dave took a step back and bumped into Sami, who he hadn't
realized was standing right behind him.

Sami placed the end of his leathery tail on Dave's left shoulder and
leaned his head over his right. "They grow up so fast."

Trista tapped the tip of her tail on the nearest naglet's head. "This is
Tami."

Tami hissed and snapped at her mother's tail.

Trista continued. "And that's Suna, Tasha, Bolo, Mavi, and Poe."

Dave couldn't wrench his gaze away from the half-devoured dwarf
leg. He forced out the words, "They're adorable."

Cooper looked at his wrist. "Holy shit. Look at the time."

"You have a lovely family, Trista," said Julian. "Thank you for
everything, but we really should be on our way."

"Before you go," said Trista, slithering up to Julian. She put her
face right in front of his, so close that Dave feared it might inspire

jealousy in Sami. "Could I bother you for a small favor?"

Julian stared back at her, slack-jawed, like he was in a trance. "Anything."

It wasn't enough for these sadistic monsters to just kill them outright. They had to make a game out of it. She was going to ask Julian to choose one of his friends to leave behind. Dave was fucked.

Trista grinned. Her forked tongue flicked out between her horrible white teeth. She broke eye contact with Julian and retreated back to her babies. "Your life changes when you have children."

Dave and Tim exchanged puzzled glances.

"Yes," said Julian.

"Your priorities change," Trista continued. "You have new responsibilities. You can't just go on living carefree like there's no tomorrow."

"Yes," said Julian. He wasn't really flexing his Diplomacy muscles like the situation required.

"I'm sorry," said Cooper. "I'm confused. What the fuck is going on here?"

Sami hissed, sending shivers up Dave's spine.

Tim punched Cooper in the leg. "Shut the fuck up and let her talk."

"A stream runs just outside our home," said Trista.

"Yes," said Julian.

"That's right," said Tim, picking up Julian's slack. "We followed it up to the lake."

"We made our home here for that very reason," said Trista. "Wandering travelers ensured us a steady supply of food and entertainment, which was just fine when it was only Sami and myself. There is little in the forest which could threaten us. But, like any mother, I fear for my children's sake. I want them to be able to play outside without fear of being killed. There's far too much foot traffic along that stream. It fills me with anxiety."

"Yes," said Julian.

Dave wished he could walk over and slap Julian, but he was frozen in place with fear.

"What would you like us to do about it?" asked Tim.

Trista looked at Tim with sad, grateful eyes. "If it's not too much of

41

a bother, we'd like you to travel back up to the lake and divert the course of the stream."

"Is *that* all?" said Cooper, his voice heavy with relief. "Naga please. We are *on* that shit."

"Wonderful!" Trista smiled in a way that might have looked perky if her mouth wasn't bristling with nightmare fuel. "Stop by again anytime!"

Julian clapped his hands together. "Daylight's a-wastin'. Let's get moving."

Dave willed up the courage to speak. "So we can just go then?"

Sami slithered around him and joined his family. "Of course. You can't very well divert the course of a stream from here, now *can* you?"

Julian walked casually out of the cave. Tim and Cooper backed out more cautiously.

Sami and Trista stared down at Dave. He took a tentative step backwards. When they failed to jump on him and tear his face off, he took another. With his third step, he turned around and waddled completely out of the cave to join his friends on the other side of the camouflaging greenery.

"Way to step up to the plate," Cooper said to Tim as the four of them made their way back to the stream. "You bought us four tickets to *the fuck out of there*. Stupid nagas."

Julian winced. "I really wish you'd stop saying things like that."

"And I wish you would have said something other than *Yes. Yes. Yes*," said Tim. "You sounded like a goddamn robot. What the hell was that all about?"

"I guess I just choked," said Julian. "They were scary."

Cooper snorted. "The way she was looking at you, I was sure she was going to make you do weird snake sex things with her in front of her husband."

"Ew," said Julian. "And her kids?"

"Who knows what kind of freaky shit nagas are into?"

Julian sighed. "Look. I understand that's what they're called, but it still sounds really wrong when you say it."

"Hey," said Cooper. "Where are you going?"

Dave wanted nothing more than to put as much distance between himself and Sami as possible, and thus found himself in the rare position of leading the party when they reached the stream. He stopped and turned around. While he, Tim, and Cooper had turned downstream, Julian was headed back up the hill.

Julian stared back at the rest of them like they were aliens. "I'm going back up to the lake."

"What the fuck for?"

Julian furrowed his eyebrows as he stared at Cooper. He then looked at Tim and Dave. The four spent a moment in a stalemate of confusion.

"Don't you remember? We're supposed to divert the stream."

"Fuck that," said Cooper. "We're in the clear. Let's go get some food before we have to eat Dave."

Dave was moderately certain that Cooper was joking, but still shivered at the memory of naglets tearing apart a dwarf leg.

"But we said we were going to."

"And if they'd asked, I would have said that I *wasn't* going to jerk off to Trista's big snake titties later on, but that doesn't make it fucking true."

"Seriously," said Tim. "Let's just remember to never come up this hill again, and we should be okay."

Julian put his hands on his hips and glared down at them. "Do your words mean nothing? Dave?"

Dave frowned. "I didn't actually say any words."

"Tim?"

"We were afraid for our lives," said Tim. "We're not honor bound to keep promises made under duress."

"Cooper?"

Cooper looked down at his loincloth, then back up at Julian. "I, too, was underdressed."

Julian shook his head. "Shame on all of you." He turned around and began stomping his way upstream.

"What the fuck, man?" Cooper called out after him. "Is this some kind of white guilt thing?"

"Screw you, Cooper!" Julian called back without turning around.

"Have fun jerking off!"

"I will!"

Tim threw his hands in the air. "What kind of bullshit was that?"

"Okay, you caught me," said Cooper. "I was bluffing. I won't be able to concentrate properly while Julian's out here alone."

"No," said Tim. "I meant when did Julian turn into such a sanctimonious little shit?"

Dave stroked his beard. "He didn't." The pieces were beginning to fall into place inside his head.

"Were you not paying attention just now?"

"He's not honor bound," said Dave. "He's spellbound."

"What are you talking about?"

"Trista wasn't getting all up in his face to make sexy-eyes at him. She was casting a spell on him."

"How do you know?"

"It just makes sense. That's why he kept saying yes to everything she said. That's why they just let us up and leave. They knew the rest of us would ditch them the first chance we got, but Julian would move that stream or die trying. It's a Quest spell. Tim, you used it when we were playing C&C back at the Chicken Hut last Christmas. Remember when you made the town sheriff piss the lyrics to *Jingle Bells* in the snow?"

Tim grinned. "That asshole was drunk off his tits for a week."

Dave sighed. "I guess there's only one thing we can do."

"Club him over the head and drag him back to town?" suggested Cooper.

"I was thinking more along the lines of helping him divert the stream."

"That's another valid option."

"Fuck," said Tim. "Let's go and get this over with."

Dave, Cooper, and Tim trudged back up the hill until they found Julian, soaking wet from the waist down, struggling to carry a rock as big as his head.

"What do you think you're doing?" asked Dave.

Kersplunk. Julian dropped the rock into the stream at a point just before it widened into the lake. He didn't even give them a glance as he searched the bank for another rock. "I'm doing just what I said I was going to do."

Ravenus provided what little contribution to the cause that he could, flying over the stream and dropping pebbles.

Tim rolled his eyes.

"I know," said Dave. "We're here to help you."

"Wait, what?" said Cooper. "When did my plan get taken off the table?"

"More specifically," Dave continued. "What are you doing?"

Julian stopped what he was doing and turned to face him. "I'm damming up the stream."

"That's a terrible idea."

Julian wagged his finger at Dave. "If you thought you were going to come up here and talk me out of this, you wasted a trip. Integrity means something to me. Tomorrow *I'll* look at myself in the mirror and not be ashamed of the face looking back at me."

Tim cupped his hand over the side of his mouth. "Cooper's plan is starting to grow on me."

"I'm not trying to talk you out of it," said Dave. "I just think you're going about it the wrong way."

Julian wiped the sweat from his brow with his palm and sat on the bank. "I'm listening."

Ravenus fell to the ground like a sack of potatoes. "Thank heavens!" he said between labored breaths.

"You can throw all the rocks you want in there," said Dave. "The water's just going to go around them and work its way back to the stream long before it gets to the naga cave. It's got to go somewhere, right?"

"Yeah," said Julian. "So what are you suggesting?"

"I'm suggesting that, before you try to stop the water flowing through here, you give it somewhere else to go."

Julian nodded. "That makes a lot of sense. Thanks for coming back."

Dave willed himself to ignore the rumble in his stomach. "Don't mention it." Not recalling any great locations to the right of the stream where they had been fishing, he started walking clockwise along the edge of the lake. "We'll want to find a spot a good distance from here, so that the water doesn't just work its way back into the stream bed."

Julian sent Ravenus off to go scavenge, and then he, Tim, and Cooper followed Dave for a good forty-five minutes. Dave stopped several times to assess potential locations for a new stream, but nothing jumped out at him as being terribly convenient. Either the ground didn't slope the right way, or there was a big tree they'd have to uproot, or they'd have to dig through solid rock. Dave had packed for fishing that morning, not for creating and destroying ecosystems.

And then he saw it. It was like Mother Nature herself was lying naked on a bed and begging to get fucked. A perfect storm of natural anomalies. A single boulder, about as big as a cow, was all that stood between the water and a sheer, thirty foot drop in elevation. For how many centuries had this unlikely chunk of stone denied the creatures which inhabited this hilly forest the beauty of another small waterfall?

Dave placed his palm on the boulder. "It's perfect."

Cooper frowned. "What am I looking at?"

Dave hopped down into the shallow water. "If we can push this boulder off the ledge, our problems are solved! Hell, we probably won't even need to go back and dam the other stream." He leaned his shoulder into the stone and pushed with his legs. It didn't budge. "Cooper? A little help?"

Cooper jumped into the water. He and Dave shoved as hard as they could, but to no avail.

"Maybe you should try pulling instead of pushing," suggested Tim.

Julian tugged at his long ears. "What difference would that make?"

"Objects are easier to pull than they are to push," said Tim. "It's basic physics. Why do you think you put a horse in front of a wagon, rather than behind?"

"Umm," said Cooper. He abandoned his effort against the boulder and looked up at Tim. "So it can see where the fuck it's going?"

"Remind me," said Tim. "Who's got the highest Intelligence score here?"

"Well let me explain some basic fucking physics to you, Professor. Even if I could climb over that rock, secure a grip on it, and pull it free, that leaves me with a thirty foot free fall, hugging a goddamn boulder."

"Who said I was talking about you?"

"No?" said Cooper. "In that case, sweet. Dave, I'll push. You pull."

Dave looked at Tim. "What?"

Tim raked his fingers through his curly hair. "Jesus Christ. I'm talking about a horse!" He pulled a coil of rope out of his bag. "Julian climbs down there and summons a horse. We tie one end of the rope to the horse and the other end to the boulder. Horse pulls. We push. Problem solved. We all go back to town and get some fucking dinner."

Julian rubbed his chin thoughtfully. "It could work."

Tim raised his hands out to his sides. "Any objections?"

Dave shrugged. Cooper farted.

"Okay then. Julian, work your magic."

Julian hopped and skidded down the side of the hill where it wasn't quite as steep while Tim got busy tying an adjustable knot on one end of his rope.

"Horse!" said Julian from down below.

Dave peeked over the edge. Sure enough, Julian was combing his fingers through the mane of a sturdy-looking white horse.

"Here," said Tim, tossing the looped end of his rope to Cooper. "Loop this around the rock, and throw the other end down to Julian.

Cooper did as he was told.

Julian caught the loose end. "It's too short!"

"What are you talking about?" Cooper shouted down at him. "You're holding it!"

"But I don't have enough rope to tie it to the horse."

"Shit," said Tim. "I probably should have tested the rope length before I had him go down there and summon the horse."

"Now what are we going to do?" asked Dave.

Cooper leaned over the edge and looked down. "I say we eat the horse."

Tim groaned and rubbed his belly. "Don't even talk about that."

"What's wrong with that?" asked Cooper. "Lots of cultures eat horse meat."

"Hey, I'm with you, man. I would murder a pile of horse steaks

47

right now. That's not the problem."

"So what then?"

Tim glared up at Cooper. "Come on, man! You know those magical horses disappear as soon as they die!"

"That's right," said Cooper. "I've considered that. But how much of it do you think we could eat without actually killing it?"

Tim bit his lower lip and peeked down over the boulder.

"Tim!" said Dave. "Tell me you're not actually considering this."

"I'm so fucking hungry," said Tim.

"I'm hungry, too," said Dave. "But come on, man. You want to rip the flesh off of a living, breathing creature? That's fucking barbaric is what that is."

Tim looked at Dave with wide eyes. "That's it!"

"Oh shit, what?" Dave was not comforted by Tim's sudden manic grin.

"Cooper!" cried Tim. "You big fucking retard!" He punched Cooper in the leg.

"Hey, man," said Cooper. "What the fuck?"

"Use your Barbarian Rage!"

"Oh." Cooper pursed his big lips. "Yeah, I could do that." He stood up. "Take a step back, Dave."

Dave hurried out of Cooper's way.

"Hey guys," said Julian, scrambling back up the slope. "Tim got me thinking about physics. What if we made some levers out of –"

"I'M REALLY ANGRY!" Cooper's muscles ballooned out like time-lapse video of baking   bread.

Julian laughed and rolled his eyes. "Doh! Why didn't we think of that before? It could have saved me a –" His smile suddenly vanished. "Wait, Cooper! No!"

Cooper roared like the T-Rex from Jurassic Park as he hugged the bottom of the boulder and pushed up with his legs. Even with the Strength bonus from his Barbarian Rage, he struggled to move the big stone. But he kept roaring, and the boulder finally broke free. Once he had it dislodged, the weight of an entire lake's worth of water helped him push it over the edge.

Dave leaned over to watch the boulder fall, spotted Julian's horse grazing just below, and turned his head away just in time to hear, but not see, the crash. The lack of accompanying horse screams suggested that at least it went quickly.

"Goddammit, Cooper," said Julian.

"What?" asked Cooper, deflating to his normal form as the Barbarian Rage ceased.

"You killed my horse."

"Oh shit. My bad."

Water rushed out of the breach like a god taking a piss after having held it in during a long bus ride. Once the lake reached an equilibrium, the force of the water would likely subside, but for now –

"FISH!" cried Julian, pointing down to the water.

Try as they may, the fish which got caught too close to the edge of the lake couldn't outswim the sudden current. Cooper immediately squatted down and began scooping them out of the water just before they made it to the breach.

Julian, Dave, and Tim waited eagerly to catch whatever Cooper flung from the water. Julian caught a nice, fat, shiny pink fish. It was eyeless, and had tentacles growing out of its face. It looked delicious.

Dave caught a blue fish with its pectoral fins on the bottom.

Tim caught a naked green woman.

"JESUS!" screamed Tim, flailing his arms and legs about wildly. "GET IT OFF ME! GET IT OFF ME!"

Dave stepped back and caught himself just short of falling off the ledge. The fish, flopping and twisting out of Dave's grasp, wasn't so lucky.

Tim's Catch-of-the-Day slapped him in the face with her green, webbed hand before rolling off him. "How dare you toss me around like an oyster shell!"

"That fucking hurt," said Tim, rubbing his red cheek.

The woman's hair was a darker shade of green than her skin, and hung down like seaweed to cover her small breasts. The rage in her aquamarine eyes turned to fear as she backed away, finding herself outnumbered four to one.

"We didn't mean you any harm," said Julian. "Actually, Cooper here probably just saved your life." He nodded at the water rushing out of the breach, then stared curiously at the woman. "What are you? Some kind of sea-elf?"

"I'm a nixie."

"A nixie?"

"They're like pixies," Tim explained. "But without –"

"Kim Deal?"

"…wings."

The nixie glared at Tim. "That may be the most insulting oversimplification of our kind that I've ever heard. Who are you people? What do you want? Why did you –" She backed into their bags and fishing rods. "You're the fishermen from earlier this morning, aren't you?" Her tone was accusatory.

So that was the reason they couldn't catch anything. These people must have a special relationship with the fish in the lake. Dave whispered to Julian, "Surrender your fish."

"Huh?" Julian looked down at the fish in his hands. "Oh, okay." He knelt before the nixie and held up the squirming fish. "Please accept our humble apologies."

"Very well," she said, cautiously accepting Julian's offering. Gripping the fish firmly by face and tail, she savagely bit into its side, tearing away a large chunk of flesh. Blood dripped from her mouth as she chewed.

Dave frowned. "You eat fish?"

The nixie stared quizzically at Dave while she chewed. After she swallowed she said, "We live in a lake. What do you expect us to eat?"

Dave felt blood rush to his face, both from the implied stupidity of his question, and from the fact that he'd just given away their only food for no reason.

Tim was glaring at him, and he could sense Cooper's eyes burning a hole in his back as well.

"I just thought maybe the fish were your friends or something."

The nixie held up her dead fish so that she was staring it in the face. "Hello, Mr. Fish. Tell me about yourself. Do you have a family?"

She pinched the sides of the fish's mouth so that its lips moved, and spoke in a deeper voice. "Well, Lana. I don't really know, on account of I'm a fish. I suppose if I did have a family, I'd probably try to eat them, because I'm a stupid fish."

Dave folded his arms. "You've made your point."

"Oh dear," said the nixie, Lana, to her fish. "I don't think I could be friends with someone who would eat their own children."

"That's okay, Lana," she responded in her fish voice. "I don't have the emotional capacity for friendship anyway, because I'm a godsdamned fish."

Tim grinned. "I like her. She's fun."

Dave felt he'd suffered enough ridicule for one day. "So what have you got against fishermen?"

"Aside from the fact that they come here specifically to steal our food?" said Lana. "Well there's also the matter of the garbage they dump in the lake."

"That was you then!" said Tim. "You were the ones who put all those boots and helmets and shit on our hooks!"

Lana flashed him a quick grin before continuing. "And sometimes, just *sometimes*, a group of particularly witless bastards will up and try to destroy our home outright." She was staring at the water rushing out of the breach.

"Ummm…" said Cooper. "Sorry about that."

"That wasn't our fault," said Dave. "The nagas made us do it."

Lana raised an eyebrow. "Sami and Trista? Why would they want you to do that?"

"They wanted us to dry up the stream running by their cave to keep travelers away from their children."

Lana's eyes lit up. "Trista had her babies? That's wonderful! I'll have to send her some fish."

"You're friends with *nagas*?" asked Cooper.

"Jesus, Cooper!" said Julian. "Can you hear yourself?"

"Not friends, exactly," said Lana. "But we appreciate them keeping travelers away from our lake."

Images of the dwarf leg in the naga cave flashed in Dave's mind. "You are aware of how they do that, right?"

"Uh-oh," said Lana, her eyes focused on something beyond Dave.

51

"What is the meaning of this?" demanded a booming male voice from the direction Lana was looking.

Dave turned around. Trotting up the slope was a creature that Dave recognized from fantasy literature other than Caverns and Creatures. The creature's lower half resembled the body of a horse, but it had the upper body of a muscular, hairy man. A centaur. In his hands he carried a large, wooden spear. The pristine steel tip glistened in the sunlight, but the wood just beneath it was stained brown, suggesting he was no stranger to its use.

"Who's that?" asked Julian as the centaur approached.

Tim rolled his eyes at having to explain yet another fantasy creature to Julian. "It's a centaur. Half man, half horse."

"How dare you, insolent halfling!" shouted the centaur, thrusting the end of his spear about a quarter inch from Tim's nose. "Retract your words at once!"

Tim dropped to his knees. "I retract! I retract!"

The centaur likewise retracted his spear. "I am no part man, no part horse. I am *all* centaur. We are a proud and noble race, and I will not have our name besmirched by the likes of a sniveling halfling coward like yourself."

"You should have heard what he had to say about nixies," said Lana.

"For the record," said Julian. "I know what a centaur is. I read Harry Potter." He paused to raise his eyebrows smugly at Tim, still on his knees. "I asked *who* this was, not *what*."

"Gentlemen," said Lana. "This is Gallus. Gallus, I haven't actually had the time to learn their names yet. I imagine you're here about the breach in the wall."

"My rutabagas are flooding! I demand an explanation!"

"You'll probably want to talk to Finn. I'll be right back. Talk amongst yourselves."

"Huh?" said Dave. "Don't leave us alone with…" When he turned to look at Lana, she had already disappeared into the lake. "Shit."

The centaur, Gallus, eyed the four of them with obvious distaste. If normal centaurs were supposed to be comparable in size to their human and equine counterparts, he was a large specimen indeed. He stood a full head taller than Cooper even, and was nearly as broad across the shoulders. His chest was crisscrossed with scars, some of which were clearly earned in battle. But a row of smaller scars across the top right of his chest were too uniform to have not been put there intentionally. Dave guessed they were trophies he'd been awarded for some sort of tribal victories.

Julian bowed his head slightly. "I'm Julian. It's a pleasure to meet you."

Gallus stood tall and proud, his wild mane swaying in the breeze. He sniffed the air. "And the one who smells of fresh urine?"

Dave, Tim, and Cooper blurted out their own names simultaneously.

"Are you the ones responsible for the breech in our forefathers' dam?"

In spite of his inexplicable knowledge of stonemasonry, Dave had assumed the wall keeping this lake in was a product of nature. He was impressed.

"You mean to tell me this was man made?"

Gallus's spear point was suddenly in Dave's face.

"Man had no part in its construction. We are centaurs, a fact I encourage you not to forget a third time. Now did you or did you not remove the crown stone from atop the dam?"

"Not me personally," Dave whimpered.

"Who then?" demanded Gallus. "Who is responsible?"

"None of them are," said a voice from behind the centaur. Almost as high in pitch as Lana's, this voice sounded older and more wizened.

Gallus turned around. "Finnean." He addressed the nixie accompanying Lana out of the lake with a respect that Dave guessed was formally expected, if not entirely sincere.

Lana escorted Finnean to a rock where he sat down. His skin was a paler shade of green than hers, and hung loosely on his old nixie bones. His seaweed-like hair was long in the back, but absent on top of his head.

"Lana has told me the whole story, as it was related to her," said the old nixie. "These young men cannot be held accountable for their actions. They were coerced by the nagas."

"That is no excuse!" said Gallus. He turned his back to Finnean and faced Dave. "Your reasons are not important to me. You are responsible for your own actions, and must live with the consequences of those actions."

It was beginning to feel like being back in middle school, getting a lecture from another kid's dad, where you were only going to listen to a little more of it before you just gave him the finger and ran away laughing. It didn't help that Lana was standing behind Finnean the whole time moving her dead fish's mouth in time with Gallus's words. Cooper and Tim were trying to maintain their serious faces, but neither of them were doing a very good job of it.

"Now I'm going to ask you one more time," Gallus continued.

Lana shook the fish slightly to make its mouth tentacles jiggle when it talked. Cooper couldn't contain it anymore. He snorted and farted at the same time.

Gallus looked back at Lana, who quickly put the fish behind her back and smiled innocently. He turned to face Cooper. "Who is responsible?"

"Like Mr. Finnean said," Julian spoke up. "The nagas –"

"The nagas didn't break our dam!" Gallus shouted. "Once I have dealt with you, I shall deal with the nagas. But until then, I must –"

"And just how do you sssuppose you'll *deal with the nagas*?" Sami slithered up along the edge of the lake.

Dave could only think of one explanation to account for his timing. He'd noticed the reduction of water flowing in his stream, and that concluded the usefulness he had for the four of them. *He's here to hunt.*

Sami grinned at Dave, sending a wave of shivers down his spine. *Was the naga reading his mind?*

Trying to remain casual and not move his lips, Dave spoke quietly enough so that hopefully only Julian would be able to hear him. "We have to get out of here. Summon some hor-"

A ray of darkness shot out of the nagas tail, hitting Julian squarely in the chest.

"Fuck!" shouted Cooper, grabbing his greataxe from off his back and stepping in front of Julian.

Dave supposed that confirmed the naga's mind reading ability. "Are

54

you okay?"

Julian patted his chest. He looked startled, but unhurt. "I don't feel any different."

"These are my prisoners, naga!" said Gallus. "And if their story is true, you have your own crimes to answer for."

"Sssunflowers will bloom in the Abyss before I answer to a horse-man."

Gallus brandished his spear at the naga. He was positively shaking with rage. "You take that back, by the gods, or I'll –"

"You'll what?" said Sami. "You whinny like a foal."

"You filthy, stinking naga!"

"Whoahohohoho!" said Julian. "Come on, man. No need for that."

Tim and Cooper glared at him.

Julian raised his hands apologetically. "I know, I know. I'm sorry. It just still sounds wrong to me. The seed was planted, and I... Carry on with what you were doing."

Gallus stomped his hooves like he was warming up for a run. "I've sent greater foes than you to the Abyss, naga. Prepare yourself!"

Sami bared his teeth and flicked his tongue. His dark hood expanded. He pointed the tip of his tail at Gallus and fired a bolt of purple lightning.

Seemingly ready for just such an attack, Gallus deftly leaped out of the way. The lightning flew harmlessly past him and struck the dam next to the breach. Moss-covered stones exploded, revealing them for the façade they were. Dave took half a second to appreciate the exposed masonry.

Gallus, too, glanced back at the dam. "My wall!" he cried. "My rutabagas!" The ground shook as he charged at Sami.

Sami coiled up and sprang out of the way just in time to miss the full force of Gallus's charge, but the spear sliced a six inch gash into his underbelly, spilling a trickle of black blood. He hissed in pain.

As Gallus slowed and turned around for a second charge, Sami turned tail and slithered hurriedly toward the wall. Was he retreating?

"Stand your ground and fight, craven naga!" Gallus shouted. "I can outrun you on two hooves!"

Having reached the edge of the lake next to the wall, Sami turned around and flashed a toothy grin at Gallus. His tail crackled with purple lightning.

"No!" cried Gallus, breaking into full gallop toward Sami.

Sami fired his lightning directly at the wall, widening the breach another four inches as the stonework exploded into coarse dust.

"Well that's just mean," said Julian. He was right. Sami was either trying to demonstrate how little a threat he took Gallus for, or he just cared more about being cruel than he did for his own survival. Either way, it was a dick move.

"What happened to the nixies?" asked Tim. Dave glanced at where he had last seen Lana and Finnean. Sure enough, they had disappeared. It was probably the wisest course of action.

Sami coiled up and grinned as Gallus approached, slowing down so as not to charge right over the edge of the dam. When Sami tried to spring over his head again, Gallus reared up on his hind legs and plunged the spear deep into the naga's chest.

Sami screamed in pain, and probably no small amount of surprise. Gallus obviously had quite a few fighter levels on him.

"Vile beast!" Gallus shouted as he drove the impaled naga down into the water. "I damn you to the depths!"

Sami's tail flailed about wildly as Gallus held his spear firm, pinning him under the water.

The naga's panic eventually ceded way to reason, and his tail coiled around Gallus's humanlike torso and horselike abdomen. Gallus grunted as Sami squeezed him, but he continued to hold his ground. The battle appeared to be at its unlikely conclusion when Sami pulled out one last surprise.

An inky black stinger emerged from the end of the naga's tail, and he plunged it into Gallus's rear. Gallus howled in pain, losing his grip on the spear. Sami's head emerged from the water. His gasps for air were interrupted by Gallus repeatedly punching him in the face.

Sami pulled his stinger out of Gallus's side and relinquished his hold on the centaur. Gallus hobbled backward on shaky horse legs while Sami stayed in the lake to catch his breath, black blood still leaking from his chest wound. The flowing water posed little danger to him, as he was too large to fit through the breach. The combatants stood panting, facing each other. Tired, haggard, and bleeding as they were, both appeared ready to react if the other should strike, but neither of them seemed to be in any great hurry to make the first move.

"Should we, um… help?" asked Julian.

"Which one?" said Tim. "I'm pretty sure they both want to kill us."

"We should get out of here while we have the chance," said Dave. "Julian?"

"Right," said Julian. "I'm on it." He pointed at the ground in front of him. "Horse!" A small squirt of glowing sparkles spat out of his finger, but no horse appeared.

"I warned you, elf!" shouted Gallus, turning around to face Julian.

Dave tried to stay focused on the problem at hand. Why didn't Julian's spell work? Sami must have cast some magic-nullifying spell on him.

"I will not be mocked!" Gallus continued shouting at Julian. "My people are an ancient and proud race! We have dwelled in this forest for countless gener—"

"Holy fucking shit!" said Cooper.

Dave looked up. Sami stood triumphant over Gallus, whose head was conspicuously absent from atop his neck.

Crimson blood gurgled out of the centaur's neck like a science fair volcano. His wobbly horse legs buckled, and he collapsed to the ground, spilling blood into the lake.

"Damn," said Cooper, shaking his head. "That's the wrong naga to fuck with."

Julian jabbed Cooper in the side with his quarterstaff. "Don't even try to tell me that one wasn't on purpose."

Sami spit Gallus's head out next to his body. "Thank you, elf." He smiled, showing off his blood-soaked teeth. "Who's next?"

"What should we do?" asked Julian.

"We could ask him to go halfsies on the centaur," suggested Cooper. "Would it be weird if we ate the horse half?"

"Dude," said Tim. "He's going to kill us. We need to run."

"No," Dave said flatly. That naga could outpace any of them. He wanted them to run, just for the thrill of the chase. Dave's stubby dwarf legs didn't have much of a chase to offer. He repeated the phrase 'Kill naga' in his mind to block the telepathic transmission of the last ditch idea that had just occurred to him. "Stay here. I've got this." Holding his mace firmly with both hands, he charged toward the naga.

"Dave!" Cooper called after him. "What the fuck are you doing?"

"BWAAAAAAHHHHHH!" *Kill naga. Kill naga. Kill naga.*

Sami looked genuinely perplexed as Dave waddled huriedly toward him.

"BWAAAAAAHHHHHH!" *Kill naga. Kill naga. Kill naga.*

Sami's malicious grin faltered as he broke into a yawn.

He was almost there. *Kill naga. Kill naga. Kill naga.* Sami backed up a couple of feet; a nice extra bit of cruelty. He didn't want to tear Dave's head off right away. It would be more fun to watch him sink and drown in his armor. *Kill naga. Kill naga. Kill naga.* Just keep it going a little... bit... longer... "BWAAAAAAHHHHHH!" *Kill naga. Kill naga. Destroy wall.*

"Huh?" said Sami as Dave changed his course.

Just as Dave had expected, the naga's lightning bolts had severely weakened the mortar of the ancient masonry. The top of the dam was days, if not hours, away from crumbling apart. He'd just give it a little help.

"No!" cried Sami. He tried to coil, but he was a lot less bouncy in the water.

Dave's dwarven knowledge of masonry, which he was only now discovering he had, allowed him to judge where the most stable part of the wall was for him to stand on, and which part of the wall was best to strike in order to help the water destroy the largest part of it. Gripping his mace firmly with both hands, he struck a particular block of exposed stone that he was certain none of his friends would have seen any special structural importance in.

The result was both immediate and catastrophic. A solid square meter of wall disintegrated into individual blocks and collapsed under the enormous pressure of the lake water, which gushed out with renewed fervor, dragging a helpless Sami over the edge.

The breach was wide enough now that the water no longer shot horizontally out of it, but rather flowed straight down along what was left of the dam. It was likely that Sami survived the initial fall, but Dave didn't like his odds against the loosening blocks of stone that continued to rain down on top of him.

The stone beneath his feet started to wobble, reminding Dave that he was standing on a collapsing dam. *Shit!* Time slowed down as he pivoted around, trying to save himself. He wasn't going to make it. He didn't need his dwarven knowledge of stonemasonry to tell him he was fucked, but he had it just the same, and it only reinforced his conclusion. Dave needed a miracle, and in his experience, miracles were just – *right above his head?*

He didn't question the loop of rope sailing through the air toward him. He just reached for it, catching it below the knot in his left hand. As the stone he had been standing on fell away, the rope tightened around the leopard fur of his forearm. It hurt like a motherfucker.

"Fuck, you're heavy!" said Cooper as Dave did his best to avoid scraping his face against stone and jagged mortar.

When he crawled up onto solid, stable land, Cooper, Tim, and Julian were right there to greet him.

Dave loosened the rope around his arm and tried to wring out some of the burn. "How did you guys get here so fast?"

"We were walking behind you," said Julian.

"You're kinda slow," added Tim.

Cooper scratched his balls under his loincloth. "That was seriously the most piss-poor battle charge I've ever seen. You should be embarrassed by that."

"I only have a base 20 Movement Speed," Dave explained. "And I can't run while I'm wearing my –"

"Ravenus!" shouted Julian. He ran off toward Gallus's dead body, where Ravenus was greedily slurping back one of the dead centaur's eyes. "Stop that! It's disrespectful."

Ravenus swallowed what he already had in his beak. "I'm very sorry, sir. You can have the other one, if you like."

"That's not what I meant. I just don't think –"

"Fuck it," said Cooper. "We're all starving. Let the bird eat. I'm still open to thoughts about chopping up this dude's bottom half. Anyone with me?"

"That would be… inadvisable," said Finnean as Lana escorted him slowly toward the party. Lana had a satchel over her shoulder. It was made of kelp and adorned with shells and fish scales.

"Oh, hey," said Dave. He looked back at the dam. The breech had grown to about three meters wide. "Umm… sorry about your lake."

"Don't be," said Lana cheerfully. "It's supposed to be down there. The centaurs stole that land from us over a century ago."

"Aren't they going to be pissed at you?"

Lana put her webbed hands up defensively. "Hey, we weren't even here."

Tim scowled at her. "Yeah, we noticed that."

"So what are you going to tell them?" asked Dave.

Lana shrugged. "We'll blame it on the nagas."

Cooper folded his arms and shook his head. "Brothas can't catch a *break*!"

Julian elbowed him in the side. "Knock it off."

"Still," said Finnean. "It would be prudent for you to leave this place before the other centaurs show up."

Dave didn't need to be told twice. "Well, thank you for everything. Good luck."

"I got you something," said Lana. She pulled a fat green fish out of her satchel and tossed it to Dave. It was slippery and flapping, and a little heavier than he expected, but Dave managed to hang onto it.

"Oh Lana, you don't know how much –" Dave had an idea. He held the fish up, pinched the sides of its mouth, and did his best Lana-fish impersonation. "Thank you, Lana!"

Instead of a laugh, his effort earned him a sympathetic smile from Lana and narrow-eyed puzzlement from Finnean.

Dave decided to have one more try. He pinched the fish's lips again. "Well, I guess I'll see you *lake*-er!"

Lana looked away, her pale green skin turning pink in the face. "I, um… I just remembered. I've got a… thing." She turned around and dove into the lake.

Noticing that none of his friends would make eye contact with him either, Dave lowered his fish.

"Sorry Dave," said Julian. "It's just not as funny when the fish is actually gasping for its life."

"See you *lake*-er?" said Tim. "Jesus, Dave. Was that even a joke?"

Cooper cradled his head in his hands. "Ugh... I feel like my brain just got kicked in the nuts."

Dave tucked the fish under his arm. "You guys can all go to hell. I'm not sharing this." He turned around and started the long walk back to Cardinia.

He ate the fish raw on his way back to town, but took little comfort in his spiteful selfishness, as his friends walked behind him the entire time, laughing and making water-and-fish-related puns, every one of them better than his.

The End

Elf Inflicted

(Original Publication Date: November 10, 2014)

Tim sucked the froth off the top of his beer glass, savoring the evening's first hint of alcohol. Soon he would be blissfully oblivious to everything in this shitty, shitty game world.

"It's nice to get out of the Whore's Head every now and again," said Julian, presumably just to fill the silence. The tips of his long ears were already pink from his first sip of beer.

Dave downed a shot of stonepiss. "Yeah, real nice. Drinking in *this* dingy tavern is so much better than drinking in the dingy tavern we usually drink at."

Tim stared into his beer. Julian had made a vacuously cheerful remark. Dave had bitched about something. All that was missing now was –

"Hey Dave," said Cooper, trying to flick a half-orc booger at him. It was too sticky, and he eventually gave up and licked it off his finger. "Your mom's a whore."

Dave rolled his beady dwarf eyes. "Not really your best effort."

"That's what a hundred guys who might be your dad said."

Dave puffed his bearded cheeks and exhaled. "Seriously, what are we doing here? There's literally no difference between this place and the Whore's Head, except that we can drink for free there."

It was Tim's idea to come out, so he was expected to answer. "I can rest my brain here. It's not so noisy."

"It's plenty noisy in here."

Dave wasn't technically wrong. The lizard people at the next table were particularly rowdy, slurping their drinks and chatting loudly in their clicky reptilian language.

"Oh," Dave continued, looking at the lizard people. "And everyone at the Whore's Head speaks English."

Tim gulped back some beer and licked away his frothy mustache. "And *that's* why we're here."

"You lost me."

"I'm so sick and tired of listening to everyone. Yeah, it's noisy in here, but everybody's speaking a different language that I don't understand. Back there it's all about how they miss their shitty lives back in the real world, or Doctor Who quotes."

Dave pouted. "I like Doctor Who."

"Bullshit," said Cooper. "Nobody likes Doctor Who. Everyone just watches it for geek cred. It's like going to church for nerds."

"You don't know what the hell you're talking about," said Dave. "Have you ever even watched an episode?"

"Fuck no."

"Then how do you know you don't like it?"

"Because I'm not retarded."

"Easy, Coop," said Tim. "You're kind of on the fence there."

"Fuck you nerds," said Cooper, standing up. "I'm going outside to take a shit."

"Did everyone catch that?" said Julian as the lizard people stopped their conversation to look up at Cooper. "Oh good. Thanks for the update, Cooper. Don't forget to wipe."

Cooper gave the rest of them a middle finger as he walked out of the tavern.

"Greetings," said a cloaked figure stepping behind Cooper's empty chair. He wore a neatly trimmed blond goatee, and his icy blue eyes shone out from the shadow of his hood.

Julian smiled up at him. "Hi there!"

Dave let out a heavy sigh. "Not interested."

"I beg your pardon?"

"Dave!" said Julian. "You're being rude."

Dave looked up at the stranger. "Let me guess. You've got some sort of quest you'd like us to go on."

The man looked baffled. "Well, yes but –"

"You'd go yourself, but it's dangerous, and you have a wife and a sick child to think of."

"That's true, but –"

"But you promise to make it worth our while."

"Of course, but how do you –"

"This is Caverns and Creatures," said Dave. "We're in a tavern, and you're a mysterious stranger. That's how the game works."

"You speak in riddles, dwarf."

Tim had to hand it to Dave. He'd made an astute observation which would probably save them all a big headache. It was time to end this conversation.

Tim cleared his throat. "I'm sorry, sir. My friend is right. We've had a long day, and we really don't want anything more than a quiet drink."

The stranger pulled back his hood, revealing some of the cleanest blond hair Tim had yet seen in Cardinia. He looked like a Sunday school picture of Jesus. "If peace and intoxication are what you desire, these things I can provide. I have a private room in the back of the tavern, and I thought you might be interested in a finer vintage than the goblin piss you're drinking now."

Tim raised his glass and his eyebrows. "Listen, buddy. This is no goblin piss. Believe me. I know. I've …" He suddenly became aware of everyone staring at him. "…said too much, haven't I?"

"Um…" Julian broke the awkward silence that followed. "You said something about good booze?"

Dave glared at him. "Julian, no!"

The stranger smiled down at Julian. "All I ask is for you to hear my tale."

Dave shook his head.

Julian raised a reassuring hand to Dave and looked up at the stranger. "What if we tell you up front that there is no way we will do whatever it is you want us to do?"

"If that is your choice, so be it."

"I mean really," Julian continued. "No matter how heartbreaking the sob story you've got for us, we're just going to drink your booze, listen to what you have to say, and be on our way."

"I probably won't even listen," added Tim. He liked where Julian was going with this, and hoped his superfluous display of callousness might help convince Dave.

Dave frowned so hard that his head trembled. "I don't like this."

"I seek only to unburden myself of my woeful tale," said the stranger. "I expect nothing from you but a sympathetic ear, even if your sympathy is not genuine."

Tim looked up at the stranger. "Even if all you need us to do is run down to the market and fetch you a loaf of bread to feed your starving family, I'm going to say no."

"I understand."

"I'm serious," said Tim. "Even if your kids are on fucking fire, and you ask me to walk across the street and piss on them, I'm going to tell you to kiss my little halfling ass."

"Jesus, Tim," said Dave. "You've made your point. Take it down a notch."

"Your overzealous lack of compassion is noted and accepted," said the stranger. "This world is rife with charlatans and ne'er-do-wells. You are wise to steel yourself against false appeals to tender hearts."

"I'm smart," Tim corrected him. "Dave's the wise one." It didn't hurt to butter up Dave just a bit more. "What do you say, Dave? We've made it perfectly clear that we have every intention of abusing this man's generosity and ignoring his pleas for help. Do you feel better now?"

"Not really."

"That's not a *no*."

"Actually, it kinda –"

"It's settled, then," said Tim. "Lead us, tall stranger, into drunken oblivion."

The stranger smiled. "When you've settled your affairs here, you may join me in booth number five. I'll be waiting." He turned his back to them and gracefully strode between tables full of drunk humans, quasi-humans, and straight up monsters toward the curtained booths at the back of the tavern.

Tim sucked down the rest of his skunky warm beer, spilling at least half as much down his shirt as he was spilling down his esophagus.

Dave took another shot of stonepiss. "This is so stupid. There is no way this will end well."

"That's it," said Tim. "No more bitching and moaning until I'm drunk enough to ignore it. Now go pay the tab and I'll meet you in booth five."

"Where are you going?" asked Julian.

"I've got to take a piss, and let Cooper know where we are."

"Check on Ravenus for me?"

Tim sighed. "Fine."

He walked out of the front entrance, not nearly drunk enough to call out to a bird in a British accent without feeling silly. But when free booze or sex was at stake, sometimes you just need to check your pride at the door.

"Ello! Ello!" Tim called into the darkening purple sky.

"Ho there, halfling!" said an elf passing by on the other side of the street. He was one of a group of five. With their wild hairstyles and black leather clothes, they looked like teenage ruffians, but you could never tell with an elf. They could have been three hundred years old for all Tim knew. "Are you talking to me?"

"Oh no," said Tim, instinctively reverting back to the Common tongue. "I was talking to a friend."

The leader of the elf pack made a show of looking left, then right, then back at Tim. "I don't see no friends." He continued to speak in his native Elven language, or British as far as Tim was concerned. "Is your *friend* an elf?"

"No!" said Tim, not quite sure of why he said it so abruptly. "He's a… bird." From the confused and angry looks on their faces, he guessed he wasn't helping his situation.

The leader tilted his head until his neck cracked. "He's a bird?"

The conversation was slipping away from Tim. If he wanted to avoid getting his ass kicked by The Cure, he needed to try an unskilled Diplomacy check. "I mean, it's not that I don't have elf friends. I have elf friends. Well *an* elf friend, but –"

"I don't see no birds neither, mate," said the leader, stepping into the street toward Tim. "And if your friend is a bird, that still don't explain why you was shoutin' out in Elven."

"I think he's takin' the piss out of us, Derrick," said one of the subordinate elves, the one with the green curtain of hair hanging down over the right side of his face.

"Is that right, halfling?" said the leader, Derrick. "Are you takin' the piss?"

Tim sighed with relief. "That's precisely what I came out here to do."

Derrick stopped in his tracks right in the middle of the street. He turned back to his friends and laughed. "Do you *believe* this guy?"

"He fancies himself a jester," said the green-haired elf.

Derrick pointed at Tim. "You's a funny little guy."

Tim wanted to take the words at face value, but sensed they were more menacing than that. "Um... thank you?"

Derrick glanced up and down the empty street, then scowled at Tim. "Let's see how funny you are with no tongue." He flicked his wrist, and there was suddenly six inches of shiny steel in his hand.

Tim felt a rush of warmth in his crotch area as he made good on his word to take *the* piss.

"Is there a problem here?" said a voice from behind, and significantly above, Tim's head.

Cooper. Tim relaxed, but made no effort to stem the flow of urine down his left leg. There was really no point now.

Derrick, staring up past Tim, took a step back and retracted his blade. "Who are you?"

Tim crossed his arms over his chest, confident in spite of his soaked pants. "This is my friend, Cooper."

"That ain't no bird, mate."

"What the fuck is he talking about?" asked Cooper.

"Hullo then!" said Ravenus, flapping down to perch atop a parked wagon. "What's the trouble?"

Tim was uncomfortable speaking in a British accent around actual elves, but fuck it. These guys were assholes, and his dignity was already puddled around his feet.

"Julian wanted me to make sure you were okay."

"Couldn't be better, sir!" said Ravenus. "There's a sickly dire rat around the back of the pub. He's not quite dead, but he's nearly there. Whatever he's dying from is causing his skin to rot, so he tastes about right. I've been pecking away at him a bit, you see."

"That's lovely," said Tim. "I'll be sure and let Julian know."

"Very good then," said Ravenus. "Toodle pip!" He flew out of sight over the roof of the building.

"Well I'll be," said the green-haired elf. "He was tellin' the truth about the bird after all."

"I beg your pardon, mate," said Derrick, backing further away still.

"Fuck off," said Tim. "Come on, Coop. We're getting the V.I.P. treatment in here."

Tim led Cooper back through the crowded tavern, past the table they had been sitting at, which was now occupied by a group of gnolls, and finally to the curtained private rooms at the rear of the establishment.

"Booth number five," said Tim. He pulled back the curtain.

Soft pink and green light emanated from sconces near the ceiling, casting a soft, multi-colored glow on the table and benches below, reflecting and refracting on the fancy glassware.

That was as much as Tim had time to notice before Dave shouted, "YOOOOOOOOO!"

He was standing on the bench, opposite Julian and the stranger, his left hand raised over his head in devil horns, and his right hand holding an empty glass bottle upside down like a microphone.

"His name is Cooper! He's always in a stupor! He's late for the party cuz he was in the pooper!"

"Please make this stop," said Tim, as Dave made a poor attempt at beatbox noises.

"His strength is super! So call a state trooper! If you wanna battle him, you can –"

Cooper ended Dave's rap career with a swift, controlled punch in the face. Dave collapsed neatly into a sitting position. Cooper shoved his unconscious body to the side and took a seat next to him.

"Can someone please fill me in on what's been going on since I went out for a dump?"

Tim gestured at the stranger. "This man, Mr…"

"Please, just call me Colin."

"He's buying us drinks in exchange for us listening to his bullshit."

Cooper scratched behind his ear. "Is this like a timeshare pitch?"

"No," said Tim. "It's something about his sick kid who we're absolutely not going to help."

"Fuck," said Cooper. "That sounds depressing as shit. Better hook me up with some of whatever Dave was drinking."

Julian stuck to beer, either genuinely interested in Colin's blathering about curses and witches and drinking water, or doing a hell of a job of feigning it.

Tim was tempted to join Cooper in drinking whatever Dave had gotten so trashed on, but he didn't have as high a Constitution score as either of those two. Any drink that made Dave think he could rap was sure to put Tim in a coma. He wasn't quite ready for that just yet, so he also stuck to beer.

The night carried on and the drinks kept flowing. Julian held the party true to their word by listening to Colin drone on about his problems while Tim and Cooper looked through the half-open curtain and discussed which of the tavern's patrons they'd most like to have sex with.

Without an abundance of mammalian females in the establishment, Tim and Cooper's conversation devolved into which of the patrons they'd be willing to have sex with in a pinch, and then if continued civilization depended on it.

"That's not what I said," Cooper explained as he poured the remaining contents of a bottle into his glass. "I said it's not gay if you get halfway through before you find out it's a dude, like in Thailand."

Tim, halfway through his fifth mug of beer, forgot what argument he had been trying to make, and nodded his surrender to Cooper. The beer was taking its toll, and Tim's eyelids were getting heavy.

"Dude!" said Cooper. "Don't fall asleep! This is important, man!" He lightly slapped Tim on the cheek.

Tim shook himself out of sleep's grasp. "I'm awake! I'm awake!"

Cooper gulped back the rest of his drink. "I know what you need."

"Huh?"

"Some music."

"No, I don't –"

Cooper pulled the curtain all the way open and stepped out of the booth. "Let's get this party started!"

"What is he doing?" cried Colin. "Get him back in here this instant!"

The tavern's patrons watched in stunned silence as Cooper tried to sing *YMCA*. He obviously didn't know any of the lyrics. The only words he articulated were "Young man" and "YMCA." Being illiterate, he didn't even know what the letters looked like, so his accompanying dance resembled something more like PTX4. He made it all the way to a second X before a glass flew out of the crowd and smashed him in the forehead. Cooper went down like a chopped tree, and conversations picked up where they'd left off.

Colin and Julian dragged Cooper back inside and sat him down next to Dave.

Colin pulled the curtain shut. "Well, that was… interesting."

"Maybe it's time we call it a night," said Julian.

"But I have not yet finished my tale."

"I think we've heard enough."

"I haven't heard shit," said Tim. There was no way he was leaving without having a taste of whatever this stuff was that made Dave and Cooper think they could sing. Dave still had a nearly full glass in front of him. "Let him talk a bit more."

"How am I supposed to get all of you assholes back to the Whore's Head?"

"Just one more drink," said Tim, eyeing Dave's glass.

Julian sighed. "Fine, but that's it."

As Colin started talking again, Tim sniffed Dave's drink. It smelled like citrus. He took a sip. It was sweet and made his mouth tingle.

"Fantastic," he mumbled to himself before gulping back the rest of the glass.

"Okay," said Julian. "That was nice and quick. Now let's get out of here. Thank you for a wonderful night, Mr. Colin. We're sorry we can't help youuuuuuuuuuuu…"

Time slowed down. Tim's vision was suddenly in polarized shades of blue and orange. The rest of the night was like a series of shuffled photographs.

Julian screamed, clutching his forearm.

Colin's face elongated and became covered in fur. He had fangs and glowing red eyes. *Sweet!*

Ravenus was flapping around, scratching Colin in the face. Blue feathers everywhere.

Tim was standing on top of the table, singing *My Sharona*.

Gnolls carried them all outside and dumped them on the street.

*

Tim awoke to the sound of a loud, hacking cough. He was wet and cold and uncomfortable. He opened his eyes and found that his vision was no longer made up of vivid oranges and blues. In fact, he may have lost all sense of color completely. All he could see was grey. The sky. It was raining.

The cough again.

Tim turned his head, and his face came in contact with Cooper's slimy wet skin. *Ew.* He turned his head the other way, and his nose rubbed against rough wood. The sound of wooden wheels rolling through mud registered in his mind. They were in the back of a cart. He sat up.

A muddy trail flowed beneath them like a river. After a second's consideration, Tim reasoned that they, rather than the trail, were the ones moving.

Cough. Cough.

It was Dave. He was lying on Cooper's arm, hacking like a two-pack-a-day smoker and reaching down for a nonexistent blanket.

Tim stretched his back and neck to look behind him and saw that Julian was riding the horse that was pulling the cart. At least it looked like Julian from behind. The brim of his sombrero sagged down with water, obscuring his head. Tim had no reason to believe it wasn't Julian, but could think of no reason for them all to be on a cart headed for who-knew-where at the ass crack of dawn in the rain.

"Dave!" Tim whispered.

"I'm ready when you are, baby," said Dave. He gave up on the blanket and placed a hand over Cooper's nipple.

When Tim got over his initial fit of gagging, he retrieved his dagger from the sheath beneath his vest, held it by the blade, and reached over to clonk Dave on the helmet with the pommel.

"What!" said Dave. "Okay, I'm up. I'm just... give me a sec, okay."

"Oh good," said Julian. "You guys are awake? Hold on. I've only got maybe thirty minutes left on this Mount spell. I'm going to pick up the pace a bit."

"Jesus!" cried Dave, coming to terms that he'd been caressing Cooper's man-tit in his sleep. He sprang to his feet like reverse footage of a marionette being dropped. The cart jolted forward, and Dave lost his balance. He fell right off the back, splashing into the mud.

"Julian!" shouted Tim. "Stop the cart! We lost Dave!"

"Dammit!" said Julian. "Whoa!" The cart stopped moving and Julian turned around. "I told you guys to hang on."

Cooper sat up. "What's going on? Why is my nipple hard?" His eyes went wide. "Shit! Mudman!" He leapt off the back of the cart and tackled Dave, who was covered in mud and stumbling toward them.

"Get off me!" said Dave, struggling under Cooper's weight.

"Knock it off, Cooper," said Tim. "That's Dave, and you know it."

Cooper stood up. "It could've been a mudman."

"That's not even a thing."

"I hope you guys are happy," said Julian, his boots squishing in the mud as he joined the others at the rear of the cart. "Our first horse just timed out."

Dave sat up in his muddy puddle. "Where are we? What are we even doing out here?" He glared up at Julian. "We're on a quest, aren't we? I told you this would happen! I said let's go back to the Whore's Head, but nobody listened to me. You and your stupid bleeding heart had to –"

"It's not my heart that's bleeding, Vanilla Ice," said Julian. "It's my arm." He pulled his left arm out from beneath his serape. He had a purple bruise, about the size of a baseball, on the underside of his forearm. In the middle of it was a football-shaped pattern of puncture wounds. He'd been bitten.

"Ouch," said Tim. "That looks bad." Fractured memories of the previous night flashed in his head.

"Ya think?"

"That Colin guy. Did he turn into a wolf at some point? Or did I dream that?"

"He's a werewolf," said Julian. "And if we don't bring him some golden figurine from some stupid ancient shrine before the next full moon, I'm going to be a werewolf too."

"Sweet!" said Cooper.

"It's not sweet," said Julian. "I don't want to be a fucking werewolf!"

"Why not? Think about it." Cooper counted off the justifications for his position on his fingers. "You'd have a super sense of smell. Girls would line up for miles to ride your wolf dick. Ummm... you'd be awesome at basketball."

"Cooper," said Tim. "Could you please shut the fuck up for a minute."

"Yeah, all right."

Tim wiped the rain off of his face and looked up at Julian. "Don't listen to Cooper. You most certainly do *not* want to be a werewolf. You'll have to make a whole bunch of Saving Throws every time there's a full moon, or you'll lose control of yourself and go on a murderous rampage. That's almost certainly grounds for Frank kicking us out of the Whore's Head."

"You guys," said Dave, still sitting in the mud. "If there's a remedy available, why don't we just go back into town and buy it?"

Tim and Cooper looked at Julian.

"You honestly think that wouldn't occur to me?" asked Julian. "Colin said the only cure was to drink a vial of blood from the same creature who bit me. I guess it works like a vaccine or something."

"Something's not right," said Dave. "I don't remember anything about that from the Monster Manual."

"What *do* you remember?"

"Not much," Dave admitted. "Lycanthropy was complicated. You had to keep track of moon cycles, Saving Throws, Willpower checks, and a whole bunch of other shit, so we never really used them much in our games."

"Come on," said Julian. "You guys have been playing this game for years. One of you must remember something about werewolves."

Tim thought hard, grasping for any recollection. "I remember they have Damage Resistance to anything but silver or magical weapons."

"Okay great! Now how about something useful?"

Tim, Dave, and Cooper exchanged shameful glances before turning back to Julian.

"Seriously? Nothing?"

"Dave's right," said Cooper. "The lycanthropy rules are too complicated. Who wants to keep track of all that shit? We just wanted to drink beer and roll dice."

Julian shook his head. "You must be the worst group of gamers in the history of Caverns and Creatures."

Tim squished some mud between his toes. "How much time do we have? When's the next full moon?"

"What do I look like?" Julian snapped. "A fucking astrologer?"

"I'm just trying to help."

"I know. I'm sorry. I'm just a little freaked out by all this. A dude bit me, and I've got his infected spit flowing around in my blood."

"Yeah, that's fucked up," said Cooper.

Julian looked skyward. "I couldn't see the moon because of the clouds. I could have anywhere from a day to the better part of a month."

Tim nodded. "Best not take any chances."

"Right. So everyone hop back on the cart, and I'll summon another horse."

Dave stood up. "When did we get a cart?"

"I think we stole it," said Julian. "It was parked on the street outside the tavern when we got thrown out. Colin helped me load you guys onto it and told me to take it. I wasn't exactly in a position to argue."

The rain continued to fall as Julian used up the rest of his Mount spells. The trail led into dense jungle that no party of low level adventurers had any business going into. The trees themselves looked like they might reach out and grab Tim if he let his guard down for a second. The roots slowed the cart to almost walking speed. The one nice thing about the rain was that he didn't have to step off the trail in order to pee. His clothes were already soaking wet, and he could piss himself without anyone knowing. Then again, judging by the hours they'd spent on the trail already with no one calling for a pee break, his friends had likely come to the same conclusion.

When the last magical horse disappeared, they had to abandon the cart and continue on foot. The jungle was alive with strange noises. Creatures snarled, slithered, and hissed from just beyond where Tim could see. His eyes darted left and right as he pointed his trembling crossbow toward every sound he heard.

"Great news, gents!"

Thwang.

"FUCK!"

"Shit," said Tim. "Sorry, man. I didn't –"

"Put that thing away!" said Cooper, plucking the bolt out of his ass. He flung it into the dark jungle.

"You found something?" Julian asked Ravenus, who had been the one who'd scared the shit out of Tim.

Ravenus perched atop Julian's quarterstaff. "A tree decorated with skulls."

"Under what set of circumstances would that ever be considered *great news*?" asked Dave.

"It's the last of the landmarks Colin told me about," said Julian. "It means we're almost there. Good work, Ravenus. Stay close, okay?"

After another ten minutes of trudging through the mud, they saw it. Ravenus's description had not adequately prepared Tim for the horror standing before them. This wasn't just some lazy goth kid's Christmas tree. It was a living nightmare.

The trunk was thick and black. Low-hanging branches reached out like tentacles, the ends of which sprouted smaller tentacle fingers tipped with dark purple heart-shaped leaves. Blue-green vines covered the trunk like varicose veins, wrapping around branches, worming through the eyes, noses, and mouths of the skulls.

And there were so many skulls. Different shapes and sizes. Some were human sized. Some were smaller or bigger, ranging from halfling to half-orc. A curious number of them had no eye sockets. Just flat bone where eyes should be.

As disturbing as that was, the thing that frightened Tim most was a relatively fresh dwarven head. It hung upside down by its long, brown beard, staring at Tim with its cloudy hazel eyes.

"This is amazing!" said Julian. "I wish I could take these back home to show my anthropology professor."

"Yeah," said Tim. "Me, too. Like, right now." He felt Julian wasn't appreciating the message implied by a tree full of skulls. If his anthropology professor was here, he might suggest it was a warning that they should all get the fuck away from this place as quickly as possible.

"I've found it, sir," said Ravenus, settling on the branch under the dwarf head. "There's a clearing to the southeast with a man-made structure at the center." He pecked out one of the hazel eyes.

"Jesus!" said Dave.

Julian looked away. "Good work, Ravenus."

Julian led them off the trail, into the thick undergrowth of the jungle. Not a single plant let them pass by without either taking something (blood, skin, bits of fabric from their clothes) or giving something (powder, slime, barbed seeds). They swam through a sea of vegetation, easy prey for anyone, or anything, that might call this place home.

Tim didn't know if they'd traveled mere yards or full miles when they finally broke free of the jungle's grasp. The sky, still cloudy as it was, was a welcome sight. It was brighter than Tim expected. How long had they been traveling? How long had it been since he'd slept, the time spent passed out drunk notwithstanding?

"That's it?" said Cooper.

The clearing was perfectly circular, probably the same area as a football field. The soil was as dark and rich as that of the surrounding jungle, but not a single plant grew within it. At the center of the clearing stood a modest stone structure about the size of a shipping container. It was mostly unadorned, except for a symbol above the entrance, which looked like an empty Venn diagram. The only other thing in the clearing was a large log, about two feet thick and twelve feet long, lying on the ground next to it.

"It's not much of a temple," said Julian.

Tim scanned the clearing and put his hand on the grip of his crossbow. "At least it should be easy enough to search."

"I don't think so," said Dave. "That symbol above the doorway. Those are the double rings of Yulu Hari, the goddess of Life and Death. Any temple to her would be round. My guess is this is one of several entrances. The temple itself is underground."

"Shit," said Cooper, Julian, and Tim.

"Get down!" Julian whispered.

The four of them crouched at the edge of the jungle as a pale, muscular, almost naked man emerged from the structure. He wore a loincloth nearly as ratty as Cooper's. His scraggly grey hair hung over his face. He was carrying a wooden pail.

"Do you think he saw us?" whispered Dave.

"I don't think he *saw* shit," said Cooper. "Look at him."

A small gust of wind blew the hair out of the man's face for a second, revealing his lack of eyes.

"I know these guys!" Julian whispered excitedly. "We saw some of their skulls in the tree."

"That's really fucking interesting," said Tim. "Now keep your voice down."

The eyeless creature sniffed the air, turning his head left and right. Could he smell intruders? Would he soon have four new decorations for his tree? Tim held his breath. The creature walked vaguely, but not directly, toward them, stopping once again to sniff the air when he was about a quarter of the way between the temple entrance and the edge of the jungle. He dumped the contents of his bucket, a lumpy brown liquid, on the ground.

Tim thought he heard faint scratching and clawing sounds, but couldn't see anything to account for them.

The creature lifted the front of his loincloth and started to piss. The sound of his urine hitting the ground seemed off by a fraction of a second. Were Tim's ears playing tricks on him? Then there was a hiss. Tim was sure he heard that, but couldn't account for the source. The only candidate was the creepy blind guy taking a leak, and he looked like he was really enjoying it because he was laughing. His laughter was deep and throaty. Whatever had hissed, it certainly wasn't him. Having finished his business, he picked up his pail and went back inside.

Tim exhaled. "Hey Dave. This goddess, Yolo Honey."

"Yulu Hari," said Dave.

"Whatever. Is she a good goddess or an evil goddess."

"She's neutral."

"That figures." Tim stood up and looked into the clearing. "I suppose hoping she was good was a longshot. Not that it matters much. These guys aren't going to – Wait a second."

"What's wrong?" asked Julian.

"Where's that dude's piss puddle? And the shit he dumped on the ground?" The clearing was flat and featureless.

Julian shrugged. "Is that really the most interesting thing you feel you've seen today?"

"I just think it's strange that it's not there. Don't you?"

"I don't know," said Julian. "Maybe he kicked some dirt over it."

Cooper rubbed his belly. "I've got a good one brewing if you want to watch."

"Jesus, Cooper!" said Tim. "Why would you even –" His whole body shuddered. "I really didn't need that image in my head."

"Listen guys," said Julian. "We don't know how much daylight we've got left, or when the next full moon is. So maybe we should stop screwing around."

"We need a plan," said Tim. "We can't just walk in there blindly."

Julian grinned and nudged Cooper with his elbow. "I think we all just witnessed evidence to the contrary."

Everyone frowned at Julian.

"'Cause he's got no eyes," Julian explained. "He walked in there *blindly*."

"Meh," said Cooper. "It's funnier than a Dave joke."

"Hey!" said Dave.

Tim put his hands on his hips and glared at Julian. "Wasn't someone just saying something about how we should stop screwing around?"

"Sorry."

"Let's get to the entrance first and figure out how to proceed from there. Keep your voices down. These things are blind, which probably means they have an excellent sense of hearing. So stay close, and stay quiet."

Tim started walking into the clearing as silently as he could. Julian walked ahead with him, while Cooper and Dave lagged behind a few yards.

"That guy was sniffing the air a lot," Julian whispered to Tim. "They probably have a good sense of smell as well."

"Speaking of which, do you smell that?" The air was suddenly ripe with the stench of sewage. It was like they just walked into a cloud of concentrated Cooper. "Where the fuck is that coming frooooo—"

Splat.

Tim turned over. He'd fallen at least ten feet and landed on his face, but he wasn't hurt. His fall had been broken by a soft layer of... He looked at his hands, then at the ground around him. "Shit!"

"Tim?" said Julian. He was standing on the side of the trench, staring down, but not at Tim. The ground was an illusion. Tim could see out, having fallen through it, but Julian couldn't see in.

"Shit! Shit! Shit!" said Tim. He was covered in soupy excrement. He could feel it seeping into the hundreds of tiny cuts the jungle plants had given him.

"Where are you?" Julian asked. He turned around. "I don't know. He just disappeared. He's around here somewhere. He keeps saying *Shit*."

Tim was about to break down and start crying when he saw a familiar face. About twenty feet away from him, a dire rat snarled and bared its brown, shit-stained teeth. Behind it, two more giant rats stared at him through their beady little demon eyes. The largest of the three had a face full of wet fur, and looked none too pleased about it. Tim had faced stronger, more objectively terrifying creatures than these Rottweiler-sized rodents, but since one of their kind had been the first creature in this world to nearly kill him, he had a special terror reserved just for them.

"Ro – Ro – Ro –"

"...your boat?" asked Julian.

"Rope!" Tim remembered he had a rope in his bag. He reached

inside, grabbed the coil of rope, wrapped his wrist with one end, and threw the rest of the coil up out of the trench.

"Hey," said Julian. "That's incredible. How did you do that?"

"Pull the goddamn rope!"

The rope pulled him up by the arm just in time to avoid the first rat lunge. The piss-face rat jumped up at him, though, catching his left pant leg.

Tim's vision went wonky as Julian and the dire rat played tug-of-war with him. His head kept bobbing up over the surface of the illusory ground, making it appear as if he was buried up to the neck. And then the rat would pull harder, and he'd see the horrifying reality below.

Dave tipped the scales in the tug-of-war game. He and Julian pulled Tim up out of the trench. The rat's head was now the one bobbing above and below the surface of the illusion as it held on to Tim's pant leg. It looked like a glitchy computer game.

Cooper finally grabbed the dire rat, pulled it away from Tim, and body slammed it back into the trench.

Julian wiped sweat off his forehead. "I guess that explains what the log is for."

"Cooper," said Tim. "This trench is about ten feet wide. Do you think you could jump that?"

"No sweat," said Cooper. "There aren't a whole lot of Strength based skills, so I put all my points into Swim, Climb, and Jump. I could make that jump with Dave's mom hanging on my dick."

Dave shook his head. "That doesn't even mean anything. That was just purposeless vulgarity."

Tim got on his hands and knees and pawed at the ground until he found the edge. "Okay, Cooper. Get a running start. The edge is here where my hand is."

Cooper ran, jumped, and landed easily on the other side of the invisible trench. As strong as he was, it took every point of Strength he had to lift that log up to a standing position. He carefully felt for the edge of the trench with his foot as he rolled the vertical log into place, then let it fall to the other side, bridging the trench.

Tim and Julian crossed the log with ease. Dave had a tougher time of it, and nearly lost his balance at the end, but Cooper caught him by the arm and pulled him safely the rest of the way.

"Well here we are," said Julian. "Who wants to go in first?"

"I'm going in alone," said Tim. "Can you make me a light?"

"That's crazy," said Cooper. "You almost got killed by a fucking rat just now. How are you gonna take on an army of eyeless assholes?"

"I'm not going to take them on. I'm going to sneak in, get what we came for, and sneak back out again."

Julian shook his head. "I can't let you do that. I'm the reason we're here. At least I've got to go in with you. I can be quiet."

"I'm a rogue," said Tim. "This is what I'm made for. I've got a bunch of ranks in the Move Silently skill. Those are all for nothing if I have you guys tagging along. You're a sorcerer. Now sorcer me up a light."

Julian touched Tim's crossbow. "Light." The weapon glowed with a soft, white light.

"I'm just going to take a peek inside first," said Tim. "Give me ten minutes." He stepped into the open entrance, then turned to his friends. "Or until I start screaming."

Taking his first steps down the stone stairs, Tim felt strange to be Moving Silently while carrying a glowing weapon. It seemed counterintuitive. He'd be the most visible thing in the whole temple. *They don't have eyes. Light means nothing to them.*

He descended about fifty more steps before he came to his first obstacle. A set of black velvet curtains with the goddess's symbol embroidered in gold thread. *The double rings of whatever the fuck her name was.*

Tim licked his dry lips. They tasted like shit. Should he go back and report this? No. This wasn't information that would serve a purpose. Whatever was on the other side of that curtain was what was important. If he turned back now, it would only be because he was too scared to look. *Come on, Tim.*

Trying not to think about what he was doing, he felt for the edge of the left curtain. The glowing crossbow, loaded and cocked, felt heavy in his right hand. His heart was racing and he knew that he'd shoot at anything he saw, whether it was a threat or not. With his luck, it would probably be a gong, or a set of wind chimes. He moved his finger away from the trigger.

On one. Ready? One!

He pulled back the curtain and thrust his crossbow inside to reveal…

More stairs?

Tim sighed silently, trying to force his heart rate to slow. Why the hell would they even put a curtain there? It's not much of a defense. But then, this wasn't meant to be a fortress. It was a place of worship.

The stairway beyond the curtain curved gently to the right. Twenty steps later, Tim arrived at another set of curtains, identical to the first. He pulled the left curtain back and was not surprised to see more stairs. He was surprised, however, to hear faint chanting. It wasn't in any language he understood, but it must have been at least a hundred voices strong.

That's what the curtains were for, to absorb sound. Tim followed the stairs down in an increasingly tighter spiral until he reached a third and, from the clarity of sound on the other side, final set of curtains.

His heart was beating fast again. He pulled the curtains apart very slowly, just enough to peek through. As he expected, it was too dark on the other side without the aid of his glowing crossbow to see much, but he appeared to be on the edge of an enormous pit, with orange light coming from somewhere below.

Reminding himself again that these creatures had no eyes, he worked up the courage to step through the curtains. The chamber was vast. Tim found himself on the top tier of something like a Greek theater. Concentric circles formed ten foot high steps that eventually led down to a fire pit with a stone dais raised out of the flames at its center. A lone figure stood atop the dais, chanting words that Tim couldn't understand. Above his eyeless head, he held a six inch golden statue, no doubt the item they had been tasked with stealing. A congregation of at least two hundred worshipers stood on the second tier, repeating the chant. *How the fuck were they going to pull this off?*

"Guard!" shouted a voice from the tier below Tim. "Guard! I'm hungry! I'm so hungry!"

Tim got on his knees and peeked over the edge. The upper tiers of the temple were much less populated than the lower ones, but this asshole was calling a lot of attention to himself, and potentially to Tim as well.

One of the eyeless creatures – Tim was almost certain it was the same one they'd seen outside – stomped toward the source of the pleading voice. He didn't look pleased. He paused briefly as he passed under Tim's position and sniffed the air. He raised his upper lip in disgust, showing off his rotten teeth as he faced Tim directly. Tim remained perfectly still, holding his breath and trying not to piss himself again.

"Guard!" shouted the voice again. "I'm hungry!"

The creature broke his non-gaze away from Tim and continued stomping toward the prisoner.

"No food!" said the creature. "You. Eat. Morning!"

"Oh," said the prisoner. "Okay."

That's it? Okay? How hungry could you be, you fat fucker? You nearly got me killed!

Then it occurred to him. The prisoner wasn't trying to get the guard's attention. He was trying to get *his* attention. He'd seen the light from the crossbow, and wanted to let Tim know he was there. But he couldn't very well shout *Hey! Come help me!* Not bad thinking on his part.

Normally, Tim would look at this as another chore to heap on the pile, but this guy might actually be useful. There were a hell of a lot of those things between him and the golden statue. Tim was ready to take whatever help he could get.

He crawled back to the curtains leading to the staircase, in case he needed to make a run for it, and waited for the guard to go away. Grumbling as he left, the guard proved easy to keep track of by sound.

When Tim deemed it safe enough, he sneaked to just above where he estimated the prisoner's voice to have been coming from. The tiers were interrupted by staircases every couple of hundred feet, and

Tim was right in the middle of two of them. Each one had a few of the eyeless creatures milling about, so he decided to take the fast way down. He crept up to the edge of the tier he was standing on, and lowered himself down until he was hanging by his fingertips. There was still about six feet of empty space between his feet and the next tier, but he didn't think that would amount to any loss of Hit Points. He let go.

As soon as he landed, two meaty hands lunged out at him, grabbed his upper arms, and pulled him up against iron bars. The dwarf on the other side of the bars averted his eyes as if in pain.

"You have to help me!" he whispered.

"That's what I'm trying to do, fucktard," said Tim. "Let go of me so I can get you out of there. And for fuck's sake, keep your voice down."

The dwarf released Tim's arms. While Tim dug through his bag for his thieves' tools, the dwarf hunkered down next to him.

"They killed my brother two days ago," said the dwarf, wringing his hands. "I fear they will come for me tonight."

Tim unrolled his picks and chose the one he thought best suited to this particular lock. "Your brother didn't have hazel eyes, did he?"

A tear rolled down the dwarf's dirty, haggard face. "Aye, and a beautiful pair of eyes they were. How is it you come to guess that?"

Tim tried to remain focused on the lock. He felt around inside for the tumblers. "Just lucky. I've got a really high Intelligence."

"I won't argue that," said the dwarf. "It was right smart of you to cover yourself in grimlock excrement."

"Grimlock!" said Tim. Since he saw the first one outside, he had been trying to remember what these things were called.

"They can find an outsider by scent."

The lock popped, more loudly than Tim would have preferred. "Shit!" What was he doing? This wasn't part of the plan.

"Olag will have heard that," said the dwarf.

"Who the fuck is Olag?"

"He's the grimlock in charge of guarding me. Real nasty feller."

"Yeah," said Tim. "I think I know the one." The door creaked when Tim pushed it. Figuring it best to avoid a prolonged noise, Tim relied on ripping-off-a-Band-Aid logic and gave it a good hard push. Noisy as the door was, it was surprisingly light on the hinges. The scream of iron on iron was loud enough to interrupt the chanting a hundred feet below them, and the clang of door against cage didn't help matters either.

"Olag will certainly have heard that."

"Shit," said Tim. He'd fucked up trying to rescue this stupid dwarf. The statue was going to have to wait. "Let's move."

He took a step toward the stairway on the right, but there was Olag, running at them with a raised battleaxe, screaming like an enraged chimpanzee. Tim fired his crossbow. The sphere of light which had been surrounding him was now surrounding the grimlock.

"That fucking idiot!" said Tim. "He enchanted the bolt!"

Olag fell, and the light turned dim and pink as blood gushed out of his throat. It was a Critical Hit for sure, which was nice, but left Tim and his fugitive dwarf in the dark. Hostile voices barked orders and angry battle cries. The chanting from below turned to chaos.

"Boost me up!" said the dwarf.

"I need to get my bolt back," said Tim. "I can't see without it!"

"Well I *can* see, halfling. And I'm telling you, there's no time. We must flee now!"

Tim believed him. The howls and barks that made up whatever language the grimlocks spoke were getting louder by the second. He locked his fingers together for the dwarf to step onto. The dwarf climbed from Tim's hands to the horizontal cell bar, then to the top of the tier and disappeared from Tim's view.

"Hey!" shouted Tim, no longer making any effort to keep quiet. "Don't you fuck off on me now!"

"Hurry!" said the dwarf, his hand reaching down as far as it could go. These were not the two most ideal races to be attempting such a maneuver.

Tim had always thought it kind of dumb that halflings got a +2 bonus to Jump checks, considering they got a -2 penalty for Strength, which is the ability score that the Jump skill depends on. But he was grateful for that bonus when he grabbed a cell bar, sprang into the air, and caught the dwarf's hand.

Olag's blood had obscured most of the light Tim's bolt was giving off, leaving Tim as good as blind.

"Hurry!" the dwarf repeated, grabbing Tim's arm and taking off in the direction of the stairwell Tim had entered from. Tim stumbled along blindly, trying to keep up as best as he could.

A particularly enraged roar, much closer than the general cacophony of roars currently echoing all over the temple, came from right in front of them.

"Get down!" said the dwarf. Tim was already on the floor with his arms wrapped over the top of his head. Sparks flashed as steel clanged against stone, but thankfully without the preceding sound of cutting through dwarf.

"Hnnng!" said the nearby grimlock. Tim could only assume that was Grimlockian for *I just got uppercutted in the nuts by a pissed off dwarf*. It's similar in any language.

The grimlock's axe fell to the floor. The next sound Tim heard was a dwarven grunt, followed by a grimlock scream, which fell away and abruptly stopped about ten feet below them.

"Come, halfling!" said the dwarf. "I have his axe, but dozens more approach." Tim felt the dwarf grab his arm and jerk him forward again. "We can't outrun them. Our only hope is to retreat to the stairwell and take them two at a time. We'll take as many of the eyeless bastards to the Abyss with us as we can!"

Tim felt the velvet brush over him as they passed through the curtain. The dwarf dragged him up a few stairs, then stopped.

"Have you considered *not dying* as an option?"

"Alas, my boy. I fear it be too late for that. They run far swifter than the likes of us."

The angry howling and barking was growing closer. A mob of angry grimlocks was nearly upon them. Tim crouched on the stairs and felt around in his bag.

"Stand up, lad! Die bravely!"

"I'd rather live cravenly," said Tim. He pulled his caltrop sack out of his bag. "Let's go!" He grabbed the surprised dwarf by the arm and gave him a shove up the stairs.

"Huh?"

"Just move your ass, man!" Tim tossed a single caltrop over his shoulder as he scrambled up the stairs behind the dwarf. A few steps later, he tossed a second.

"Just dump the bag already, and let's be on our way!"

"No," said Tim, continuing his routine of climbing and tossing. "If I shoot my load right now, they'll have it cleared away and be up on our asses long before we reach the –"

A grimlock howled out in pain about twenty feet below them.

"They're right behind us!" said the dwarf, continuing up the stairs.

Tim tossed another caltrop and kept climbing. "But that one fucker with the punctured foot will slow down the whole mob."

Climb. Toss. Climb. Toss.

"They have two choices," Tim continued. "They can proceed very slowly and carefully, not being able to see, hear, or smell these. Or they can risk a hole in the foot. Either way, they're –"

"Hwaaaahhh!" screamed another grimlock, this one maybe thirty feet below them.

It's working!

Tim felt the second curtain brush by him.

"Ho there!" shouted the dwarf. "State your business!"

A long, wet fart squirted out from above.

"They're with me!" said Tim.

"Tim?" said Cooper. "Is that you?"

"Yeah, I'm behind the dwarf. Turn around and start running!"

The five of them hurried up the gradually curving staircase. Dave, being unable to run in his armor, soon fell behind until even Tim had to slow down to avoid hobbling him with caltrops.

Another grimlock screamed in pain. They were somewhere between twenty and thirty feet behind Tim. The lead they had been gaining was now limited by Dave's sluggish Movement Speed.

Ahead, Tim was relieved to see the first faint flashes of light as the rest of his friends passed through the final set of curtains. Cooper was even thoughtful – or clumsy – enough to tear them down on his way through. Finally, Tim could actually see where he was going.

Climb. Toss. Climb. Toss. The bag was getting lighter. He'd be out of caltrops soon.

They were still maintaining their short lead, and Tim guessed they'd probably reach the surface unscathed, but what then? There were still a couple of hundred grimlocks after them. Should they stand and fight at the entrance of the temple? Between the five of them, they'd be able to take down quite a few of these assholes if they kept coming out only two at a time, but they'd only be prolonging the inevitable. They couldn't outrun them either. Making a break for open ground was only asking to be surrounded and more quickly slaughtered. Their only hope was that someone else was working on a third option.

The light of day, grim and grey as it was, widened as Tim approached the top of the staircase.

"We're almost there, Dave," said Tim, trying to be encouraging. "Move your ass!"

Dave huffed as he marched up the stairs. "You know I'm going as fast as I can!"

Tim dumped the few remaining caltrops from his sack and bolted past Dave to the surface, where Julian was standing impatiently with an open scroll.

"Get out of the way!" said Julian. "Dave, move to the right!" He looked at the scroll, the parchment trembling in his hands. "Horse!"

Tim dove out of the way as a hefty black steed materialized next to Julian.

"Yah!" said Julian, slapping the beast on the rump. It obediently charged blindly into the temple entrance.

"Fuck!" Dave shouted from within. The clash of metal, stone, and probably hoof, echoed out from the darkness of the staircase.

"Shit," said Julian. He called down to Dave, "I meant *my* right. I should have specified. My bad."

Dave finally emerged, among the screams of angry grimlocks and the whinny of a surprised horse, trudging up the last few stairs. He had a black left eye, his face was all scraped up, and his nose was bleeding into his beard. He didn't say a word as he limp-waddled past Tim, toward the log bridge, revealing a fresh hoof print on the backplate of his armor.

"I'm really angry!" said Cooper when Dave, Julian, Tim, and the other dwarf had crossed to the outer edge of the invisible trench. His body grew thick with four Strength Points' worth of muscle, and he picked the log up off the ground with ease.

"Good idea, Coop," said Tim. "Cut off their means of follow— What the fuck are you doing?"

Cooper turned around to face the temple entrance.

"Bwaaahhh!" said the first grimlock to reach the surface. He brandished his battleaxe as he sniffed the air for someone to hit with it. His nose wrinkled as he faced Cooper, but his disgust didn't last long. Cooper sent him back downstairs with a log to the chest. Several grimlocks just behind him screamed as they were forced back.

Cooper ran and jumped a good five feet before reaching the edge of the trench, but still landed about five feet beyond the other side.

"Julian, Dave, new guy!" said Tim. "Start running. We'll catch up with you at the skull tree."

"What are you going to do?" asked Julian.

"We have to stay back and fix Cooper's latest blunder."

Julian needed no further explanation. He, Ravenus, and the two dwarves bolted toward the jungle.

"You said it was a good idea," said Cooper, who had recovered from his Barbarian Rage.

"That's because I thought you were going to throw the log into the trench," said Tim. "I didn't think you were going to hand them their bridge."

"But did you see the look on that dude's face when I hit him with the log?"

Tim grinned as he loaded a bolt into his crossbow. "Yeah, that was pretty epic."

"So," said Cooper. "What are we doing?"

Tim trained his crossbow on the temple entrance as angry grimlock voices once again approached the surface. "As soon as they lay down that log, you're going to shove it into the trench."

The first two grimlocks emerged unburdened by their log. Tim chose a target, but held his fire, waiting to see what they would do. Both of them sniffed the air, homed in on Tim and Cooper, and started running for the trench.

Tim waited for his chosen target to get within about ten feet of where he'd have to jump from before firing his crossbow. As he'd hoped, the bolt interrupted his jump, but not his inertia. The injured grimlock stumbled, fell, and disappeared beneath the illusory ground.

The other grimlock cleared the trench, swinging his axe down at Cooper as he landed on the other side. Cooper ducked the blow and punched the grimlock in its eyeless face. It fell backwards into the trench. Invisible though they were, both grimlocks could be heard screaming as they tried to fend off what sounded like an army of hungry dire rats.

The next four grimlocks emerged with the log. The two at the front stood at the edge of the trench. With rehearsed timing, the four of them swung the log twice before releasing it, forming a perfect bridge, which they quickly used.

They were so efficient, in fact, that the first two were already on top of Cooper by the time he got a hold on the log. They tried to wrestle him away from it, but Cooper held on.

Tim drew his dagger, ran up, and stabbed one of the grimlocks in the small of the back. It let out a single, sharp cry, but Tim knew it was dead before it fell over and disappeared into the trench.

As the second pair of grimlocks stepped onto the bridge, Cooper gave up his struggle and concentrated fully on the log. While he succeeded in neutralizing the bridge, he did so at the cost of falling into the trench with it. Dire rats shrieked under the sudden weight of a log, a half-orc, and three more grimlocks.

"Cooper!" cried Tim, loading his crossbow again.

"I'm okay," Cooper called up. "Give me a minute!"

"We don't have a minute!" said Tim as two more grimlocks came limping out of the temple entrance. These two had obviously fallen victim to his caltrops. As pissed off as they appeared, Tim reasoned that they were no immediate threat. They didn't look to be in any state for trench-jumping.

The next two, however, looked perfectly nimble, as did the two that followed them.

There was a hell of a fight going on just below Tim's feet. Axes clanged against rocks. Rats squealed and hissed. Grimlocks grunted, growled, and barked. Cooper swore a lot. Tim wanted to help out, shoot something that wasn't Cooper, but he couldn't see anything beneath the façade of still, featureless earth.

Firing his crossbow might also give his position away. Tim couldn't be sure, but he didn't think the gathering crowd of grimlocks was paying any attention to him. His scent must still be masked. They looked to be far more interested in the fight below.

More than a dozen grimlocks crowded at the edge of their side of the trench, eagerly cheering whenever they heard a dire rat squeal. Tim got the feeling that they did this sort of thing for recreation. It reminded him of listening to a boxing match on the radio. Still more grimlocks filed out of the stairwell, some limping, some not, all eager to listen to the battle raging on below.

"Fuck! No! Get that one!" Cooper sounded as though he'd formed a temporary alliance with the surviving grimlocks. Getting trapped in a shit pit full of dire rats makes unlikely bedfellows.

Tim wanted to call out for his friends to come back, or call for Cooper to hurry up and do whatever he had planned. Keeping silent was driving him nuts.

"Ha ha!" said Cooper as one of the grimlocks below grunted. "Stupid fucker." One of the dire rats gave a particularly agitated squeal before flying out of the ground like it had been launched with a catapult.

The dire rat landed in the middle of the crowd of about fifty grimlocks, who then proceeded to freak the fuck out. The chaos that erupted was beautiful. Grimlocks screamed, shoved, and started swinging their axes with wild abandon. At least eight of them, who had been too close to the edge, fell into the trench, where they were met with more bloodthirsty rats and Cooper.

"Fuck! You!"

Two seconds later, a grimlock head flew into the crowd. This neither stemmed nor bolstered the panic-driven madness, as none of them could see it. *Nice try, Cooper.*

A second dire rat thrown into the fray, however, bolstered the madness quite nicely. Then Cooper's hands popped out of the ground, followed by the rest of him. He was scraped up, bloodied, and covered in shit, but he'd looked worse.

"Let's get the fuck out of here," said Cooper, climbing the rest of the way out of the trench. He picked up Tim and started running.

Tim fired his crossbow into the crowd of rat-crazed grimlocks because *why the fuck not?* He didn't know if he hit any of them or not. They were all screaming.

"How did you get out of the pit?" Tim asked, bouncing under Cooper's arm as they crashed through jungle foliage.

"I piled up a few grimlock bodies, climbed on those, and used my Jump skill."

"It's more useful than I'd given it credit for."

Before long, Cooper and Tim caught up to the others at the skull tree. Cooper set Tim on the ground.

The dwarf sat against the black trunk of the skull tree, cradling the head of his dead brother. "O Baelrick, sweet brother. What beautiful eyes you once had. How I hoped to gaze upon them one last time as I say goodbye. But alas, those savage devils deny me even that!" He turned the head outward to show how his brother's eyes had been removed.

"Pfft," said Cooper. "That was no savage devil. That –"

Julian clonked him on the head with his quarterstaff. "Shut up, Cooper!"

"What the fuck!"

Tim watched curiously as Julian attempted to cover what Cooper had already blabbed while simultaneously justifying his own outburst.

"The man is grieving," Julian explained slowly and deliberately. "The *grimlocks* ripped out this man's eyes. If that isn't savagery, then I don't know what is. This isn't the time for one of your lectures on racial harmony."

Well played, Julian. Would Cooper pick up the innuendo?

"Did you get hit in the fucking head? What the fuck are you talking about?"

Apparently not.

"We can talk about this later," said Julian, holding his staff like he

93

was ready to hit Cooper with it again. "Let the man grieve."

"I'm a dwarf," said the dwarf. "In case you haven't noticed." He stood up. "My name is Dodwynn. I thank you, halfling, for rescuing me."

Tim lowered his head. "I'm sorry we didn't arrive in time to save your brother as well."

"Don't be," said Dodwynn. "The grimlocks did him a kindness, believe it or not. I feared he was destined for a worse fate, which would have claimed both our lives."

"What's that?" asked Julian.

"Lycanthropy."

"You don't say."

"It was torture," said Dodwynn. "Every day we were locked in that cage, not knowing when he would turn. We nearly went mad trying to keep track of how much time had passed, trying to remember when we last saw the moon, and what phase it was in."

"How long were you down there?"

"It's impossible to say for sure. Based on my beard growth, close to a month. Baelrick must have been bitten just after a full moon."

"So if he was still alive," said Julian. "And he hadn't turned by now..."

"Then tonight would almost certainly be the night."

"We have to go back for that statue," said Cooper.

"Statue?" said Dodwynn. "You sought the holy figure? That was our quest as well. Were one of you bitten?"

"There's no time for that," said Julian. "If it's his blood I need, I'll just go and get it. Werewolf or not, how strong could he be? Surely the five of us can hold the bastard down while I bite him back, right?" He turned to Dodwynn. "That is, if you'll join us."

"I believe we seek the same creature," said Dodwynn. "For my brother's honor, I shall join you."

"Any objections?"

Tim shook his head. "I like our odds against one werewolf better than two hundred angry grimlocks."

Evening brought more rain, which fell on them even harder once they emerged from the jungle. Once night fell, everyone kept a sharp eye on Julian, looking for signs of his turning. The rain felt great to Tim. It washed away the crust of grimlock shit from his skin and clothes. He'd never felt so alive, and so ready to kill someone. Tim's desire to hunt down Colin was neither altruistic nor borne of his friendship for Julian. It was straight up vengeance.

It was still raining when they reached the main road leading back to Cardinia. Julian had made it through the night thus far with no hint of change, as evidenced by his answers to Dodwynn's continuous questions.

"Do you feel anything?"

"No."

"Not even a little tingle?"

"No."

"Do you feel maybe you've grown a bit more hair in your genital area?"

"NO!"

"It just don't make no sense." Dodwynn looked up, letting the rain splash on his face. "If only we could see through those clouds."

Julian stopped walking. "Of course! Why didn't I think of that before?" He looked at Ravenus, tucked under his serape. "Why didn't *you* think of that before?"

"Think of what, sir?" said Ravenus. "I've only been privy to the part of this conversation where you keep saying 'No.' It's a tad hard to follow."

"Ravenus, I need you to go up and look at the moon for me. Can you do that?"

"If you like, sir. But I'd much rather this be a moment we could share."

"Stay focused, Ravenus! This is important. I need you to go look at the moon, and then come back here and report. Got it?"

Ravenus nodded resolutely. "Right away, sir!" He launched himself from Julian's bosom and climbed into the night.

"I don't know what you expect to gain by this," said Dave.

"What are you talking about?" said Julian. "I'd like to have at least some idea of when I'm going to turn into a goddamn dog!"

"Does it change what we've got to do tonight?"

95

"It might."

"Suppose Ravenus comes back and tells us we've got two weeks left."

"Impossible," said Dodwynn.

"But what if?" Dave continued. "Are any of us really going to rest while there's the potential for you wolfing out on us? Whatever we're going to do, we've got to –"

Ravenus returned, spraying the group as he shook the water out of his feathers.

"Did you see it?" asked Julian.

"Yes, sir."

"And?"

"Well, I'm not sure what you're expecting, sir. I'm hardly a poet, and you haven't given me much time to –"

"What phase is it in?"

"Phase, sir?"

"Is it waxing, waning, full, new?"

"Oh," said Ravenus. "It's full."

"Full?"

"Quite full, sir." Ravenus cleared his throat and flapped his wings. "Like the eye of a goddess, it shines down on –"

"What does he mean, *it's full*?" asked Dodwynn. "That can't be. Why haven't you changed?"

"Could it be the cloud cover?" asked Tim. "Maybe you have to be exposed directly to the moonlight, like a vampire is only affected by the sun if the light actually touches him."

"Dunno," said Dodwynn. "T'wouldn't seem like all that big of an issue if it could be managed by staying indoors a couple of nights a month."

"I disagree," said Julian. "It still feels like a pretty big issue to me. I'd much rather bring the odds of me involuntarily killing all of my friends down from slim to none."

Dodwynn stroked his beard. "Could explain why my brother never turned."

Tim looked up at the sky. The clouds were still thick in the sky, but who knew how fast that could change? "We have to get you into town, like, pronto. You don't have any more Mount spells?"

Julian shook his head. "I used all I had to get us to the temple, and then I used my emergency scroll to send a horse down the stairs."

"Shit," said Tim. "You might still have a chance to fix this if you get back to Colin before you change. But if the weather clears up before we get there..." Tim bit his lower lip, trying to think of a way to move faster.

"I can dig a hole," said Cooper. "We'll bury Julian until the sun comes up."

Julian frowned. "Anyone feel free to jump in with an Option B."

"Is it after midnight?" asked Dave.

Cooper snorted. "If it isn't, then your fairy godmother fucked you over bigtime."

"If it's technically a new day, all of our one-use-per-day abilities reset. Julian can get his spells back. Cooper gets his Barbarian Rage. We've been through this before."

"I'm really angry!" said Cooper.

"Cooper!" said Tim, turning around. "You don't have to waste –"

But Cooper had already hulked out. He ran over to a young pine tree about as thick around as one of Tim's legs.

"Fuck you, tree!" He punched it in the trunk, felling it in one blow. He twisted and tore the top of the tree from the stump and hurled it like a harpoon into the meadow

"That wasn't strictly necessary," said Dave. "Sorcerers only need a few minutes of meditation to prepare their spells. We could have just waited for Julian to try."

Dodwynn scratched his head. "You all are a peculiar lot. The elf seems less affected by the moon than any of you."

While Cooper spent the remainder of his Barbarian Rage using various parts of his body to break up the tree trunk into smaller pieces, Julian sat on the wet road and meditated.

Tim watched the sky nervously for ten minutes. Every time the rain seemed to let up just a little bit, he clutched his dagger hilt, for all the good it would do him against a werewolf. He didn't know as much as he should about werewolves, but he knew that attacking one without a silver or enchanted weapon was tantamount to jumping the queue to have your throat ripped out.

Finally, Julian stood up. "Horse." And just like that, there was a gorgeous white stallion glistening in the rain next to him. Julian was still limited to four Level 1 spells, so Tim doubled up with him.

"These will only last a couple of hours, but that should be enough time to get back to town if we ride fast."

Once they were all mounted, they galloped as fast as their magical steeds would take them. It was thrilling at first, but Tim's arms soon became sore from holding on so tightly to Julian, and his ass started to ache from bouncing up and down on the horse. He was cold and wet and tired and sore. He wished he could just curl up and go to sleep.

"There are the walls!" Julian finally cried out. "We made it!"

Tim didn't know what he was so excited about. Making it back to town was the easy part. Drawing blood from a werewolf might prove a bit more challenging. He wished Cooper hadn't blown his Barbarian Rage already.

The main gates were closed at this time of night, but as long as you weren't leading a hostile army or a horde of zombies, the guards were pretty lax about letting folks in through a small door on the side.

Julian dismissed his magical steeds outside the city walls. "It feels good to end that spell without some act of horrible butchery."

Within the walls, the cobbled streets of Cardinia were cool and slick as Tim sloshed through the puddles. Having no idea what time it was, he had no way of knowing whether the lack of activity was due to the rain or the late hour. His answer came as the group neared the Collapsed Sewer District. Lights shone through several tavern windows, flickering where the source was fire, and steady where the source was enchanted. Tim judged the hour to be around two in the morning. The bars were still open, but the noise level suggested that things were beginning to die down.

Nobody remembered the exact location or the name of the pub they had met Colin in, so they wandered around aimlessly until Tim recognized the gang of elves that had almost kicked his ass the night before. They were huddled together, three of them barely able to stand up. The two lucid-looking elves looked scared. When one of them shifted their stance, Tim caught a glimpse of what they were all looking at. Steely blue eyes peered out of a black, hooded cloak. Colin, that werewolf motherfucker himself.

Tim stopped walking and waved for his friends to duck into an alley across the street.

"He's there," Tim whispered. "He's talking to a group of elves. They look drunk and scared. He's probably pulling the same shit on them that he did with us."

"Let's go jump him," said Cooper excitedly. "If the other group joins in, our odds will be even better."

"Bad idea," said Dave. "They're scared, confused, and drunk. They might just as easily try to defend him if they think he holds the cure for their affliction. We're not going to have time to explain our case before all hell breaks loose."

Tim and Julian peeked around the corner. Colin was showing the group a vial of red liquid.

"That's his pitch," said Julian. "He's sending them off to find the statue, and his blood is their reward."

"What a dick," said Tim.

Julian pulled back into the alley. "He's got the vial on him. Let's pretend we've got the statue, and I'll see if I can't use Diplomacy to get him to give up the blood first, like a measure of good faith or something. I'd rather drink it from a vial than bite into him."

"Oh," said Cooper. "I was thinking we'd just stab him and you could lap up the blood off the street."

"I'm still liking the vial option better."

Tim kept watching until Colin's newest marks skulked away, the two lucid ones clutching bloody handkerchiefs around their wrists.

"He's alone!" Tim whispered. "Now's the time."

"Would you mind staying behind for a minute?" Julian asked Dodwynn. "I'd like to try to settle this without a fight. You can put your vengeance off for another minute, can't you?"

"My brother, Baelrick. He was a good dwarf. He would want you to be free of this curse."

Julian nodded, took a step forward, then stopped. "Of course, if things do turn violent, feel free to jump in."

Dodwynn grinned, though Tim suspected the streaks running down the sides of his face consisted of more than rain. "Aye, lad. You can count on it."

Julian looked under his serape. "Ravenus, I need you to keep still."

"Still, sir?"

"As still *as a statue.*"

"Ah, I see, sir." He nodded his head once, then became as rigid as if he'd been carved out of wood.

Julian covered his bird and addressed the group... specifically Cooper. "*I* do the talking. Got it?" After everyone nodded, Julian led them out into the street.

Colin was sitting on a crate in the alley, smoking a pipe. The second story of the building he sat next to was built slightly wider than the first. The overhang kept him out of the rain.

When the group was halfway across the street, Colin looked up, startled. He stood quickly and tapped out his pipe against the wall, as if it was the high school principal who had just caught him smoking.

Julian halted and raised his hands slowly.

Colin's face relaxed into a smirk. "I wasn't expecting to see you boys again... so soon."

Julian lowered his hands. "We don't like to waste time running other people's errands."

Cold. Businesslike. Not Julian's normal M.O., but Tim could see it being an effective diplomatic strategy.

Colin pulled down his hood and stepped out into the rain. He still had a scratch on his face that Tim thought he remembered Ravenus giving him. His smirk was gone.

"Do you have the statue?"

Julian tapped the bulge beneath his serape on his left breast. "Do you have the vial?"

Something was strange. One thing Tim was pretty sure about was that lycanthropes could only be harmed by silver or enchanted weapons. A bird claw wound should have healed almost instantaneously, unless... *Ravenus was Julian's familiar. Did that make him magical? Did his claws count as enchanted weapons? That would be cool.*

Colin pulled back the left side of his cloak about an inch, and raised his right hand as if he was going to grab something, but stopped short of doing so.

In turn, Julian pulled back the left side of his serape. A high-pitched screech and a storm of black feathers exploded out of it.

"NO!" Julian cried.

Colin yelped like a scared puppy, raising his arms to shield his face, but Ravenus was already on him, scratching and pecking and cawing.

"So," said Cooper. "The plan…?"

"Get him!" shouted Julian.

"Sweet!" Cooper bolted forward and tackled Colin to the ground, instantly pinning him in a sleeper hold.

"You… double… crossing… bastards!" Colin choked the words out.

"Where is the vial?" Julian demanded. Ravenus continued to flap and claw and peck.

"Take it!" said Colin. "It's inside my cloak!"

"Ravenus!" said Julian. "Stand down." The bird flew to Julian's shoulder, leaving Colin's face a blood-streaked mess. "You were supposed to stay put. Like a statue, remember?"

"Apologies, sir," said Ravenus. "You didn't fill me in on the whole plan. When you tapped me and opened your serape, I assumed it was a call to action."

"You're right," said Julian. "I should have been clearer. But look at that. You kicked his ass."

"I do what I can, sir."

Julian took a knee next to Colin. "Let's get this over with."

Cooper loosened his hold on Colin, but did not let go.

Julian reached under Colin's cloak and felt around until he found what he was looking for. He pulled out a small glass vial of red liquid.

"Take it and go!" said Colin. "Leave me alone before I call for the Kingsgua—"

Cooper slapped a hand over Colin's mouth.

Julian unstoppered the vial and sucked down the contents. His face contorted like he had just bitten into a lemon. He looked closely at the vial. "This isn't blood." He glared down at Colin. "What the hell did I just drink?"

Cooper released his hold on Colin's face.

Colin spit a few times, no doubt trying to rid himself of the taste of Cooper. His eyes darted back and forth, like he was searching for an exit. "It's p-p-p-pomegranate juice."

"What the fuck, man?"

"That's good for you," said Cooper. "It's got, like, antioxygens and shit in it."

Julian glared down at Colin. "Are you expecting me to believe that the cure for lycanthropy is pomegranate juice?"

Colin shook his head. "No. I just used that because it looks like blood. It was all for show."

"Hmmm…" said Julian. "I guess I could just lick your face, but that would be weird."

"I beg your pardon?"

"Okay, here's the plan. Cooper, Dave, hold him down. Tim, give him a little jab in the neck with your dagger."

"Wait, WHAT?"

"I need your blood, right? Pomegranate juice just isn't going to cut it."

"No no no no no," said Colin, laughing shallowly. "You don't understand."

"What, *exactly*, don't I understand?"

"It was all a sham," said Colin. "The affliction, the cure. I made all of that up. I'm not even a werewolf."

"Bullshit," said Tim. "I saw you change."

"I did too," said Julian. "And I was pretty lucid."

"It was a simple Alter Self spell," said Colin. "I'm an apprentice wizard. My professor is a devout disciple of Yulu Hari. I thought if I could get that statue, you know…"

"That's what this whole scheme was about?" asked Julian. "You trying to impress your wizard professor?"

"I'm sorry," Colin pleaded. "Really, I am. But hey, nobody got hurt, right? No harm done. Please don't kill me."

Julian shook his head. "You're a good looking guy, Colin. You should have taken up sorcery."

Colin frowned. "I don't know how those two sentences are related to one another, but thanks."

"I don't know either, Colin. And you're welcome."

"Does that mean you're not going to kill me?"

Julian smiled. "Of course we're not going to kill you."

"You'll let me go then?"

Tim was impressed with the uncharacteristic streak of cruelty Julian was demonstrating. He didn't know what Julian had in mind, but he was pretty sure he was toying with this guy.

"Sure," said Julian. "We'll let you go, but we'd like to introduce you to a friend we met along the way." He turned toward where Tim and Dave were standing and waved them aside.

Tim hadn't realized that Dodwynn had been standing right behind them.

"Dodwynn!" said Colin, trying to mask his panic. "I didn't think you... Where's your brother?"

"You two have obviously got some catching up to do," said Julian. "We'll just leave you to it."

Dodwynn stared gravely at Colin. "You promised my brother some of your blood. I'm here to collect."

Julian relaxed his cold, hard demeanor. "Would you mind giving us some time before you settle up? I really don't want to see or hear any of this."

"Don't worry about that, elf." Dodwynn cracked his knuckles. "I'm planning on taking me time with him. I've got a place in mind where no one will hear him."

Julian winced. "Yeah, see, I'd rather not know anything like that either."

Dodwynn looked down at Colin. "On your feet, boy."

Cooper released Colin, who promptly scrambled to his feet toward the alley.

Dodwynn kicked him in the ass before he had his balance, and Colin's face smashed down hard into the wet cobblestones. Dodwynn looked at Tim, raising his hand to his eyebrow in a casual salute. "I thank you again, halfling. Now you boys run along. I got this under control."

Tim didn't need to be asked twice. He did an about face and started walking away. It wasn't long before his friends caught up to him.

"Do you guys feel right about leaving that guy to be torture-murdered?" asked Dave.

"Absolutely," said Tim.

"Fuck him," said Cooper.

Julian said nothing, so Dave started up again.

"I expect that from Tim and Cooper. But I'm a little surprised at you, Julian."

Julian stopped in his tracks. "I didn't see you jumping in to save the day."

"Hey hey," said Dave, raising his hands defensively. "I'm not accusing you. You're right. I didn't help the guy either."

When Julian started walking again, Dave finished his thought. "Of course, I also didn't deliberately serve him up for the slaughter."

"You know what?" said Julian. "Screw you, Dave. I was angry, yeah. And if we had more time, I might have tried to talk Dodwynn out of killing the guy, or at least doing it quickly. But I had a decision to make."

"If we had more time?" Dave scoffed. "Where the hell do we have to be at this hour?"

"I had to choose between hanging out and reasoning with Dodwynn, or trying to catch up to those elves Colin just sent to the temple."

"Aw fuck," said Cooper. "Is that where we're going? I'm tired, and I need a drink."

Dave folded his arms incredulously. "It sounds like you're rationalizing to me. Were you really thinking that at the time, or is this something you're pulling out of your ass right now?"

"You'll be pulling my foot out of yours if you don't shut up."

"I'm with Cooper," said Tim. "Those guys are assholes. I'm exhausted, and wet, and sober. That's just no way to feel. Let's give them some credit, huh? They're probably not as stupid as we are."

"You think?"

"Sure. They'll take one look at that skull tree, and decide to come back to town for reinforcements. Or maybe they'll just decide to cope with lycanthropy – build a cage, buy some manacles, whatever – and be pleasantly surprised in a month."

Julian tugged on his ears. "I guess it could play out that way. That makes more sense than just charging unprepared into a temple full of grimlocks."

A bell rang out from a nearby tavern. *Last call.* Tim tried not to look too hopeful.

"Heck," Julian continued rationalizing. "They might even know what phase the moon is in, and know that they have a full month to prepare. Or they might have horses. We probably wouldn't catch up to them. They could be anywhere. I still feel kind of bad though."

"I've got a cure for that," said Tim. "Let's hurry before they close the bar."

The End.

The Land Before Tim

(Original Publication Date: February 23, 2015)

"Where the fuck are we?" said Tim. It was not an unusual question for him to ask upon waking up in the morning, but the potential answers were usually limited to piss-filled gutters outside taverns in the city of Cardinia. He couldn't recall ever waking up on a bed of giant ferns.

The air smelled of sea-salt and… "Eggs?"

Tim stood and oriented himself toward the scent and sizzle of frying eggs. Even jumping, he wouldn't be able to see over the ferns. Being a halfling sucked. He struggled for a few meters through the dense vegetation until he emerged onto a white, sandy beach.

"Hey!" said Dave. "You're up." He was bare-chested, pale, and hairy. His dwarven man-tits poked out from either side of his beard like fish eyes, jiggling in the tropical sunlight.

Tim averted his eyes. "Jesus, dude. Where the hell is your armor?"

"Cooper and Julian are using my breastplate to cook with."

Tim looked past Dave. Halfway between the jungle and the sea, Cooper and Julian were tending a homemade stove. Rocks and sticks held Dave's breastplate above a small fire. Where Dave's tits would normally reside, a gooey yellow substance bubbled. Julian stirred it with a stick.

"Where are we?" Tim repeated now that there were people around to answer. "How did we get here?"

"Fuck," said Cooper. "He's still drunk." He pulled his finger out of his snout. "Listen, buddy. We've been magically transported into the Caverns and Creatures world. Don't freak out, dude, but you're a halfling."

"I know that, shithead," said Tim. "I'm not talking about this world. I'm talking about this goddamn beach."

"Oh right," said Cooper. "Fuck if I know."

"Go wash your hands."

Cooper stomped toward the water, leaving giant half-orc footprints, and a turd, in his wake.

Tim clapped his hands over his face, trying to contain his massive headache. Julian was still tending the eggs. "Do you know anything about this?"

"I've been trying to figure it out," said Julian. "What do you remember from last night?"

Tim thought hard. "We went out to that new tavern."

"I keep telling you guys we need to stop doing that," said Dave.

Tim looked back at him and winced. "Could you maybe spread your beard out to cover your nipples? I'm feeling kinda rough this morning."

Julian poked some of the cooked egg on the edge into the still-liquid center. "I don't remember that much. I was already pretty trashed when we left the Whore's Head."

"Which we absolutely shouldn't have done," said Dave.

"Dude," said Tim. "You're not helping." Memories teased his brain, like they were apprehensive about returning. "Why did we leave the Whore's Head anyway?"

Dave rolled his eyes. "You and Cooper kept going on about *A Quest for Big Titties*."

Tim laughed. "Oh yeah. I remember that. Did we see any?"

"I don't think so. The new place was a total sausage fest."

"We should try to introduce the concept of Ladies' Night to this world," said Julian.

Tim focused on Dave's forehead to avoid looking at his hairy man-boobs. "You've got a high Constitution score. Do you remember anything else?"

"You spent most of the night making out with a dwarf in the corner."

"Oh Jesus," said Tim. He pulled a blonde hair out of his mouth as a vague recollection started to form in his mind. "She had a fucking beard, didn't she?"

"Most dwarven women do."

Tim tried to shake the memory out of his head. It only became clearer. "Was she at least hot by dwarf standards?"

"Nah," said Dave. "She was pretty dumpy. I wouldn't have touched her with Cooper's dick."

"How could you let me do that? Where the fuck were you guys?"

"Cooper and I got caught up in a drinking contest with a table of wizards."

"That sounds bad."

"It was fucking epic!" said Cooper, returning from the sea.

"Cooper," said Tim. "I want you to think real hard. Did you say anything to piss off those wizards? Anything, for instance, that might make one of them want to teleport you and your friends to an uncharted island?"

"No way," said Cooper. "Those dudes thought I was hilarious."

"Come on, Cooper," said Tim. "We didn't get lost on the way home and wind up on a fucking beach. I need you to put all seven points of your Intelligence score to work here. Are you absolutely sure you didn't say anything to offend any of them?"

"Well that one guy with the forked beard got a little bent out of shape when I made a crack about him bringing his grandma out to the bar."

"You said *what*?" Dave was actually a shade paler. "To Boswell the Grand?"

"I don't know," said Julian. "As far as Cooper jokes go, that sounds pretty tame."

"I know, right?" said Cooper. "I was on fire last night. And of course everyone's going to laugh the hardest at some lame, throwaway joke. Fucking Philistines."

"Dude," said Dave. "That wasn't his grandma. That was his *wife*."

"Oh," said Cooper. "I can see now how that was unintentionally hilarious."

"Jesus Christ, Cooper," said Tim. "What the fuck were you thinking?"

"I don't know. You'd think a guy named Boswell the Grand might be able to do a little better for himself."

"He's an elf," said Julian. He smacked himself on the forehead as realization dawned on him. "She's human. That's why she's aging so much faster than he is. No wonder he took it so hard. That's like making bald jokes in a cancer ward."

"You need to keep your big stupid mouth shut, Cooper!" Tim shook his head. "Man, you really fucked us over good this time."

"Well maybe you should have told me that last night," said Cooper. "But you were wrist deep in dwarf snatch."

"Wha?" said Tim. "Did I...?"

Dave gave him a sympathetic nod.

Tim sniffed the fingers on his right hand. He wasn't certain what they were supposed to smell like, given the standard of hygiene in this world, but he was pretty sure they were a little off. "I've got to... I'll be right back."

"Hurry up," said Julian. "The egg's almost done."

Tim ran as fast as his tiny legs would take him toward the sea. He deftly leaped over Cooper's turd and dove headfirst into the salty water. He grabbed a handful of wet sand and scrubbed the shame and dried vag-juice from his right hand. He gargled salt water a little too eagerly and wound up swallowing some. His body was quick to reject the seawater, sending it, along with whatever he had eaten and drunk the night before, exploding out of his mouth.

When he was done vomiting, he rested on his hands and knees, tears in his eyes and salty snot dripping from his nose, thankful that he was a million miles away from the scene of his indiscretion.

There were no camera phones in this world. All he needed was some good booze, and he could forget he ever… he wasn't quite sure just how far he'd gone last night. He scooped up another handful of wet sand, reached into his pants, and scrubbed his crotch clean as well. Can't be too safe.

After his genitals were scrubbed raw, Tim began to feel better about the events of the night before. So he'd hooked up with an ugly dwarf. He'd probably had lower points in his life. He knew for a certainty that Cooper had. The guys wouldn't be able to bust his balls too bad over this. And as for her, she would soon be a distant memory. Just lay low at the Whore's Head for a few weeks, and he'd never have to see her hairy face– *Why were there four people standing around the fire?* Cooper was easy to pick out. Julian was still tending the eggs. Dave was still shirtless. The fourth one looked like Dave in stature and girth, but had blonde hair and slightly bigger tits.

Dave pointed at Tim. Tim stopped in his tracks. With nothing but sparkling blue sea and sandy white shore, there was nowhere to hide. He wished Cooper's turd was bigger so that he might cower behind it. He was stuck, defenseless, trapped. The she-dwarf looked at him and smiled, a gap between her two front teeth wide enough for Ravenus to fly through. Tim wanted to throw up again, but he had nothing left to give.

He looked down at his right hand and whispered, "You've been in that creature's cavern."

"Hi, Tim!" Her enthusiasm made Tim's testicles shrivel. What the hell was she doing here?

"Um… Hi,…"

Her smile faltered. "Gilda."

"I know. I'm sorry. Still a little drunk is all." He had no choice but to keep walking toward her. He felt like the Millennium Falcon being pulled toward the Death Star. He glanced at each of his friends, looking for a snicker. To his surprise, everyone's face was blank. They were all either too curious or hungry to care about Tim's involvement with this she-beast. "What are you doing here?"

"I challenged that wizard to a duel for sending you away from me," said Gilda. "He laughed and sent me after you."

Tim buried his face in his hands. This was so much worse.

"What's wrong with your arm?" asked Gilda.

"Huh?" said Tim, looking at his right arm. It was scraped pink and raw almost up to his elbow. He'd been pretty aggressive with the sand. "Oh, that's nothing. Just a rash."

Gilda swallowed hard. "Nothing *contagious*, I hope."

Tim panicked. "Wait! What? No! It's not… um… It's nothing, really."

It became obvious that Dave, Julian, and Cooper had been holding their laughter and ridicule back in an effort to be decent human beings, or whatever. The walls started to crumble as snorts of laughter burst through the cracks.

Gilda's face turned red.

Julian covered his laugh with a fake cough. "Who wants eggs?"

"Me!" cried Tim. Food and an exit from that conversation were just what he needed.

"I made some spoons out of bamboo," said Dave. "They're nothing special, but they should work." He held up four five-inch lengths of bamboo, the end of each cut diagonally.

Julian nodded. "Well done, Dave." He kneeled on the ground and smothered the fire with sand.

Dave passed spoons to Julian, Cooper, and Tim before frowning at Gilda. "I'm sorry. I wasn't cxpccting company." He fumbled with the spoon in his hands for a bit, then offered it to her. "Here, take mine."

"I'll just share with Tim, thanks." She waddled into Tim's comfort zone while Cooper kept his lips shut as tight as a frog's asshole. He looked like he was about to explode. Fortunately, his release came from the other end.

"Jesus, Cooper!" said Dave. "We're about to eat, man!"

Tim had never been so relieved to bask in a cloud of Cooper's ass vapor. "Here," he said to Gilda, offering her his spoon. "You have your fill first."

"I couldn't."

"Okay then." Tim had been as gentlemanly as he was prepared to be. He scooped up a spoonful of egg and shoved it into his mouth. It was warm and wonderful. "This is fantastic," he said to Julian through his full mouth. "Where did you get the eggs?"

"Egg," Julian corrected him. "Ravenus found it and Cooper climbed up the tree to get it."

Tim swallowed the egg in his mouth. "What do you mean, *it*? There have got to be more than a dozen eggs in here."

"No," said Julian. "Just the one. We would have had more, but Cooper broke all the others when he fell through the nest."

"Birds are shitty builders," said Cooper. "I almost broke my ass."

"How big was this egg?" asked Tim.

Julian picked something up off the ground. It looked like a deflated basketball. "This is the shell."

"Holy shit, man!" said Tim. "That's big enough to fit over Cooper's head."

"Sweet!" said Cooper. "Hand it over."

Julian shrugged and gave Cooper the empty leathery eggshell.

"I'll cut some eyeholes in it, draw some flames on the side. This will be my alter ego. El Cupo."

Tim shook his head. "Come on, guys. Think about this. Can you imagine a bird passing Cooper's head through its vagina?"

"I guess I *could*," said Julian. "But ew."

"Do birds have vaginas?" asked Gilda.

"Good question. Ravenus?"

113

"Yes sir?"

"Oh right, sorry. Do birds have a vagina?"

"This isn't important right now," said Tim.

"It's important if you want Cooper to put his head in one."

"What's a vagina, sir?"

"Hmm…" said Julian. "How to explain. It's the female reproductive… orifice? I don't like that word."

"Tell him it looks like Dave's face when he yawns," suggested Cooper.

"The vagina is the whole organ," said Gilda. "Not just the orifice."

"Sorry," said Julian. "My sex-ed teacher was a nervous gym coach."

"It's like a cloaca then, is it?" asked Ravenus.

"I guess?"

"Fine!" said Tim. "Then imagine a bird that could pass Cooper's head through its cloaca. How big –"

"What the fuck is a cloaca?" asked Cooper.

"It's like a vagina," said Julian. "But for birds."

"Then why don't they just call it a vagina?"

"I tried to explain," said Gilda. "The vagina is the whole organ. It extends from the uterus to –"

"Yeah, yeah, to Tim's elbow," said Cooper. "We've got it."

Everyone stopped eating. Gilda stood, horrorstruck and open-mouthed, staring at Cooper.

Tim had suffered through some awkward silences before, but this one seemed to last forever. He looked at Julian and mouthed the word *Diplomacy*.

Julian raised his eyebrows as if to say *IIow the fuck is Diplomacy going to fix that?*

Julian's eyebrows had a point. Diplomacy was just about as likely to help as murdering a horse would, but Tim would still reserve the latter option as a backup plan. Tim raised his own eyebrows back at

Julian to convey the message, *Come on, man. At least give it a try.*

Julian pursed his lips and furrowed his eyebrows. The message was clearly *Goddammit!* But instead of turning to Gilda, he turned to Cooper.

"Also," Julian squeaked. He cleared his throat. "Both male and female birds have a cloaca, so it's not really synonymous with vagina at all."

Brilliant. If all parties agreed to pretend Cooper hadn't spoken, the slate could be wiped clean. Or at least covered over with a tarp or something.

Tim followed Julian's lead. "Let me just make my point. I shouldn't have beaten around the bush."

Cooper snorted. "I don't think anyone would accuse you of doing that after –"

"I will fucking end you!"

"Sorry."

Tim took a deep breath. "Here it is. Something pretty fucking big must have laid those eggs, right? What if it comes looking for vengeance?"

Dave hurriedly shoved another spoonful of egg into his mouth, like he might not have much more time.

Julian's eyes widened. "Holy shit, you're right!"

Cooper licked his lips. "We'd eat like fucking kings!"

Tim pulled at his hair and sighed. "Yeah, we would... or *it* would."

Dave licked the tip of his finger and touched his breastplate. Judging it cool enough, he tossed his spoon aside and started shoveling egg into his mouth with his bare hands. Tim suspected he was less concerned with eating at this point, and more concerned with getting his armor back on.

"Dude, relax," said Cooper. "I don't care how big it is. We can handle a fucking bird."

"But what if it's not a bird?" said Tim. "This is C&C. What if it's

115

a *dragon*?"

"Whoa!" said Julian, taking a step back.

Dave paused from his frenzy to glance up at the sky.

Even Cooper seemed to finally pick up on the gravity of what Tim was saying. He frowned for a second, and then joined Dave in a race to gobble up the most egg.

"Wait a minute," said Julian. "Do dragons live in nests?"

It was a good question. A nest seemed like kind of a humble abode for one of the most prominent creatures in the game. "I don't know."

Dave and Cooper stopped eating. Everyone turned to Gilda.

Gilda nervously wiped at her beard like she thought she might have had a piece of food stuck in it. "What? Why are you all looking at me?"

"We thought maybe you knew something about dragons," said Julian.

"Why would you think that?"

"Well, because you're from here."

Gilda looked at Julian as if he'd just yodeled his last sentence. "I don't even know where *here* is! I'm from the Griffon Valley."

"I'm sorry. I should have been clearer. What I meant was –"

A sound erupted, like a thousand screaming Ravenuses, from above the jungle trees. It might have been avian. It might have been reptilian. It was certainly pissed off.

"Ravenus?" said Julian. "Can you translate that?"

"It's a dialect I'm unfamiliar with, sir. It almost sounds like –"

"I'll translate for you," said Tim. "It said 'What the fuck happened to my eggs?' Head for the trees *now*!"

Tim led by example, racing up the beach toward the treeline, his feet pounding into the hot white sand. He'd only run about five yards when a shadow passed over him. He had to know. He stopped running and looked up.

"HO," said Julian.

116

"LEE," said Dave.

"FUCKBALLS," said Cooper.

Everyone but Gilda, who kept running toward the trees, stood mesmerized by the creature gliding out over the water. Its head was narrow, crested at the top, and at least as long as the rest of its body. As it banked over the water, sunlight shone through its translucent, pink, bat-like wings, which had a span of at least thirty feet.

Tim felt a zeal for life that he hadn't felt since childhood. Every indignity he'd ever suffered, every endeavor he'd ever abandoned, every asshole he'd ever served a bucket of fried chicken to. None of that mattered now, because he was looking at a goddamn dinosaur.

"What are you fools doing?" cried Gilda. "Run!"

Tim snapped out of his fascination. The pteranodon had arced completely around and was flying back toward them. More specifically, toward Dave, who was still trying to scrape egg out of his breastplate. It opened its mouth like a giant pair of scissors and repeated its terrible, prehistoric scream.

"Drop the armor and run!" Tim shouted.

Dave dropped his armor, but he didn't run. Instead, he picked up his mace. That was probably for the best. Dave couldn't outrun a three-legged cow. There was no way he'd outrun a giant flying reptile.

"Shit!" Cooper unstrapped his battleaxe and ran toward Dave.

Tim started running around toward the water. He'd miss the first pass, but hopefully he'd be able to line up a pretty good crossbow shot when it swooped down at Dave a second time.

"Magic Missile!" said Julian. A white bolt of energy hit the creature just before it reached Dave, sending it crashing into the sand.

Cooper slowed down to a jog. "What the fuck?"

"Oh yeah!" said Julian. "Magic Missile for the win!"

"That's some bullshit," said Cooper. "No wonder those fuckers are extinct."

The pteranodon sprang back to life, crawling surprisingly quickly toward Dave on its feet and wings like some ungodly combination of pelican and tent. For all Tim knew, Julian's Magic Missile hadn't hurt it at all. It was just a clumsy flyer.

Sand flew in every direction as the pteranodon closed in on Dave, snapping its massive beak. Dave helplessly stumbled backwards, shielding his eyes.

Cooper started running again, and Tim approached as stealthily as he could from behind. The crossbow was his preferred weapon to deal with monsters that could bite him in half if he got too close, but with all the sand flying around, he might just as easily hit Cooper or Dave. Tim set his crossbow down, unsheathed his dagger, and hoped that what he was about to do wasn't an extremely stupid mistake.

Dave screamed and dropped his mace as the pteranodon bit down on his right forearm.

Cooper ran at it with his battleaxe raised over his head. "Back to the tarpits with you, fossil fool!" He caught a facefull of sand and fell to his knees. "Fuck!"

Confident that his bare feet on the sand couldn't make more noise than Dave's screams or Cooper's swearing, Tim sprinted at the pteranodon and leapt onto its back.

"Sneak attack, motherfucker!" He grabbed the bony crest at the top of the creature's head and stabbed it in the side of the face with his dagger.

The pteranodon shrieked, letting go of Dave, and spread its great wings.

"Shit!" said Tim, wishing it had occurred to him that the beast might try to flee, and the possible ramifications that might have for him. He shoved the crest back and forth like the gearshift of a stubborn car, slamming the creature's beak down repeatedly on Dave's head.

"Hey, man!" said Dave. "Knock it off!"

The wings flapped down, and Tim felt himself ascend a couple of feet off the ground. He held on more tightly to the crest and wrapped his dagger arm around the pteranodon's neck in a stranglehold. "Help me!"

Another flap and another jolt upward. Tim was shit scared. He squeezed his arm around the pteranodon's neck even harder, and jerked its head from side to side with the crest. He wasn't sure what the desired outcome of the latter move was, but he was working with the tools he had at hand.

The third flap failed to take them any higher. That was good, but why –

"I've got his feet!" said Cooper. "Jump off!"

Fuck that. It was time to end this. Reassured by the fact that the creature was anchored to the ground, and Cooper's reminder that he could have jumped off at any time prior to now, Tim released his hold on the pteranodon's neck and plunged his dagger into its eye.

Its scream was deafening. It flapped harder, and Tim felt himself starting to ascend again.

"Come on, man!" Cooper shouted. "Just let go! I can't hold on much longer!"

Tim barely heard him. His head was pulsing with adrenaline and dinosaur bloodlust. He stabbed and stabbed, cracking cartilage and gouging soupy chunks of flesh, blood, and eye goo.

The pteranodon broke free of Cooper's grasp, and Tim was no longer tethered to the ground.

Stab. Stab. Stab. Where is that walnut fucking brain? Tim shoved his dagger as far as he could into the pteranodon's significantly widened ocular cavity and twisted its head around by the crest. His rage was beginning to give way to fear and exhaustion. "Just fucking die already!"

The pteranodon made a hard downward spiral, causing Tim to slip. When he leaned right, it straightened out. It was done. He'd killed the fucker. He was steering the dead beast as it glided to the ground.

"YEAH!" Tim cried, punching into the air with one hand and yanking the dead pteranodon's crest toward him with the other.

He was pretty far up. His friends on the beach didn't look quite so small as ants. Large cockroaches, maybe, and heading quickly toward squirrels as he rushed down toward them.

"Um… Hello there."

Tim jerked his head to the right. He hadn't been expecting company. "Ravenus?" He forced out a British accent. "What are you doing here?"

"Julian sent me here to see if I could be of any assistance. Frankly, I'm not sure what I'd be able to do."

"Got any tips for hitting the ground without dying?"

"Grow wings?"

"Thanks for the advice." Judging by the rate at which he was descending, Tim reckoned he was going to hit the ground hard. Not fatally hard, but it wasn't going to feel good. Unless… "I'll jump off."

"If you don't mind me saying so, sir. That sounds like a remarkably bad idea."

"Not now," said Tim, picturing the dismount in his mind. "Just before I land."

"Are you sure you're not still drunk, sir?"

It was a stupid idea, sure. But how many times in life does one get such an opportunity? With a combination of his Jump bonus, his high Dexterity score, and the fact that his style of landing wouldn't have any game consequences outside of potentially being awesome. If you can't do a backflip off the body of a dead pteranodon as you plummet to the ground, then what the hell are you even playing C&C for?

Tim felt an unnatural surge of confidence in his decision, as if the game itself was nodding its approval.

Keeping one hand firmly wrapped around the crest, Tim carefully got to his feet. His flight path should have him crashing just beyond where his friends were gaping up at him.

"Tim!" cried Dave. "What the hell are you doing?"

"Hang on, buddy!" said Cooper. "I'll catch you!"

Tim swatted the air with his free hand. "Get the fuck out of the way!"

Cooper stepped aside.

The ground was rushing at him, closer and closer.

"WOOOOOOOOOO!" *Fuck.*

Tim let go of the crest and pushed hard with his legs. The world somersaulted around him, then stopped suddenly as his feet planted into the hot sand. *Perfect execution.*

A second later, the dead pteranodon made a decidedly less graceful landing. Its lower beak, which had been hanging open, snapped back as it hit the sand, sending the rest of the creature tumbling crest over feet. Tim was relieved that he'd decided to bail. Even if he'd fucked up his own landing, it would have hurt a lot less than staying mounted would have.

He turned around to face his friends. "What wiped out the dinosaurs? *Tim wiped out the dinosaurs!*"

"I aborted a few," said Cooper. "Does that count?"

"Well done," said Julian.

"Actually," said Dave. "Pterosaurs aren't technically considered dinosaurs."

"Screw you, Dave. I'm a fucking meteor!"

"Very impressive." Gilda's voice from behind him sent a shiver up Tim's spine.

Dave and Cooper looked at their feet.

"I'm going to check on Ravenus!" said Julian, walking hurriedly past Tim toward the pteranodon carcass.

Tim would have preferred to face a pack of hungry tyrannosauruses than the tubby, bearded dwarf he'd so thoroughly explored last night. He turned around.

"Thank you." The words came out like he'd been drinking sand.

"I underestimated you," said Gilda. Her widely far apart eyes were sad. "I'm sorry. I shouldn't have run."

"No!" said Tim. He already had enough guilt and shame on his plate. If she started crying, he'd just have to run into the ocean and hope sharks ate him before he drowned. "Running was the right thing to do. What I did was stupid."

"You're smart and brave." Her words hit Tim like a punch in the gut. These were not descriptors he was accustomed to hearing about himself back in the real world.

Tim looked down at the sand between his toes. "I'm not really all that smart. It's just in the game."

"I don't know what that means."

"Never mind."

"Start putting that high Intelligence score of yours to work," said Dave. "Try to think of a way out of here. If there are pteranodons around, this place is bound to be some kind of *Lost World* themed island, and that means –"

"I've got it!" said Tim. "We'll build a raft."

"Building a raft is hardly a novel idea for getting off an island," said Dave. "Why do you look so excited about it?"

"Because our raft is going to be awesome. We can use the pteranodon wings for sails. Its head will make a good rudder, and we can eat the rest of it as we go. All we need to do is –"

"We don't even know where we are," said Gilda. "Why don't we just use the portal?"

Tim halted the part of his brain that was busily constructing a dino-powered escape boat. "What portal?"

Gilda folded her arms across her chest. "You really don't remember *anything* about last night?"

Tim averted his eyes. "Bits and pieces."

"You don't remember telling Boswell the Grand that you were going to 'pop a bolt in yo ass' if he didn't bring your friends back?"

"I went gangsta?"

Cooper nodded approvingly. "Pop a bolt. I like it."

Gilda shook her head. "He said we were all acting disgraceful."

Cooper snorted. "He kind of had a point with you two."

Gilda glared at Cooper. She looked like she was deciding whether to cry or kick him in the junk.

"Shut the fuck up, Cooper," said Tim. "Go on, Gilda. What about the portal?"

"He said a nice long walk would sober us up. He said there's a portal leading back to Cardinia on the other side of this island."

Tim rubbed his hands together. "Okay, cool. So let's get to the other side of the island and find this portal. Should we stick to the beach, or try to cut through the jungle?"

"I like the beach," said Gilda. "Now that we know pteranodons are relatively harmless. We can always retreat into the ocean if anything bigger comes after us."

"Relatively harmless?" said Dave. "That thing nearly ripped my arm off!"

"It doesn't look so bad to me."

"That's because I used two healing spells!"

Tim put his hands on his hips. "That pteranodon probably wouldn't have bothered us if you idiots hadn't gone and destroyed all of her eggs. I'm with Gilda."

Gilda's scornful look at Cooper evaporated as she jerked her fat head toward Tim.

Shit. "I mean, I like her beach idea. The circumference of the island is longer than the diameter, but we'll cover it faster on the sand than we will in the jungle."

"What if the island isn't circular?" asked Dave. "What if it's sausage shaped? We might be on the other side in an hour by cutting

123

across it, rather than spend days walking around it."

"It's safer on the beach," said Tim. "We can spot danger from farther away, and I'd rather face another pteranodon on the beach than a stegosaurus in the jungle."

"Stegosaurus was an herbivore."

"That doesn't mean he won't fuck your shit up," said Tim. "I don't think he evolved that spiky tail to use as a salad fork. Anyway, what if the island is sausage shaped, and we're at one end of the sausage? Then we'll have eliminated virtually none of the distance, but increased our travel time by three or four hundred percent. Without knowing the layout of the island, our best bet is –"

"What if we knew the layout of the island?" Dave was wearing his sudden revelation face.

"What?" said Tim. "Did Boswell give you a map?"

"We don't need a map," said Dave. He looked past Tim. "We've got a Ravenus."

Tim slapped himself on the forehead. "Why don't these things ever occur to me?" He turned around to face the dead pteranodon. Julian was watching Ravenus gorge himself on the eye that Tim hadn't gouged out. "Julian! Get over here! Bring your bird."

"I'm going to go scrub the rest of the egg out of my armor," said Dave.

"I'll give you a hand," said Gilda. She walked after Dave.

Tim watched the two dwarves walk off together. It would be a real weight off his back if Gilda fell for one of her own kind. Was that a horribly racist thought to have? Probably, but it would still be a huge relief.

"What's up?" asked Julian.

"We need to figure out the layout of the island," said Tim. "Ravenus, do you think you could scout the island for us?"

Ravenus let out a small belch. His face was sticky with eyeball goo. "You're speaking gibberish again, sir."

124

"Oh, right. Sorry." Tim repeated his request in a British accent. "We need to know the shape and size. And let us know if you spot any dinosaurs, or anything else you think we might want to know about."

"Like eggs?"

"No!" said Tim. "Leave the eggs alone! I mean like terrain features that might facilitate or hinder our trek across the island. Rivers, mountains, magical portals, that sort of thing."

"One of those things sounded decidedly different, sir."

Julian wiped some of the goo off Ravenus's face with the edge of his serape. "Just do your best, buddy."

"Right-O, sir!"

It took Ravenus a few sluggish flaps to lift himself into the air. Pteranodons have big eyes. Tim, Julian, and Cooper watched him until he disappeared over the trees.

"Hey," said Tim. "Thanks for not giving me too much shit about last night."

"Don't sweat it, dude," said Cooper. "I've done worse in my day."

Tim glared at Cooper. "I wasn't talking to you, fuckhead! You need to keep your goddamn pie-hole shut. That hairy she-beast has feelings!"

"That was touching," said Julian, pretending to wipe tears from his eyes. "Your humanity is an inspiration to us all."

"What the fuck are you guys even talking about?" asked Cooper. "I was just joking. I'm not any worse to her than I am to any of you."

"I'm talking about empathy," said Julian.

Cooper rolled his eyes. "Here we go."

"Don't you roll your eyes at me. You need to hear this. I'm talking about considering how your words affect other people. Yeah, it's fine for you to bust our balls. We all know each other and have an established rapport, and so nobody takes what you say to heart. But you don't know that dwarf girl. She looked really hurt by some of your *jokes*. You have to consider what kind of life she's led that would culminate in her all but screwing a midget in the middle of a crowded tavern."

"Halfling," said Tim.

"And giving Tim shit about it is even worse. Think of the context. She's not the prettiest girl in the world. She's probably been getting dumped on for that her whole life. You're not laughing at Tim for the act itself, but instead for the girl he's doing it with. That only multiplies the shame and humiliation she feels. And don't give me that low Intelligence and Charisma score excuse. I know you're capable of empathy. I've seen it in you. I want you to think about that, okay?"

Cooper exhaled through pursed lips. "Yeah, okay."

The sullen silence which followed only lasted a minute before Ravenus returned.

"Ready to report, sir!" he said just before crashing into the sand. "Oh dear. Seems I'm a bit heavier than I'm used to."

"That was fast," said Julian.

"It's not a terribly large island, sir. You might walk across it in a day."

"What shape is it?" asked Tim, remembering to use the Elven tongue.

"It's roughly circular."

Tim nodded. "That's it then. Beach it is."

"Not so sure about that," said Ravenus. "Eastward there's a thick lava flow. Probably not something you'd want to cross on foot."

"And to the west?"

"There's an inlct."

Julian squinted. "So?"

"So it's a lot more coastline to cover," said Tim. "We'll be walking west, and then doubling back east again." He looked at Ravenus. "It looks like Pac Man, right?"

126

"I'm afraid I'm unfamiliar with the gentleman in question, sir."

Tim drew a left-facing Pac Man in the sand. "Is this about right?"

Ravenus bobbed his head. "The inlet isn't quite so triangular, and doesn't quite reach the center of the island, but you've got the gist of it."

"I say we head west along the coast for a couple of miles, then cut north by northwest through the jungle until we reach the coast here." He drew a line along his proposed path through Pac Man's lower jaw. "We'll take a break on the beach for lunch, and then head north by northeast to the northern most point of the island." He looked at Ravenus again. "You didn't spot any magic portals, did you?"

"No, sir. I'm afraid not."

"Dinosaurs?" asked Julian.

"I'm sorry, sir. The jungle canopy was too thick for me to make out any wildlife."

"Don't apologize, Ravenus," said Julian. "You done good."

"You might even find shelter at the mouth of the inlet," said Ravenus.

Julian raised his eyebrows. "Is there a cave?"

"No, it's more of a humanoid-built structure."

"Wait a minute," said Tim. "Are you saying there are other people on this island?"

"Cannibals," said Cooper.

"The Others," said Julian.

"What's it like?" asked Tim.

"It's very nice," said Ravenus. "It's made of wood. It has a lovely view of the beach, and an attractive vegetable garden in the front yard. It's not dissimilar to what you might find along the north end of the Bluerun River."

Tim stood up to give Ravenus a stern look. "Why wasn't that the first fucking thing you mentioned?"

"What's up?" asked Dave. Neither he nor Gilda appeared to shine with the afterglow of hot, sweaty dwarf sex. Pity. His armor, however, while still scarred with various dents and hoofprints, was shinier than it had ever been, scrubbed clean with sand and salt water.

Tim pointed down at his Pac Man map. "We're here. Ravenus says there's some kind of wooden, man-made structure here." He pointed at the top of Pac Man's head. "The magic portal leading back to Cardinia should be somewhere around here. I say we check out the house first. Maybe whoever lives there can lead us to the portal. You're the wise one, Dave. What do you think?"

Dave nodded slowly before speaking. "I think this is very good news."

"How's that?"

"That pteranodon was probably a one-off random encounter. Think about it. How long would you expect some rickety wooden shack to last if this place was crawling with dinosaurs?"

"That sounds reasonable," said Julian. "But we're in the game, and game logic doesn't always reflect real-world logic. What if that house is only there because Mordred drew it on a map without considering –" He froze.

"Without considering what?" asked Dave.

"Shut up for a second."

Dave folded his arms. "No, I won't shut up. If you're so keen to poke holes in my logic, at least –"

"Dude, shut the fuck up!" Julian's voice was a panicked whisper. "Did you feel that?"

Tim, Dave, Cooper, and Gilda looked at each other and shook their heads.

"There it is again!" said Julian. "Look at Cooper's piss!"

"Hey, come on, man," said Cooper. "You know I can't always hold it in. It's not my fault."

Julian waved for Cooper to stop talking as the group stared down at the puddle of urine around his left foot. "Just wait. Cooper, stand as still as you can."

A few seconds passed.

"This is making me very uncomfortable," said Cooper.

Just before the last of Cooper's pee disappeared into the sand, the surface of the puddle rippled.

Julian looked at Tim. "You don't think that means…"

Tim sighed. "Of course it fucking does."

"Holy balls," said Dave.

Tim followed the gaze of Dave's suddenly very wide eyes. About half a mile up the beach, a tyrannosaurus was waving its Volkswagen-sized head back and forth.

Tim, Julian, Dave, and Cooper froze like statues, as if they'd all been preparing for this moment since 1993.

"Let's go!" whispered Gilda, stepping toward the jungle.

"Stop!" said Dave.

"Why?" Gilda frowned at Tim. "You guys aren't thinking about trying to ride it, are you, like you did with the pteranodon?"

"Well I wasn't before," said Cooper.

"No!" said Tim. "The T-Rex can only see you if you move."

"Where did you hear that?"

"Just trust me, okay? Stand very, very still."

Gilda looked doubtful, but she nodded.

The tyrannosaurus sniffed the air, swung its massive head toward them, and roared like a stadium full of angry whales. If it was an ordinary breeze that blew their hair back in time with the roar, it was a hell of a coincidence.

The ground shook as one giant foot crashed into the sand in their direction. Then the other. Then more quickly.

"Okay," said Tim. "Fuck this. Let's go."

Not one of the others needed any further prodding.

"What happened to standing still?" asked Gilda as she ran alongside Tim.

"My source may not have been as reliable as I thought."

"These trees aren't dense enough to slow it down," said Julian. "We can't outrun it!"

"We don't have to," said Cooper. "We just have to outrun Dave!"

"Hey fuck you!" said Dave, waddling behind the rest of them.

The ground trembled in half-second intervals as Tim barreled over giant ferns.

"Keep running, sir," said Ravenus. "I'll handle the creature."

"You'll what?"

"Trust me, sir." Ravenus flew off in the opposite direction.

"Where the fuck is your bird going?" asked Cooper.

"He said he was going to handle the T-Rex."

Cooper snorted. "Sweet. Can I recommend that, for your next familiar, you choose something less stupid. Like, I don't know, a rock or a piece of toast or something?"

"Ravenus isn't stupid," said Julian, whipping branches out of his face as he ran. "And I don't sense any fear in him. He has a plan."

Julian had risked his life on more than one occasion to protect that stupid bird. The fact that he hadn't doubled back to fight a tyrannosaurus now was evidence that he had complete confidence in whatever plan Ravenus had concocted in his little bird brain. Tim only hoped that it didn't involve trying to choke the beast to death by flying into its trachea.

The tyrannosaurus roared again. It was closer this time, but the ground had suddenly stopped shaking.

Julian slowed to a jog, then stopped running altogether. Cooper, Gilda, and Tim stopped as well.

"He did it!" said Julian.

Tim searched Julian's face for signs of crushing despair, but Julian was smiling. Ravenus had clearly not gone with the trachea gambit.

Something smaller, but much closer, crashed through the tall ferns toward them.

"Shit!" said Cooper, readying his axe. Julian gripped his quarterstaff. Tim fumbled nervously while trying to load a bolt into his crossbow. Even Gilda, who Tim hadn't realized was armed, produced a dagger from her sleeve.

"Bwaah!" said Dave, stumbling into view as his companions all stopped just short of chopping, stabbing, shooting, and bludgeoning him.

"Oh shit, sorry," said Cooper. "I forgot you were behind us."

Dave stopped to catch his breath before answering. "Thanks a lot."

Tim exhaled, relieved that he hadn't been able to load his crossbow in time to shoot Dave. "Dude, I'm starting to think that armor is doing you more harm than good."

"What's going on?" asked Dave. "Why did we stop running?"

"Ravenus took care of the T-Rex," said Julian.

Another roar, and the ground started to shake again.

"The fuck he did!" said Dave, hurriedly waddling past the group.

The rest of the party soon overtook him, but Julian stopped again after about thirty feet.

"Wait," he said. "Stop."

Cooper stopped because he was stupid. Who knows why Gilda stopped. Tim stopped because he didn't fancy continuing to run into the dinosaur-infested jungle alone.

Dave caught up to them after a few seconds. "Why are we stopped again."

"Feel the tremors," said Julian. "They're getting fainter. The T-Rex is running the other way."

Gilda put her hands on the ground. "Hmm... maybe. How can you be sure?"

"Empathy," said Julian, looking at Cooper.

Cooper rolled his eyes. "Not this shit again."

"Empathy?" said Gilda. "With the tyrannosaurus?"

"No. With Ravenus. We share an empathic link. I can sense that he's quite pleased with himself right now."

"I still think we should keep moving," said Dave.

"I'm with you," said Tim. The musty jungle was alive with sounds that might have been monkeys or might have been velociraptors. He couldn't see past the ferns more than a few feet in any direction. "It's too claustrophobic in here. I feel like we're being watched."

"Bullshit," said Cooper. "You're paranoid because we just got chased by a dinosaur."

"As reasons for being paranoid go," said Julian, "that sounds like a pretty good one to me. So what do you think? Make for the shore, or make for the house?"

"The house," Gilda answered very abruptly. "The only protection the shoreline provides us is that we can see what's going to kill us from a little farther away."

"And what kind protection do you think a wooden house is going to provide?" asked Dave.

"Well we just don't know, do we? And not knowing sounds just a little bit better than certain death if you ask me."

"Sounds good to me," said Tim. "Let's move."

They continued walking in the same direction they had been going while running from the tyrannosaurus. Tim replayed himself running into the jungle in his mind, and he was pretty sure they were headed roughly north by northwest.

"What other kinds of dinosaurs do you think they have here?" asked Julian, like he was on a class field trip. "It'd be cool to see those ones that spit acid."

Tim jumped when he thought he saw a fern move in his periphery to his left. Looking in that direction revealed nothing. *Just jumpy.*

"You mean like the ones that killed Newman?" asked Cooper.

Julian laughed. "I think his name was Nedry in the movie."

"He'll always be Newman to me."

A twig snapped somewhere beyond the ferns to Tim's left. He was sure of it this time.

"Would you two just shut up about Wayne Knight for a minute?"

"Who the fuck is Wayne Knight?" asked Cooper.

"He's the actor who plays Nedry," said Dave.

"Newman," corrected Cooper.

"What are you all talking about?" asked Gilda.

"Nothing," said Tim. "Just everybody shut up for a minute. We're being followed." He raised his hands and stopped walking.

When the group stopped walking, it sounded like at least a small part of the background jungle noise fell silent.

Tim looked up at Cooper and pointed his hands in opposite directions. Cooper craned his neck to look left, then right over the ferns. He frowned and shook his head.

"Stay together," Tim whispered. "They're stalking us, waiting for one of us to fall behind for an easy kill."

"Who?" asked Gilda.

"Velociraptors."

"Sweet!" said Cooper.

"He's right," said Julian. "We need to get to that house ASAP."

"Don't you guys start running," said Dave, his voice shaking.

Gilda folded her arms. "Look at the lot of you, foolish men! You're working yourselves up into a frenzy over nothing. What makes you suspect we're being stalked?"

"We have our sources," said Tim.

"Is this the same source that told you a tyrannosaurus can only see you if you move?"

Tim looked at his feet. "Yes."

"You're all jumping at your own shadows. I'm not saying we're safe, but let's at least wait until there's a visible threat before we soil ourselves with fear."

Cooper grabbed a handful of ferns and reached under his loincloth. "I was hoping nobody noticed. That wasn't fear, by the way."

"Maybe you're right," said Tim, trying to convince himself that it was even a possibility. "But we should keep moving just the same."

They walked in silence after that, which only amplified every leaf rustle, frog croak, and bug click, each one threatening to stop Tim's heart. He wished they'd go back to talking about bullshit, but he dared not start up a conversation himself.

After about fifteen minutes, Tim's heart rate began to slow. Maybe Gilda had been right. Or maybe the raptors had given up on trying to separate them and moved on in search of easier prey.

"Look!" said Cooper.

Tim's heart nearly cracked his ribs. "WHAT?"

Cooper reached down with his shit-caked hands to grab him.

Tim ducked and tumbled away from Cooper's grasp. "Just tell me what you see."

"The jungle ends just up ahead," said Cooper. "And I can see the house."

Tim was tempted to let Cooper lift him over the ferns, but he resisted. His curiosity would soon be sated without him needing to smell like Cooper's bowels.

After a few hundred more feet, Tim finally broke through the last of the jungle undergrowth. A forest of stumps and scorched earth stretched out for another five hundred feet, leading to the house that Ravenus had discovered.

What Ravenus had failed to mention was the giant wooden fence surrounding the property. Tim guessed it was no coincidence that it was around the same height as a tyrannosaurus.

"I guess that explains how they keep the place free of dinosaurs," said Julian.

"No way," said Dave. "It's tall enough for sure, but it's just a latticework of wood and bamboo. A T-rex would tear that to splinters in a matter of seconds."

"And yet there it stands," said Julian, sounding slightly annoyed.

"I don't know what else they'd need a fence that big for."

"Why bother with all of this speculation?" asked Gilda. "The important thing to do right now is to get on the other side of it. There's the gate. Let's go."

"Wait!" said Tim. "What about the velociraptors?"

Gilda sighed. "I thought we already established that there *are* no velociraptors."

"*You* established that. I'm not convinced. I still feel like we're being stalked."

"So you want to hang out here with them?"

"I'm just saying that maybe they haven't attacked us yet because they think they can still hide in wait for an opportune moment to strike. If we go out into the open, we deny them the ability to hide, and they might just go for broke and attack us before we make it to safety."

Gilda shook her head. "I think you're giving these imaginary stalkers of yours way too much credit. So what do you propose we do?"

Tim looked up at Cooper. "You're our fastest runner. Run like a motherfucker and see if that gate is unlocked. Julian and will cover you with Magic Missiles and my crossbow."

Cooper looked down at him and snorted. "Against velociraptors?"

Tim shrugged. "It's all we've got."

Cooper nodded. "Get your shit ready."

Tim raised his crossbow to eye level and scanned a path from the edge of the unmolested jungle to the gate. "On three. One... two... THREE!"

Cooper bolted like a racehorse out of the gate, his feet pounding the burnt ground. The cloud of disturbed ash he left in his wake made him look cartoonishly fast as he darted and weaved around tree stumps.

Tim remembered he was supposed to be watching for

velociraptors and jerked his crossbow back toward the trees. Nothing had emerged from the jungle. He glanced back at Cooper, who had now made it halfway to the fence, then back at the jungle. Still nothing. When Cooper neared the gate and slowed down to a jog, Tim lowered his crossbow.

"Feel better now, dinosaur hunter?" asked Gilda.

Tim turned around. Gilda and Julian were grinning at him. Only Dave appeared to be appropriately nervous.

"You're not going to shame me for being cautious. We've been attacked by dinosaurs twice already, and I'm not about to let my guard down to –"

Something buzzed and crackled loudly. Tim looked just in time to see Cooper engulfed in a web of blue lightning emanating from the fence.

When the lightning disappeared, Cooper fell backwards, hitting the ground hard without even trying to brace himself.

"Shit!" cried Tim.

"Horse!" said Julian. A white horse speckled with brown spots appeared next to him.

"Don't waste all your spells on horses!" said Tim. "It's not that far a walk."

"I'm not wasting them all," said Julian. "Just this one."

"Real nice," said Dave. "Take off and leave the rest of us to get eaten by dinosaurs."

Julian glared down at Dave. "It's not for me, stupid. It's for you. Get over there and help Cooper."

Dave's face turned pink. "Oh, I'm sorry. I was just –"

"Just get your fat ass on the horse already."

Helping Dave mount a horse was normally a task reserved for Cooper. Without him, it took the combined efforts of Julian, Gilda, and Tim to shove Dave onto the animal's back.

Julian slapped the horse on the ass. "Go!"

Dave bounced in the saddle as the horse galloped toward Cooper, kicking up an even thicker cloud of smoky ash. Tim, Julian and Gilda ran behind, coughing their way through the cloud.

When they finally made it to Cooper and Dave, Cooper was sitting up, confused and disoriented, in a puddle of his own shit that radiated away from him like rays of the sun.

"I heal thee," said Dave.

Cooper shook his head and gently pushed Dave away. "I'm good."

"You'd better be. That was my last healing spell."

Cooper looked from the black claws on his right hand, to the quietly humming gate, to the base of the fence, which was littered with the charred and surprised-looking corpses of countless birds, frogs, and small mammals. They were all lined up neatly a foot away from the fence. A butterfly fluttered past his face toward the fence until it exploded in a tiny globe of blue lightning. Its wings vaporized instantly as its body turned to white ash and fell to the ground. "How the fuck do you electrify a wooden fence?"

"It's magic," said Julian. His eyes were glowing bright white. He was using a Detect Magic spell. "There's a powerful magical field surrounding the whole fence. It's about a foot thick on both sides."

Tim looked at Dave. "That would explain why the dinosaurs don't just knock it down. They can't get near it without getting the shit zapped out of them."

"You should have used the handle," said Julian, extending his hand cautiously toward the gate's handle. "There's a hole in the aura." Apparently satisfied that he wasn't going to kill himself, he reached all the way in, grabbed the handle, and turned it until it clicked. The gate swung open an inch toward him.

The group backed up like they were riding a shockwave, giving Julian plenty of room to swing the gate the rest of the way open.

Compared to the charred wasteland and dinosaur-infested jungle, the area inside the fence looked like a recreated Eden. There were fruit trees, a colorful vegetable garden, and separate pens for goats and pigs.

In the center stood a large, but quaint, wooden house, built eight feet above the ground, supported by four living trees. A retractable staircase, currently raised, would give the occupants some means of protection against all but the biggest dinosaurs if their fence ever failed them.

The house rested in its tree supports above what looked like a miniature version of itself, minus the porch. Judging by all the noise coming out of it, the smaller house at ground level was a chicken coop.

Julian held out some pieces of dried fig to one of the goats, which eagerly licked them right out of his hand. "Hey there. You're a hungry little guy, aren't you?"

"Why ain't you more upset about your stupid bird?" asked Cooper.

"Ravenus is fine."

"You're never away from that thing for more than five minutes at a time, and the last time you saw him was when he flew off to fight a fuckin' tyrannosaurus almost an hour ago. How can you be so sure he's *fine*?"

"I told you. Ravenus and I have an empathic link. If he was in trouble, I'd know. Right now I sense that, wherever he is, he's very content."

"Maybe he's fucking the T-rex."

"Don't be vulgar," said Julian. "He's probably just flying around, enjoying the tropical sea air." He patted the goat on the head and looked at the vegetable garden. "I love this place. This is exactly the kind of place I want to live in when I retire."

Tim thought of the Chicken Hut. Even after having stabbed a pteranodon to death, the concept of ever being able to retire was so foreign to him. He'd always pictured himself continuing to line the arteries of rednecks until his own tired old heart finally gave in to despair, and he fell face-first into the –

From just outside the gate, the all too familiar sound of screaming horse, accompanied by the snarl and growl of whatever was tearing said horse apart, ripped Tim away from his self-pitying thoughts. All but one of the chickens inside the coop immediately stopped squawking and clucking.

"Polly!" cried Julian, taking a step toward the gate.

Tim blocked his path. "Don't even think about it." As an afterthought, he added, "And stop naming them."

In order to close the gate, someone would have to go outside and carefully pull it back around so as to avoid getting electrocuted. That wasn't going to happen. Tim scanned the yard for a place to hide.

"Behind the chicken coop!" Tim analyzed his choice of hiding place while he led his friends there. It was as good a chance as they had. The coop was big enough for all of them to hide behind, and that one retarded chicken who didn't take the hint to shut up might actually end up doing them a favor. "When the raptor busts into the coop to eat all the chickens, that's when we make a break for it."

His back up against the wall of the chicken coop, Tim could hear the soft, nervous clucking of the occupants, with the exception of the one which was still squawking away without a care in the world. The rest of them sensed danger.

Gilda grabbed Tim's left hand with both of hers. Her skin felt like rhino hide. "I'm scared."

"I told you there were fucking velociraptors." Tim felt like he had just failed a Willpower saving throw, because as much as he knew he shouldn't peek around the side of the coop, he couldn't force himself to not do just that.

When one of the goats bleated, Tim took his chance. It was a raptor, all right. Unsurprisingly, it was just as terrifying in real life as it had been on the big screen. Fortunately, it was facing away from him, its cold, vicious eyes fixed on the goat Julian had been feeding.

Any giant murder-lizard would have been frightening enough, but when it took a step toward the goat, raising its foot above the potato plants which had been obscuring it from view, Tim was reminded of the most defining feature of the velociraptor; the giant, hooked claws on its feet. This one happened to be dripping with fresh horse blood as well, which didn't ease Tim's anxiety at all.

Tim gasped.

Realizing that he'd just gasped, he pulled his head back just as the raptor pivoted toward him.

"Is it a raptor?" asked Dave.

"Of course it's a fucking raptor."

Julian was tugging on his ears. "Did it see you?"

"I don't think so."

Tim strained to hear some clue as to what the dinosaur was doing. What he really hoped to hear was a goat scream, which would mean the raptor had lost interest in him. But all he could hear was that one goddamn chicken that still refused to shut the fuck up.

"Gods be damned!" came a deep male voice from the porch above them. British. Probably an elf. "Alonzo! Fetch my wand. We've got a velociraptor in the potato patch."

"How'd it get through the barrier?" another elven voice responded.

"From the looks of it, she just wandered in through the open gate."

Cooper narrowed his eyes. "Clever girl."

"Do be careful, Felix," said the voice that Tim assumed belonged to Alonzo. "I don't want to have to rub another salve into your skin."

"Indeed not!" said Felix. "I'd much prefer you to rub one *out*." The two men laughed heartily.

Tim, Cooper, Dave, and Julian stared slack-jawed at the floor above them.

"Well I'll be a mother fucker," said Cooper. "Those two are –"

"Tim!" cried Gilda. "Watch out!"

Tim turned his head to find himself staring into the nostrils of the

140

velociraptor. It sprayed his face with a steamy bloodmist. Tim rolled away as a hooked claw sliced the air above him, taking a head-sized chunk out of the corner of the chicken coop.

The only sound that could compete with the sudden explosion of clucking was Cooper going into his Barbarian Rage.

"I'm really angry!"

The raptor took a swipe at Cooper, but Cooper caught it by the ankle and punched it in the face. The combination of Cooper's Rage-enhanced punch and being caught on one leg was enough to send the raptor tumbling to the ground.

It didn't stay down for long. The raptor leapt to its feet, shook its head, and gave Cooper a hard, scrutinizing stare. Cooper jerked his head to each side, cracking his neck, and stared back at his reptilian adversary.

The raptor screamed like a pack of jaguars. Cooper screamed back like a drunk rhinoceros.

Having demonstrated an equal capacity for verbal sparring, the two beasts lunged at each other. Even with Cooper's Rage-induced extra girth, the velociraptor outweighed him considerably. The two of them rolled out into the potato garden until Cooper, combining the force of his legs and the raptor's own inertia, kicked the dinosaur off of him and sent it flying into the magically electrified fence.

Blue electricity surrounded the raptor, crackling, hissing, but ultimately releasing it.

The upper right quarter of Cooper's back bled from a series of puncture wounds that looked like a butcher's diagram of where to cut the shoulder meat. The raptor's skin was patched with smoking electrical burns. They both took a moment to breathe.

"Finish it off!" Dave called through a cloud of feathers emanating from the hole in the corner of the chicken coop.

Tim held up his crossbow and tried to line up a shot, but a dwarf ass stepped into his line of fire.

"By Lothar's hammer!" Gilda had swiped Dave's mace, and was charge-waddling toward the injured raptor.

"Get out of the way!" cried Tim. There was no way she could have heard him over her own battle cry, and the continued squawking of the chickens, which were still losing their shit inside the coop.

A long whistle pierced through the air, rising and then lowering in pitch, like a slide whistle, bringing all action in the yard to a sudden halt. Gilda stopped running. The raptor turned its head. Cooper's body deflated. Even the chickens ceased squawking and clucking, except for that one.

Tim looked for the source of the sound. A blond elf stood in front of the goat pen like an oiled god or a cover model for a trashy elven romance novel. He was naked but for a dead black mink that hung from his waist. Its hind legs were splayed out like a Y along the top of his pelvis, the tail hanging forward like a furry phallus. Tim suspected his actual phallus was running down the animal's body, and couldn't help but wonder how far down it went toward the mink's head, which swung like a pendulum below his knees.

The mink wasn't the only small, furry mammal this elf was potentially violating. Armed with nothing but a brown hare, cradling it in his left arm and stroking it between the ears with his right hand, he stared intently at the velociraptor. He raised the hare to his mouth, whispered a single word in its ear, and set it gently on the ground.

Upon being released, the hare darted out of the gate like its ass was on fire. The raptor ran after it, slapping Cooper in the face with its tail on the way out.

"Greetings, travelers!" said the elf, whose voice Tim recognized as belonging to Felix. He placed his palm atop a wooden post which stood, seemingly purposeless, between the goat pen and the gate. The top of the post glowed with a pale green light, and the gate began to swing slowly around.

Feeling safe enough to emerge from the psychological protection of the chicken coop, Tim saw that the staircase on the porch was also sliding down.

"You must be Felix?"

"I am!" said Felix. "And how may I address the young lad with such fine ears?"

Tim's face became suddenly very warm. He tore his gaze away from the swinging mink head. "Any way but that, please."

"I beg your pardon?"

"Tim's fine," said Tim. "Look, I'm sorry about the damage we've caused."

"Think nothing of it! A few potatoes is no great loss. I only hope that raptor recovers from her wounds."

"Who gives a shit about the raptor?" said Cooper. "What about –"

"You can tell a lot about a man by the way he treats animals," said Gilda.

"Especially minks," Tim muttered a little louder than he'd meant to.

Felix flashed Tim a quick grin before addressing Gilda once again. "When you take away the trappings of man, the buildings and clothes and such, we're all beasts."

"I completely agree," said Gilda, looking up at him all doe-eyed.

Tim looked away, a cocktail of negative emotions bubbling up inside him. The beast under his clothes wouldn't be able to stuff a field mouse.

"Speaking of animals," said Felix. "Something seems to be amiss with one of our chickens."

"It's been squawking like that since we got here," said Dave.

Felix opened the front door of the chicken coop.

"Jesus!" shrieked Julian. "Stay out! Stay out!"

Everyone turned to look at him. He looked like he'd just seen the ghost of his naked grandmother.

"Hey man," said Tim. "Are you okay?"

"Huh?" said Julian. His eyes returned to normal and he looked down at Tim. "Yeah. I'm sorry. I don't know what came over –" His eyes darted up toward the chicken coop. "Ravenus!"

Tim turned around. Ravenus was hobbling unsteadily out of the coop like a drunk on the deck of a ship. The front of him was covered in white feathers. Reaching the entrance, he promptly fell face-first on the ground. He didn't even try to get up.

"Ravenus!" said Julian. "Are you hurt?"

"I'll be fine, sir," said Ravenus. "Just need a bit of a nap is all."

"What happened to you?"

"Seems I bit off more than I could chew, sir. That one in there's insatiable, she is."

Julian looked into the coop, then frowned down at Ravenus. "She's a little… *huskier* than what you usually go for, eh?"

Ravenus raised a wing. "Any port in a storm, sir." He looked at Tim. "Isn't that right?"

"Wha?" said Tim. *Stupid fucking bird!* He glanced at Gilda. *Shit! Why did I do that?* Gilda glared back at him. *Abort! Abort!* "I, um… I have to go to the bathroom."

"Very well then!" said Felix. He closed up the chicken coop and started walking toward the staircase. "Come inside. Make yourselves at home. We shall provide you with food, drink, and shelter for the night."

"That sounds fantastic," said Dave, wasting no time following Felix. Julian scooped up Ravenus, tucked him under his serape, and the rest of the group followed Dave.

Having reached the top of the stairs, Felix turned around. "And you can smoke my pole."

Tim, Dave, Cooper, Julian, and Gilda stopped simultaneously, like somebody hit the 'pause' button.

Dave turned around to face the rest of them and whispered

conspiratorially. "How badly do you guys want to stay here tonight?"

Tim didn't like the idea of being torn apart and eaten by dinosaurs, but he wondered if he'd like gobbling this fucker's mink-meat even less. "Do we *all* have to smoke his pole?"

"No way," said Cooper. "I spent my birthday last year at the Lady Slipper, and wound up hitting big on one of the video poker machines at the bar."

Dave put his hands on his head. "And this is relevant how?"

Cooper ignored him. "So I walk out of the Slipper with a thousand bucks. It's my birthday. I'm feeling good, like the stars aligned or some shit, right? Naturally, I take my good fortune with me to Come to Papa's."

Tim grimaced. "That's the strip joint off 603?"

"That's right."

"The one made out of three FEMA trailers?"

"That's the one."

"What's a FEMA trailer?" asked Gilda.

"Come on guys," said Cooper. "Time is a factor here."

Tim nodded. "Just hurry up and get to the point."

"So I drop some cash, and get two of the less reputable strippers to come spend the night in a motel with me."

Julian shivered and hugged himself. "Are there really tiers of reputability among the strippers at Come to Papa's?"

"I thought I was going to be spraying jizz like Willy the Water Bug all night long."

Dave tugged on his beard. "What does any of this have to do with —"

"I'd been out of the game for a while, and I splooged as soon as the first girl put her hand down my pants."

Tim finally broke the unexpected silence to follow.

"Is that the end of your story?"

"Pretty much," said Cooper. "Those two bitches played chess

while I tried to will my dick back to life. It wasn't happening. After thirty minutes, I just went home, broke, ashamed, and sticky."

Julian cocked an eyebrow. "They had a chess board at the motel?"

"The girls brought a travel set with them, like they'd been through this sort of thing before."

"Dude!" said Dave, twisting his beard. "Does this story have a point?"

"The point is that your brain chemistry – or whatever – changes right after you shoot your load. Like, you know when you whack it to the spring break pics that your cousin posts on Facebook, and then you feel so gross about it just after the fact?"

Tim, Julian, and Dave shared awkward, silent glances. Gilda just looked confused.

"Fuck you guys!" said Cooper. "I'm telling you, no matter how much heat that dude's packing in his fucking weasel-cannon, he's only got one round in the chamber. The rest of us will get a pass."

"So just what *are* you suggesting?" asked Tim.

"I don't know," said Cooper. "We draw straws, or play Rock Paper Scissors or some shit."

"And we never speak of it again," said Julian. He grabbed Cooper by the ear and looked square into his eyes. "You don't get to give anyone shit about this. You got that?"

Cooper yanked his ear out of Julian's grasp. "Yeah, I got it."

Dave was nearly pulling his beard out. He looked like he might be about to cry. "I don't want to smoke his pole."

Gilda sighed and looked up at Felix. "I'd be happy to smoke your pole."

"Nice try, Sugarnips," said Cooper. "But I don't think you're what he –"

"Outstanding!" said Felix. "Now all of you stop lollygagging on the stairs and come inside."

Julian grinned sheepishly. "That was unexpected."

146

"Gilda," said Tim. "You don't have to do this if you don't want to."

"Dude, shut up!" said Dave. "Yes she does."

"It's okay," said Gilda, looking directly and deliberately into Tim's eyes. "I really *really* want to." She turned and continued walking up the stairs.

Tim skulked up the stairs behind the rest of the group, trying to reason with himself that this was a good thing. He was dodging a bullet, right? Why did he feel like he was losing a battle, on multiple fronts, in a war that he didn't want to be involved in?

"Is it weird if we want to watch?" asked Cooper.

The wood that the stairs were constructed from was as rough as the wood making up the outer fence and animal pens, but the porch and house proper were sanded smooth.

"Did you build all of this yourself?" asked Julian.

"Heavens no!" said Felix. "I have a partner. Alonzo. He's inside polishing his rod."

"Um..." said Dave. "If this is a bad time, we can –"

Felix waved his hand at Dave like he was trying to shake off a swarm of bees. "Don't be ridiculous! He'd love to show it to you." He slid the front door open. "Alonzooooo!"

Alonzo appeared from around a corner at the far end of the house, carrying a tray of coconut cups with little bamboo straws poking out of the tops. His curly, brown hair bounced on his shoulders in time with the spring in his step. He was rocking a 70's porn star handlebar mustache and a robe made of peacock feathers. Neither of these adornments, however, could break Tim's gaze away from yet another man's crotch.

A tiger had died to inadequately conceal this elf's genitals. The eyelids were sewn shut, but the mouth hung wide open. Tim couldn't identify the pink, scaly animal that had given its life to be this guy's dick sock. It hung out like the tongue of no tiger that ever lived.

"There you are!" said Alonzo, his mock tiger tongue swaying

147

hypnotically from knee to knee as he advanced with his refreshments. "I was expecting you to come in the back door like you usually do."

Felix wagged a finger at him. "It's not as much fun when you're expecting it."

They smiled broadly at each other, then spoke simultaneously. "Too true!"

Dave backed up a step and leaned down to whisper to Tim. "Man, we need to get the fuck out of here before we get drugged, raped, and turned into *fabulous* home décor."

"I was just boasting to them about your rod," said Felix.

Alonzo rolled his eyes. "Oh stop!" Tim's heart froze when Alonzo turned to face them. "Do you want to see it?"

Tim, Dave, Julian, and Cooper silently shook their heads.

"I'd love to!" said Gilda. She stepped into the house before Tim could try to stop her.

Alonzo addressed the rest of them. "Don't be so bashful! Come on in and have a drink. I'm afraid all we've got to offer is coconut rum."

Tim looked up at Dave and whispered. "What if you're wrong about these guys? Coconut rum sounds really good right about now."

"I'm telling you, man!" Dave was barely keeping to a whisper. "There's nothing in those cups but semen and horse tranquilizers."

Cooper sniffed the air. "What's that smell?"

"Haven't you figured out by now," said Tim, "that you're always the answer to that question?"

"It smells like…" He sniffed again. "It smells like weed." He pushed his way past their hosts, sniffing like a bloodhound as he walked down the hall.

Felix, Alonzo, and Gilda followed Cooper toward the rear of the house. Tim could feel Dave's eyes on him, pleading with him not to follow, but Tim couldn't see how they had much of a choice now. He stepped inside.

"Sweet mother of fuck!" said Cooper when he turned the corner.

"You guys have got to come check this shit out."

Tim hurried to see what could possibly get Cooper so excited. The room was sparsely furnished, with only a rough wooden chest on the left wall and some palm leaf mats in a semi-circular pattern on the floor. The main attraction, however, was the clay fireplace, in which sat a crude, stone crucible full of boiling liquid. Above the crucible was a dome made out of some tanned animal hide. And connected to the front of the dome was a ten foot long length of bamboo as wide around as Tim's arm. The other end of the shaft was capped with a coconut shell, and rested in front of the center mat. The semi-circular pattern of the mats suggested that the shaft could pivot from side to side.

Tim was so impressed that he was unable to form a coherent exclamation. "Magna *Carta!*"

"Gindo herb grows wild on this island," said Alonzo, placing one of the coconut cups in front of the nearest mat. "It's one of our few luxuries."

"Me first!" said Cooper, taking a step into the room.

"Stop right there!" said Felix, his voice uncharacteristically authoritative.

Everyone looked at Felix. Even Alonzo paused in his task of distributing coconut cups to gawk at his partner.

Felix's harsh expression melted into a warm smile. "We are not brutes in this house. Is it not the custom where you come from to offer a lady the first opportunity to partake?" He gestured down to Gilda.

Tim and Cooper hung their heads, mumbled apologies, and stepped to the side.

"That's okay, boys," said Gilda, looking very pleased with Felix's act of chivalry and making Tim feel like even more of a lowlife. "You have your fun. I don't smoke."

Felix looked quizzically down at her. "But just a few moments ago,

149

when we were outside, you said you wanted to –"

"Oh shit!" said Dave. "When you said 'smoke your pole', you were talking about *this*?"

"But of course," said Felix, looking thoroughly confused now. "What else would I have been talking about?"

Dave grinned and rubbed his hands together. "Forget it! Let's smoke some pole!" He skirted past Cooper faster than he'd run from the T-rex.

Cooper, Julian, and Tim fell in line behind him, each taking a seat on one of the palm leaf mats.

Dave uncapped the end of the bamboo shaft, releasing a cloud of white smoke which ballooned around his head. The cloud shrunk as he took a long, deep inhalation.

"Careful!" said Felix. "Go easy on the first draw!"

Dave's eyes glazed over with either inner peace or death as he fell over backward, armor and head clunking on the polished wooden floor.

"Hand it over, Dopey," said Cooper. He took the bamboo tube away from Dave, who didn't even seem to notice, and put it in front of his nose. He sniffed hard a few times, then frowned. "Dave smoked the whole goddamn thing!"

Tim crawled over and grabbed the pipe from Cooper. "Give me that, idiot." He sat back down on his mat and re-capped the end. "You have to give it a chance to build up." He sipped his rum. Exquisite. The sip turned into a gulp. When his coconut was nearly half empty, he decided enough time had passed, uncapped the pipe and inhaled.

The vapor was smooth. Tim felt immediately light headed, and the soles of his feet tingled. This was some good shit.

Passing the pipe to Julian, Tim caught sight of Alonzo smiling down at them as he rubbed an unfinished wooden scepter with a cloth. He giggled and nearly lost his balance as he tried to nudge

150

Julian's arm.

"Check it out. He's polishing his rod."

"Do you like it?" said Alonzo, holding up the rod for everyone to get a better view. "It's to be my first enchantment. Magic is a persnickety force. You can't just enchant any old stick. The magic won't take unless the rod is of Masterwork quality."

"I keep telling you guys," said Julian. "You need to get your minds out of the gutter." He uncapped the pipe and inhaled.

"Alonzo," said Felix. "Grab my sack. I wish to smear my nut butter on the half-orc."

Julian choked violently on the vapor.

Cooper sprang to his feet in a karate stance. "What the fuck, man?"

"Oh heavens!" said Felix. "Is there some kind of problem?"

"Just back away from the exit," said Cooper. "Come on, guys. It's time to go."

"Speak not such folly!" said Alonzo. "You are injured, and your dwarf friend is not even awake. You are unfit for travel."

"Oh, but I'm fit enough for your nut butter, am I? You two grab each other's sacks and squirt your nut butter all over each other, but we're getting the fuck out of here."

"You can smear me with your nut butter," said Gilda.

"My dear!" said Felix. "Are you injured?"

"Hey!" said Tim, trying to stand on wobbly legs. "You keep your nut butter away from – Wait a minute. What kind of question is that?"

Alonzo pulled a half coconut container out of a small leather pouch. Inside the coconut shell was a light brown cream. "The oil from the pukka pukka nut has medicinal properties that can help your friend's wounds."

"I'm sorry," said Cooper, cautiously sitting back down on his mat. "I was confused. Probably the Gindo herb."

Alonzo frowned. "But you've not smoked any yet."

"Quit hogging the pole, long ears." Cooper took the pipe from

Julian, who was still red in the face from coughing.

"You guys are kind of remarkable," said Tim. The Gindo herb was clouding his mind, making him say nice things. "You built this house. You planted a garden. You know about medicine and magic and shit. Are you guys some kind of geniuses?"

"Pft," said Felix. "You're too kind. Nothing of the sort. We were but a couple of humble servants in Cardinia."

"That makes sense," said Julian, swaying like it was a major feat of Dexterity to remain sitting upright.

"How's that?" asked Tim.

"They came to this island as zero-level NPCs."

"I'm afraid I don't quite follow you," said Alonzo.

If Julian heard him, he made no acknowledgement of it. "If you're lucky enough to survive your first few encounters with dinosaurs, you're bound to level up pretty quickly, right? Their Skill Points for every gained level were allotted to skills that they needed to live here."

Tim lay on the floor and stared up at the ceiling. "Far out."

"I'm sorry," said Gilda. "None of that made a shred of sense to me."

Felix frowned. "Perhaps we've had enough Gindo weed for today."

Tim sat up. "No!" He scurried over to take the pipe from Cooper. Capping the pipe, he sat on Dave's belly and tried to think of something to keep them talking. "So how did you wind up here anyway?"

Felix sighed. "Our master was Boswell the Grand, a powerful wizard. We'd only served for two days when he banished us to this island."

"What did he banish you for?"

"The gods only know," said Alonzo.

"Maybe you said something that might have been *misconstrued*?" suggested Gilda.

"I don't see how," said Felix. "We are simple men. We speak not in riddles."

"Master Boswell seemed in fine spirits just beforehand," said Alonzo. "He had recently acquired us in a wager, along with Bindle the Bard and his famous miniature piano."

"Stop," said Tim, shaking his head. "Just stop."

"Does our story displease you?" asked Alonzo.

"No," said Tim. "I've just heard it before."

Felix and Alonzo exchanged confused glances.

Alonzo refilled Tim's coconut cup from a clay jar. "That seems highly unlikely."

"You said something about his tiny pianist, didn't you?"

Gilda choked on the rum she was gulping.

"It was all complimentary," said Felix.

"I wondered aloud," said Alonzo, "how hard such a gift must come."

Gilda sprayed rum all over Felix's bronze, oiled ass.

"Oh heavens!" said Felix. "Did you not like the rum?"

"I like it just fine," said Gilda. She grabbed Felix by the hips. "In fact. Hold still and I clean that up." She opened her mouth and lunged her face toward his ass.

"Yeeeee!" Felix squealed, tearing himself free from her grasp. "Not necessary, dear. We've got plenty. I'll just run out and get some more." He ran out of the room, then poked his head back in. "I may be a moment."

"I never thought I'd say this, Alonzo," said Cooper. "But your nut butter feels great."

"Oh stop!"

"Seriously dude. I feel great." Cooper lay on his back and closed his eyes. "I just want… to stretch out and…" As a tendril of drool made its way from his mouth to the floor, a long, low fart rumbled out of his ass like an outboard motor in neutral.

"Jesus Christ," said Julian, swiping the pipe out of Tim's hand.

"Hey man!" said Tim. "I haven't taken my turn yet."

Julian ignored him, uncapped the pipe, and surrounded his face with the only air in the room that could compete with Cooper's fart. Tim had apparently been talking too long, as the cloud around Julian's face was nearly as big as the one that had dropped Dave. Unsurprisingly, Julian went down like somebody punched the bottom of a Jenga stack.

"Ha!" said Tim, taking the pipe back from Julian's unconscious body. "Stupid fucker." He downed what was left in his coconut cup and hoped Felix would return soon with the next round.

"So!" said Gilda, speaking unabashedly directly to Alonzo's tiger face crotch. "Do you guys ever miss anything from life in the big city?"

Alonzo frowned as he listlessly polished his rod. "We used to get more homesick, back when we had to fight off dinosaurs every day." He spread his arms out, showcasing his surroundings. "But now that we've made all of this, we have everything that we need." He looked down at the floor. "Almost."

"Why didn't you ever look for the portal?"

"Portal?

"Boswell didn't tell you about the portal on the north beach?"

"Master Boswell didn't say anything but a quick and angry incantation. Next thing we knew…"

"Who's thirsty!" said Felix, prancing back into the room with a fresh clay pitcher. His mink fur appeared a little scruffier than Tim remembered it looking before. He stopped when he saw the three unconscious bodies on the floor. "Oh heavens, it seems the party is winding down."

"Nonsense!" said Tim, holding up his cup.

Felix winked at him. "Ladies first." He filled Gilda's cup with coconut rum.

Alonzo looked up from his rod. "The *lady* was just saying something very interesting with regard to this island."

"Is that right?" Felix started to fill Tim's cup.

"She says there's a magic portal back to civilization."

Felix froze. The rum stopped flowing. Tim nudged the bottom up with his finger to get it going again.

Alonzo looked scrutinizingly at Felix. "She says it's on the north beach."

"Impossible," said Felix. He turned to Gilda. "We know every inch of this island. There's nothing on the north beach but ..." He pursed his lips and looked at Alonzo. "Terrence's cave?"

"Who the hell is Terrence?" asked Tim. "You mean to tell me there's another one of you guys on this island?"

"Don't be silly," said Felix, pouring himself a cup of rum. "Terrence isn't one of us."

Tim's mind tried to sort its way through a maze of booze and weed. Felix and Alonzo, for all of their eccentricities, seemed like a pretty welcoming couple of guys. Why wasn't this Terrence guy here with them, unless...

"So is he like... a homophobe or something?"

"I beg your pardon?" said Terrence, a little more sternly than Tim was expecting.

"Terrence is the nickname we've given to a peculiar tyrannosaurus that lives on the north beach."

"He lives there?" asked Gilda.

"That's right," said Felix.

"What do you mean he lives there?" asked Tim. "Like he's got a hut and a margarita bar?"

"I know it sounds strange," said Alonzo. "But he's always there, day and night, in the same spot. He steadfastly refuses to move from the entrance to this cave. He won't chase a hare. Our weapons have proven useless against him. He just stands there, staring out at the sea."

Felix raised his eyebrows. "It's almost as if he's *guarding* something."

Tim gulped down the rum in his cup. "That's some fucked up shit." At least he thought it was some fucked up shit. He knew he couldn't trust his mind in the state it was in. He looked at Gilda. She was starting to look all right, bordering on 'good enough'. *Abort! Abort!* "We shall investigate in the morning." He uncapped the end of the pipe and inhaled like he was about to get plunged into the sea. The world was beautiful. Then fuzzy. Then gone.

*

"Rise and shine!" an unwelcome voice penetrated through the warm, comfortable oblivion. "It's a beautiful new day. Time to get up and have some breakfast."

Consciousness returned slowly. Despite Tim's best efforts to shut them out, the day's realizations came to him in their standard procession.

He was still a halfling. *Shit.*

He was still stuck in this goddamn game. *Shit.*

He'd gotten high and passed out in the home of two – Tim sat bolt upright and opened his eyes wide.

He was fully clothed. *Thank fuck.*

Neither his jaw nor his asshole felt as though they'd been violated. *Thank fuck.*

Was he a terrible person for having worried about these things in the first place? Probably. Even still, he took a quick glance around to make sure his friends were all accounted for, and that Cooper was the only one covered in nut butter.

"What the hell happened last night?" asked Dave, rubbing his eyes. "I feel like I got punched in the face by a fist made out of rose petals."

Tim shook the last of the sleep out of his head. "You hit the Gindo weed too hard. We all did."

Cooper reached under his loincloth and scratched his balls. "Did I end up blowing anyone?"

"No."

"Sweet. What's for breakfast?"

"Oh heavens!" said Felix, his nose scrunched up and his eyes started to water as he made a beeline for the window on the other side of the room. He flung the shutters open, flooding the room with blinding morning light, but also with some welcome fresh air. "What's that smell?"

Cooper rolled up the mat he'd fallen asleep on, presumably to hide the evidence of him having shit on it during the night. "This mat could probably stand a wash."

"Ew!" said Felix. "Just get rid of it. I'll make a new one."

Cooper balled up the mat and chucked it at the open window. Catching the air, it opened up, hit the wall, and stuck there.

Felix gaped at the mat, his chin quivering.

"Shit," said Cooper. "Sorry about that."

Julian stifled a yawn and shook his head. "I think we've overstayed our welcome. Perhaps it's time we part ways with our gracious hosts."

Felix looked like he was torn between his desire to be the gracious host Julian had just diplomatically challenged him to continue being and his desire to throw every single one of them through the window.

He regained his composure. "At least have some breakfast before you go. Gilda and Alonzo have been up all morning preparing eggs and potatoes."

"Oh fuck!" said Cooper. All eyes in the room turned to him. "Where the hell did you get eggs?"

Felix looked at the mat stuck to the wall, then back at Cooper. He answered tentatively. "From the chicken coop?"

"Whew," said Cooper. "Good thinking." He sniffed the air, presumably picking up a scent other than his own, and followed it

157

out the door.

"Eggs," said Dave as he waddled out after Cooper.

Tim and Julian looked at each other, then at the mat on the wall.

"Should we..." said Julian. "Do you have a sponge, or –"

"I'll take care of it," said Felix, the usual gaiety absent from his voice. "Please, just go."

"Well there you are!" said Gilda as Tim and Julian walked into the kitchen. "I thought you boys would never wake up."

The table wasn't big enough to accommodate quite so many guests, and there were only two chairs. There were, however, more than enough dishes, all of which appeared to have been crafted from the same tree trunk. Seven such dishes were crowded together on the small table, each containing a generous helping of scrambled eggs, specked with chopped onions, green peppers, and chunks of potato.

Alonzo was adorning each dish with a sprig of parsley when Felix grabbed one and dumped its contents into one of the previous night's unwashed coconut cups.

"Felix!" cried Alonzo. "Have you lost your senses?"

Felix grabbed a second dish and a second dirty coconut cup. In his haste, he spilled more egg on the floor than he got in the cup. "It's a beautiful day. I thought it might be nice to dine outdoors."

The peacock feathers of Alonzo's robe were trembling. "Stop that right now, Felix!"

Felix slammed the cup and dish on the table and glared at his partner. "May I speak to you *alone*? In the other room?"

Alonzo put on his best fake calm face and turned to the rest of them. "Pardon us for just one moment." He followed Felix out of the kitchen.

Julian frowned. "Maybe we should just cut our losses and –"

"Sweet father of the gods!" Alonzo cried from the next room. He began to sob. "We'll have to burn the whole house down and rebuild."

"Now now," said Felix. "Maybe it's not as bad as all that. Let's just leave the windows open for a couple of days and see how –"

Alonzo stopped crying. "We can tie them up and burn it down with them inside!"

A night's worth of Cooper's hotboxed anal emissions was enough to break the spirit of even the most gracious host.

"Still your tongue, Alonzo. You're a better man than that. Let's just send them on their way and hope the dinosaurs eat them."

Before anyone could react beyond exchanging uncomfortable glances, Felix and Alonzo returned to the kitchen.

Alonzo's face was streaked with tears, but he wore a tremendously fake smile. "Who wants to go on a picnic!"

Tim didn't know how to respond. Their hosts hadn't even bothered to whisper their intentions to passively murder them, but he'd already determined that they'd be leaving anyway.

It didn't matter. Alonzo wasn't waiting for a response. He shoved the two egg-filled coconut cups into Dave and Julian's hands and immediately started scooping egg from dishes to cups with his own hands.

"We need a favor," said Tim.

Alonzo stopped scooping and glared down at him. "You need a *favor*?"

"Come on, Tim," said Julian. "I think we're pushing the limits of –"

Tim kept his eyes locked with Alonzo's. "We want to meet Terrence."

Alonzo's glare softened, but his eyes stayed with Tim's. "You want to meet *Terrence*?"

"Who the fuck is Terrence?" asked Cooper.

Tim held Alonzo's gaze. "Put a cork in it, Cooper."

Cooper responded with a small, squealing fart.

"Make that two corks."

The fart didn't stop. It just grew louder and higher in pitch, like a

159

slowly deflating balloon being pinched at the opening.

Tim continued to stare down Alonzo. "Escort us to Terrence, and we'll be out of your lives forever."

Alonzo's eyes watered. His porn-stache twitched. All the while, Cooper's fart continued to squeal out, meandering through the room like an invisible serpent.

Finally, Alonzo blinked and turned his head away. "Very well, halfling! We shall see you and your friends safely to the north beach. There you will find Terrence, though I know not what you hope to accomplish. Perhaps your friend's flatulence can move him as we could not."

Dave stared down into his cup of egg. "Do you guys have, like… um… a spoon or something?"

Alonzo turned to Dave with what now looked less like a fake grin and more like a genuine, feral teeth-baring.

"It's cool, man," said Dave. "I'll use my fingers."

Alonzo faced Tim again. "We leave at once!"

*

As they traveled clockwise around the circumference of the island, Tim filled in the rest of the group with what little he knew of Terrence. The tyrannosaurus, as Alonzo had described it the night before, was a peculiar beast, and Tim hypothesized that such peculiarities may have a connection, or at least reveal clues, to the whereabouts of the portal.

While no one seemed particularly impressed with his hypothesis, none of them had any better ideas, and most of them were at least mildly curious to check out Terrence, and maybe taunt him with thrown coconuts or something.

Even Felix and Alonzo's mood lightened as the fresh sea air diluted the fart in their lungs. While the rest of the party cowered by the water's edge, eyes and weapons fixed on the jungle, Felix and Alonzo walked confidently, weapons undrawn, on the hot, dry sand.

Only Ravenus, flying ahead to tear scraps off of some disease-ridden dead fish, seemed to be as carefree as those two.

Tim nudged Julian and whispered, "Go talk to them. See if you can get them to hate us a little less, just in case."

"Why aren't you guys scared?" asked Julian, braving his way to walk alongside Felix and Alonzo. "I mean, I see you're tough, and you've obviously survived this long... But come on, man. *Dinosaurs*."

Way to go, Julian. Compliment their bravery, and back it up with evidence that you're not just blowing smoke up their shiny bronze asses.

Felix spared a glance at Julian like he was doing him a favor. "The predators on this island are opportunists. There are far too many of us for them to risk attacking. But to more directly answer your question, we know fear the same as any man. Learning to mask that fear is an essential part of survival."

"Like a Bluff check?"

"I beg your pardon?"

"I'm sorry. Go on."

"If a dinosaur senses that you're afraid, she'll know it's safe to attack you. If she doesn't smell the fear on you, her tiny brain is wise enough to wonder why."

"They smell fear?"

"Worry not, young elf," said Alonzo, as if Julian was an embarrassment to his race. "However strong your fears may be, their scents are surely overpowered by your half-orc friend."

"Hey asshole," said Cooper. "I can still hear you, you know."

Tim turned his crossbow from the jungle to Cooper's loincloth. "If you say another goddamn word, I'll shoot your dick off."

"And I can still smell you!" Alonzo turned around, fists balled and trembling. His mustache twitched. He sniffed the left shoulder of his peacock feather robe. "It's all over me!"

161

"Alonzo, please." Felix tried to put his hand on Alonzo's shoulder. Alonzo shrugged him off and stomped ahead along the beach. "I'm sorry, Felix. I just can't wear it anymore!" The robe fell off of his back, a pile of blue feathers on the white sand, revealing a previously hidden accessory on his outfit. Where the sides of the tiger face wrapped around his back and met, a tiger tail ran along his crack, hanging nearly as far down as the tongue on the other side.

Cooper snorted out laughter and snot. Tim just gawked, mesmerized and unable to look away.

Alonzo twirled around, his tiger tongue and tail flying outward and upward. Tim was startled at having been caught staring, and accidentally squeezed the trigger of his crossbow.

Click.

Twang.

"YEEEAAAAAOOOOOWWW!"

"Huh?" Tim was overloaded with sensory input.

"Son of a bitch!" said Cooper, both hands over his crotch. "You shot my fucking dick off!"

"Shit, man! I'm –" Tim reconsidered, thinking he might be able to score some points. He spoke sternly at Cooper. "I warned you, didn't I?" He glanced up at Alonzo and thought he might have caught a flicker of a smile before his eyes were inevitably drawn down to the tiger crotch.

Tearing his gaze away, he turned to Dave, who appeared curiously unmoved by both Cooper's howl of pain and Alonzo's dangling accessories.

"Hey! Dave!"

Dave's eyes focused on Tim. "Yeah?"

"I just shot Cooper in the dick."

"Far out."

Not quite the response Tim was aiming for. What the hell was going on with Dave?

"Well do you think you could… Hold on. Did you pray for your spells this morning?"

Dave laughed. "I'm an atheist."

"Dude! Are you still fucking high?"

Dave put his hand on top of his head, moved it forward at the same height, then brought it down to Tim's head. "Higher than you, man."

Tim slapped Dave's hand off of his head. "No shit, dude. You're higher than the goddamn Chrysler building."

"What's a Chrysler building?" asked Gilda.

Tim looked up the beach at Felix and Alonzo. "I'm sorry guys. Do you have any more of that nut butter on you?"

"What?" said Cooper. "No, really. It's not that bad." He groaned as he reached under his loincloth to remove the bolt. "It's… just a…" He dropped to his knees, wincing and groaning at a pitch only dogs should have been able to hear. "… superficial… wound." He exhaled and victoriously lifted his blood-soaked hand, holding the bolt. "See?" He panted a few times. "Good as new."

"You waste our time with your childish antics," said Alonzo, apparently still bitter about his fart-infused robe. "My rod shan't polish itself."

Tim and Julian shared a brief glance, but inappropriate laughter, it seemed, was easier to avoid when you've just watched a man mutilate his own genitals.

"Just ahead of us," said Felix. "Under that cliff, is where you can find Terrence. Our obligation fulfilled, we wish you good day."

Tim looked ahead. The land rose gradually. In the distance, it appeared as if a chunk of the island had collapsed into the sea, leaving a rockier stretch of beach and a sheer cliff face. The way the beach curved around, however, obscured the part where Terrence must have been keeping his strange vigil. Not being able to see the dinosaur made him even more nervous.

"You're not even a little curious about what we might discover?"

Felix looked down his nose at him. "We have wasted too many hours trying to coax Terrence into turning his back so that we might penetrate his hole."

"Um…" said Cooper. "Are we all talking about the same thing?"

"We have tried everything there is to try regarding Terrence, short of letting him eat us. I have no doubt in my mind that your band of buffoons will find a way to kill yourselves without our further assistance."

Tim wasn't sure why he wanted these two to stay so badly, except that he was shit scared of facing another T-rex without them.

Julian either felt the same way Tim did, or was picking up on his panic. "Well wouldn't you want to at least see that?"

Felix looked at Alonzo, who nodded enthusiastically. "Very well."

Cooper rose shakily to his feet, leaving behind a brown and red stew on the formerly pristine white sand. "Let's get this over with. I'm feeling a little lightheaded."

"As you should," said Alonzo. "It appears you left the contents of your head on the beach."

Felix raised his eyebrows. "Alonzo!"

Alonzo grinned sheepishly, pleased with himself for what was evidently an uncharacteristic zinger.

Felix clawed at the air. "MeeYOW!"

"So…" said Tim. "Terrence?"

Felix rolled his eyes. "Come on."

As they moved further up the beach, it became clear that, if Terrence really existed and really stood in the same place all the time, they weren't going to see him until they were nearly right on top of him. Tim started to have second thoughts.

"Is no one else in the least bit concerned that there's allegedly a tyrannosaurus just on the other side of those rocks?"

Julian shrugged. "I was apprehensive about it when we were a little further back on the beach, but not so much now."

"And why is that?"

"Because there are only three ways this can play out," Julian explained. "Either Terrence doesn't exist, in which case he presents no danger."

Felix shook his head and laughed to himself.

Julian continued. "Or he exists just as these gentlemen described him, in which case he doesn't pose a threat as long as we don't get too close."

"Option C is what concerns me," said Tim.

Julian nodded. "He exists, but is not as stationary as was stated."

"That's the one."

"Yes," said Julian. "Well if that's the case, then we're just plain…"

"Fucked?" suggested Cooper.

"Thank you, Cooper," said Julian. "Precisely the word I was looking for. We passed the point at which we could still hope to have time to flee into the jungle a while back, so there's not much point in worrying about it now."

Tim was surprised to find himself actually a little comforted by that appeal to logic.

Felix stopped, turned around, and addressed the group. "Gentlemen, lady." He nodded politely to Gilda. "I present to you, Terrence." He looked to his left.

Cooper walked up to Felix and looked to the side. "Holy fucknuggets!"

Dave waddled ahead, barely aware of his own existence. He glanced up in Terrence's direction. "Sweet."

"I'm afraid," said Gilda, grasping hold of Alonzo's hand, to Tim's inexplicable annoyance.

Alonzo smiled down at her. "You needn't worry, my dear. Terrence shan't harm you if you keep your distance."

Tim stomped ahead of them and looked up, and then up some

more. As advertised, a huge tyrannosaurus stood motionless in front of the cliff face. It was at least fifty percent bigger than the one that had chased them the day before.

"Hey!" shouted Cooper. "Shithead! Down here!"

Tim's heart pounded. He gave Cooper a look like he was going to shoot him in the junk again. "Knock it off!"

"Calm yourself, halfling," said Felix. "Even your friend's abject stupidity is no match for this great beast's stubborn unwillingness to move."

Tim peered between the dinosaur's legs at a fracture at the base of the cliff. There was a gap wide enough to walk through, though the crumbly nature of the terrain made that ill-advised. Squinting harder, trying to ignore the giant carnivorous lizard looming over him, he thought he could see a faint blue glow from deep within the gap.

"Is there a light coming from in there?"

Felix hunkered down next to Tim. "Where?"

"Right there, inside the cave," said Tim. "You can only just barely make it out."

Felix squinted. "I don't think so. Maybe. It's too difficult to tell from here."

"The portal's got to be in that cave!" said Tim. "Don't you see? That's our ticket out of this hellhole. And Terrence here is a test."

"A test?"

"Yeah. He was put here to guard the portal. If we solve the puzzle, he'll move."

"Puzzle?"

"Sure!" said Tim. "I'll bet you anything that old Boswell put him here with some kind of spell."

"Let me Detect Magic on him," said Julian. His eyes glowed white as he looked up at the dinosaur. "Yeah, he's magical all right."

"Let's just kill it," said Cooper.

Tim rolled his eyes and laughed. "I don't really think the puzzle is going to be that easy to solve."

"Fuck the puzzle. I've got a hole in my sack, and I'd like to get back home and get that sorted out. We know magical creatures can be killed. Julian's killed enough magical horses to fill hell's stables ten times over."

"Just let me think about it for a moment, and if we can't come up with –"

"Eat a dick, Terrence!" Cooper shouted, and a chunk of rock about the size of his head flew forward, striking the dinosaur on the right leg. It bounced off of its skin and landed on the ground next to it. Terrence didn't even seem to notice.

"Well that's odd," said Tim. He loaded his crossbow and fired a bolt right into Terrence's undefended belly. It bounced off and landed in front of him. "He must have a hell of a flat-footed Armor Class."

"What's an Armor Class?" Gilda asked Alonzo. Alonzo shrugged.

"Ravenus!" said Tim. "Julian, where's Ravenus?"

"I left him back at that bloated whale corpse we passed half an hour ago."

"Get him over here. He got rid of the last T-rex. Maybe he can get rid of this one."

"I don't know," said Julian. "This isn't a regular dinosaur. I don't want to subject Ravenus to any unnecessary risk before we know more about what this thing is."

"There's no risk," said Tim. "We're just experimenting. Have him do a couple of fly-by's and we'll see what happens."

Julian folded his arms. "I can't reach him right now. He's out of range."

"Bullshit," said Tim. "If Cooper starts beating the shit out of you, I bet he'll come flying back."

"I'm not going to beat the shit out of Julian," said Cooper. As an afterthought, he added, "Dave should get a pet bird."

Dave nodded slowly. "That'd be awesome."

"I'm not bullshitting you," said Julian. "If we're more than a mile away from each other, we lose our empathic link."

"Julian!" screeched Ravenus, flying in from over the sea.

Julian looked at his feet. "Shit."

"Look out, sir! There's a dinosaur right in front of you!"

Julian looked up and waved. "Thank you, Ravenus. We saw him."

"No worries, sir! I'll take care of him!" He flew wide around to come at Terrence from the side and slightly above. The trajectory he was in would take him buzzing past the back of the dinosaur's head.

"No, Ravenus," Julian called out. "It's too dangerous. Wait until we –"

"BWAAAAAAHHHHHHH!" Ravenus screeched as he started his dive, apparently hoping to annoy the beast to death.

"Stop, Ravenus!" Julian yelled. "Pull up!"

"AAAAAAAAAAAHHHHHHHH—"

Terrence's head whipped around a full one hundred and eighty degrees to snatch Ravenus out of the air. In a fraction of a second, before the echoes of the bird's battle cry had faded, Terrence's head had sprung back into its proper, forward-facing position, and he stood silently again, like a giant reptilian Buddhist monk.

Tim was in some deep shit.

"He's gone," Julian finally said.

"Dude," said Tim. "I'm so sorry. I didn't think –"

"It doesn't make sense."

"I know you must be –"

"It makes perfect sense," said Dave.

"Jesus Christ, Dave," said Tim. "Not now, okay?"

"It's just like in the movie," Dave continued. "You know how the dinosaurs had the frog DNA, so they could switch gender and populate the island?"

Tim caught a glimpse of Felix and Alonzo looking questioningly down at Gilda, like maybe this was a dwarf thing. She shrugged. Dave kept talking.

"Well dinosaurs are the ancestors of modern birds, right? So it makes sense that they'd share some of the same DNA."

"Man, I don't know where you're going with this, but now is not the –"

"Some species of birds, like owls, can swivel their heads all the way around to their backs, so–"

"So who gives a fuck?" said Tim.

"Just let me finish my thought."

"No!" said Tim. "Look, I see where you're going with this, and I'll grant you it makes about as much sense as that frog DNA bullshit in the movie, but nobody gives a hot, steamy dino-shit right now about how Terrence was able to turn his head around. Our friend is in pain."

"That's the part that doesn't make sense," said Julian. "I feel fine."

Tim wasn't familiar with the recognized stages of grief that people were supposed to go through, but he didn't think 'indifference' was on the list. He wanted to proceed carefully, but also be straightforward.

"Your familiar just died, man. Maybe you're in shock or something, but when it hits you, it's gonna hit hard. And I think you'll lose some Experience Points. I just want you to know that – "

Julian looked down at Tim. "I don't think he's dead."

Denial. That was definitely one of the stages. "Dude, he just got eaten by a dinosaur. We all saw it."

"He could have been swallowed whole," suggested Cooper. "Maybe he's still being digested."

"Cooper!" snapped Tim. "*Not* helping!"

Julian shook his head. "It's not that either. If that was the case, I'd feel his pain. I'd feel him suffocating. But I don't feel anything."

"Maybe you're just a heartless son of a bitch," said Cooper.

169

Tim glared at Cooper. "*Still* not helping!"

"It feels more like when our empathic link gets cut," said Julian. "Like when he flies out of –" He dropped to his knees and grabbed Tim by the shoulders. "That's it!"

"What's it?" said Tim. "What just happened?"

Julian spun Tim around and yanked his head back, so that he was staring up at the dinosaur. "Terrence!"

Tim raised a hand and waved at Terrence. "Sup?"

"No, you fool!" said Julian, spinning Tim around to face him again. "Don't you see? Terrence isn't guarding the portal. Terrence *is* the portal!"

"I don't know, man," said Tim. "That sounds a little farfetched to me."

Julian turned to Cooper and Dave. "What do you guys think?"

"Uh…" said Cooper.

"Awesome!" said Dave.

"Who gives a shit what they think?" said Tim. "Cooper's an idiot and Dave's still high as fuck."

"I think it's a perfectly plausible theory," Alonzo called out.

"Well there you go," said Julian, looking smugly down at Tim.

"Do I have to remind you that he straight up said that he wanted to see us get eaten by dinosaurs?"

"Is there no one that you trust?"

"Enough to convince me to go leaping into a tyrannosaurus's mouth? No. No one comes to mind."

Julian looked past Tim and nodded toward the sea. "What about that guy?"

Tim turned around. The beach was empty. "Who the hell are you talk—" *Shit! He used his Bluff skill!* By the time he turned back around, Julian was sprinting, having already covered about a third of the distance between him and Terrence. Tim couldn't hope to catch Julian with his little legs, but Cooper might be able to.

"Cooper!" Tim cried. "Get him!"

Cooper was facing the wrong way, squinting toward the beach. "I can't even fucking see him. Where is he?"

"Not him! Julian!"

"Huh?" Cooper turned around. "Oh shit!" He displaced about ten pounds of sand as he took off after Julian. "Dude! Stop! Are you fucking crazy?"

For all his faults, Cooper could run like a motherfucker. It would be close, but Tim estimated that Cooper might reach Julian just in the nick of time to save him.

Julian looked back over his shoulder, and evidently came up with the same estimate. "Horse!" A second later, Julian was mounted on a beige stallion.

Cooper stopped running. "Come on, man. Don't kill yourself over a goddamn bird."

"Ravenus is alive," said Julian. "He's going to come looking for me. If I don't get there before he flies out of range, I may really lose him forever." He looked up at Terrence, aligned his horse, and whipped down the reins. "Yah!"

The horse bolted toward the dinosaur at full gallop while Tim stood helplessly and watched.

As any idiot could have predicted, as soon as Julian got close enough, the giant tyrannosaurus bent over, quick as a bolt of lightning, and ate both Julian and horse in a single bite.

Tim hurled his empty coconut shell at Terrence, who was standing upright once again. "Stupid, stubborn bastard. Died like he lived."

"How's that?" asked Cooper.

"Killing horses."

Cooper let out a small, listless snort of a laugh, and an equally unenthusiastic fart.

"I don't think he's dead," said Dave.

Tim balled up his tiny fists. "Well look who finally got his head out of the fucking clouds. Thank you *so* much for your opinion, Mr. Cheech and Chong."

"Those are actually two people, you know."

"That's exactly the sort of reasoning that just got Julian killed. What do you want to do? Keep chasing each other into Terrence's mouth like he's the old lady who swallowed the fly?"

"Ah ha!" said Dave. "And what finally did the old lady in?"

"I don't know," said Tim. "A horse?"

"That's right. And what did Terrence just swallow?"

"Terrence is a goddamn fifty foot tall tyrannosaurus! The old woman was a fucking… old woman! It stands to reason that she'd die if she tried to swallow a horse."

"The bird was stretching the limits of credibility."

"Was there a point to any of this?"

"Terrence is big, sure," said Dave. "But big enough to swallow a whole horse and an elf at the same time? No screaming? No blood? Come on."

Tim looked at the sand under Terrence. Not even a speck of red to be seen. "I want to believe he's alive. But I'm not willing to gamble my own life on it."

"I'll prove it to you. Give me your rope and crossbow."

Tim dug through his bag, pulled out his fifty foot coil of rope, and handed the rope and crossbow over to Dave. "What are you doing?"

"The Teleport rules state that all items in your possession go with you." Dave tied one end of the rope to Tim's crossbow and handed it back to him. "I'll hold the other end of this rope. The rope is clearly in my possession. The crossbow is in yours. If the rope disappears, you know I successfully teleported. If the crossbow gets yanked out of your hand, well…"

"Fuck that," said Tim, untying the rope from his crossbow.

"Where's the flaw in my plan?" asked Dave.

"No flaws," said Tim. "It's a great plan. But if you're wrong, I'm going to need my crossbow. Give me your mace."

"I wish you weren't gambling on me dying."

"I'm just hedging my bets."

"Fair enough." Dave handed over his mace.

Tim tied a simple knot around Dave's mace. "Dave, are you sure you want to do this? This is usually the sort of stupid idea that you argue with Julian about."

"Julian usually turns out to be right. I believe him."

"You're sure you're not just still high?"

"A little. So I'd like to get this done before I come down completely from the Gindo weed."

"Dave," said Cooper.

Dave looked up at Cooper. "Yeah."

"You got any coin you want to leave behind?"

Dave looked down at Tim again. "I'll give you fifteen minutes alone with him, and you'll be looking for any dinosaur's mouth to jump into."

"Oh sure," said Cooper. "When Tim says it, he's being *practical*. When I say it, I'm an asshole."

Dave inhaled and exhaled hard a few times. "Okay, I'm going to do this before I lose my nerve." He turned around and started running toward Terrence.

If time was a factor for Dave losing his nerve, he had plenty of it.

"This is excruciating," said Cooper.

"It's like ripping off a Band Aid with a glacier," said Tim.

"I feel like I should make a sandwich or something while we wait."

As the rope slowly uncoiled, Tim gripped the shaft of Dave's mace tighter. He held it out in front of him horizontally, one hand on each end, careful not to touch the knot in the middle. As Dave approached the danger zone, Tim had to force himself to watch. Though doubts crept into his mind, he also forced himself not to call out for Dave to turn back.

Just as Dave reached the end of the horse tracks, Terrence's great head swooped down to pick him up. And just like that, Tim was stuck in a fantasy world with still one less friend.

"Fuckin' A!" said Cooper.

"I know you and Dave weren't the best of friends, but it takes a special kind of piece of shit to celebrate –"

"Dude, the rope's gone!"

Tim had lost focus of the entire purpose of this exercise. He focused his teary eyes on the shaft of Dave's mace. Cooper was right. The rope was gone, and Tim hadn't felt so much as a tug.

He looked up at Cooper. "It worked!"

"Sweet! Who's next?"

"Rock Paper Scissors?"

"Sure."

Tim and Cooper each held out a fist.

"On three," said Tim. "One. Two. Three." Tim laid his hand flat, expecting Cooper to play Rock.

Cooper was nothing if not predictable, and kept his fist balled on the final count. "Shit."

"See you on the other side, Coop."

Cooper turned toward Terrence, hiked up the back of his loincloth, and grabbed both ass cheeks.

Tim averted his eyes. "Jesus, dude! What the hell are you doing?"

"Holding onto my butts."

Cooper ran toward his possible death with all of the grace and dignity that could be expected from him, ass cheeks firmly in hands and shouting obscenities. The whole island seemed awash with serenity when Terrence scooped him up.

Tim turned to Gilda, who was standing between the two scantily clad elves. "You coming?"

Gilda frowned and shook her head. "I'm staying here, with Felix and Alonzo."

174

"Are you sure?"

Gilda nodded.

"I'm just concerned they might not be able to... you know... *satisfy* you."

Alonzo took a threatening step toward him, his tiger tongue swung forward and back. "Speak plainly, halfling!" He looked pissed.

Shit. Where the hell is Julian's Diplomacy when you need it? "Look, man. I'm sorry. It's just that she's a young woman with certain... you know... needs, which I thought that maybe you two wouldn't be able to provide for, on account of being... you know..."

"Are you hearing what I'm hearing, Felix?" said Alonzo.

"His ingratitude knows no bounds."

"Hey!" said Tim. "I didn't mean to –"

"Unlace your breeches, halfling," challenged Alonzo. "I'm keen to see what *provisions* you have to offer such a woman as this."

As all of Tim's blood rushed to his face, he saw that Felix's was rushing in the other direction while Gilda caressed the inside of his thigh. The dead mink was beginning to come back to life.

"I'm sorry, Tim," said Gilda. "I didn't want you to have to find out like this, but you speak with no shame."

"Find out what?"

"Felix and Alonzo satisfied me just fine while the rest of you were sleeping last night."

"Seriously?"

Gilda nodded, her arms wrapped around Felix's leg. Felix's jaw hung open while the mink continued to rise.

"At the same time?"

Alonzo stepped back next to Gilda, who ran a hand up his leg. His tiger tongue started to inflate like a clown balloon.

"What? Like, rotisserie style?"

Gilda shot him a half-confused glare. "I think you should go now, Tim."

Tim nodded fervently. If he didn't get out of here before that mink's mouth was forced open, he'd have to claw his own eyes out. "Shit, this is awkward. I'm really sorry. I hope you all enjoy your lives together. Um... bye!"

He turned and ran for Terrence like he was the last lifeboat on a sinking ship. He didn't even see the giant maw snap him up. He just suddenly found himself floating in darkness.

Correction. He was *falling* in darkness. He flailed his little arms and legs helplessly around, grasping for something to hold onto.

"SHIIIIIIIIIII—" he stopped falling.

"Easy there, big guy," said Cooper. "I've got –"

Clunk.

"Fuck!" Cooper dropped Tim onto the hard, stone floor. "What the fuck was – Oh. Dave, I found your mace."

"Oh, good. Thanks. I was afraid you might have left it –"

Smash.

Neigh.

"Son of a...!" said Dave, from a little further away. Can you please get rid of the goddamn horse?"

"Sorry!" said Julian. "He's spooked. He just fell from a height."

"Where are we?" asked Tim. Unlike most of his friends, he was unable to see in the dark.

"It looks like some kind of disused sewer reservoir," said Dave. "If we're back in Cardinia, that probably puts us pretty close to the site of the collapse."

Tim stood up, an inch of moist, old shit squishing between his toes. "That explains the smell. You know, that fucking Boswell is a real piece of work."

"How's that?" asked Julian.

"Think about it. You insult him in the slightest way, and he sends you off to some dinosaur infested island in the middle of nowhere. He sets up the exit portal to look like a giant T-rex, so you have to be near suicidal to take advantage of it. And then if you do, you get dumped into the sewer."

"What a fucking dick," said Cooper.

Tim shook some of the shit off of his sleeves. "Well the joke's on him. The Whore's Head Inn is in the Collapsed Sewer District. He pretty much dropped us off right at home."

"Yeah," said Julian. "I'm sure learning that would give him a real sting."

"Let's just get the hell out of here. I've got some memories I need to suppress with booze."

Dave's heavy boots squished on the shit-coated brickwork. "Follow me. There's a slightly inclining tunnel this way. Should lead to the surface."

Ten minutes later, Cooper punched his way through a hastily constructed wooden barricade, and the stink of the sewer gave way to the more familiar stink of urine, vomit, and booze. They were home.

Julian released Ravenus into the grey sky, for whatever bird-related business he had to take care of.

Unlike the sun-soaked tropical paradise they had just come from, it was dreary and drizzly in Cardinia, for which Tim was thankful. He recognized the part of the neighborhood they'd surfaced in, and knew of a good broken gutter between there and the Whore's Head Inn where he could get a nice hobo shower.

"I thought you were dead back there," Cooper confided to Julian as they splashed through the puddles forming on the mostly deserted streets of the Collapsed Sewer District. "And I thought about what you said yesterday on the beach."

"Yeah?"

"Yeah," said Cooper. "So you're saying Ravenus doesn't have a dick?"

Julian sighed. "He has a cloaca."

177

"Like a vag, right?"

"Fine, Cooper. If that's how you want to think about it."

"That explains so much."

"Did you think about the other thing we talked about back on the beach? The *important* thing?"

"What?" Cooper's face scrunched up, like it was painful to try to think. "Oh, you mean that shit about MP3s?"

"When the hell did I even mention... Jesus, Cooper! I said *EMPATHY*! Did you even hear a single word I said?"

"Sorry, man!" said Cooper defensively. "I thought you were gonna start going on about some shitty band you were into, so I was tuning you out."

"Could you just not talk to me for, like, a week?" Julian stomped ahead at a faster pace.

"I said I was sorry," Cooper called after him. "I'm glad you're not dead."

"Give him some time," Tim said, taking Julian's place next to Cooper. "He's been through a lot today. We all have."

"I don't know what I would have done if he'd died for real." Cooper sniffed, but Tim couldn't tell if there was anything emotional about it, or if it was just part of the ever-present mucous that came with having a Charisma Score of 4.

Tim looked up at Cooper, searching for some betrayal of whatever he was feeling. "You okay, man?"

Cooper hung his head. "My dick hurts."

The End.

A Fistful of Gold Pieces

(Original Publication Date: March 22, 2015)

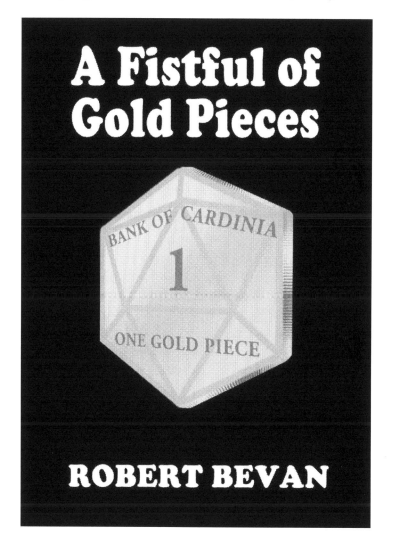

Julian squinted from beneath the brim of his sombrero and peered into the bartender's eyes. He bit his lower lip and nodded shrewdly. It was important to seem casually interested, but not too eager. A puff of cigar smoke would have rounded out the effect he was going for, but he was all out of smokes. "Please allow me a moment to discuss the matter with my companions."

The bartender was human, but as brawny as any orc. His long, greasy dark hair was pulled back into a low ponytail. Most of his chest and arms, exposed by a brown-and-yellow-stained wife beater, was covered in poorly rendered tattoos. He turned his head to spit on the floor, then faced Julian again. Something behind the bar shuffled excitedly as it lapped up the treat. Julian sometimes wished his elven ears weren't quite so keen.Ravenus, sensing his unease, dug his talons into Julian's shoulder.

Gripping the edge of his serape tightly, Julian resisted the urge to reach over the bar and wipe away beads of brown spittle still remaining on the man's beard.He concealed a shudder in the motion of a polite bow. "Excuse us."

Julian turned around to find Dave twirling the end of his beard around his finger, Tim impatiently toying with the hip flask in his pocket, and Cooper clawing at some grey gunk in his armpit. "Okay, guys. Huddle up."

When everyone leaned in, Cooper's breath hit Julian's nostrils like a garbage truck fart. Their vast differences in size meant that everyone had to bend or kneel down to Tim's height, which earned them odd looks from the bar's other patrons. Huddling wasn't going to be conducive to a productive conversation. "Second thought. Let's step outside." He turned back to the bartender. "We'll be right back"

The bartender spat on the floor again and continued looking down at it as a second creature contested the first for the prize. After a bit of hissing, scraping, and a thud which shook the stonepiss bottle on top of the bar, the victor commenced licking. The bartender grinned down at whatever it was.

Julian smiled politely before escorting his friends out the door.

"Fucking hell!" said Tim, shielding his eyes like the sun was trying to physically punch him in the face. It was easy to forget how nice a day it was outside, or even that nice days were a thing, when inside a place like the Rock Bottom pub. It had that old familiar bar musk, like centuries old wood steeped in blood, smoke, and ass.

The sight of Tim taking a swig from his flask was one that, no matter how often Julian saw it, he couldn't get used to. He looked like a stocky, alcoholic twelve-year-old.

"Don't look at me like that," said Tim. "It's bound to be afternoon by now."

"I guess I should thank you for not actually drinking that inside the establishment." He looked up at Cooper. "And thank you all for not talking while I was conducting business."

"What's the job?" asked Dave, already sounding suspicious.

"It sounds absolutely perfect for us," said Julian, trying to sound chipper. "He'll pay us fifty gold pieces to bring him this guy named…" He cleared his throat before mumbling,"Barlow the Butcher."

Tim choked on his stonepiss. "Are you out of your fucking mind? What about any of what you just said sounds *perfect*?"

"He wants the guy alive," said Julian. "It's good money, and we don't have to get our hands dirty."

"Barlow the goddamn *Butcher*?"

"I asked about that. It turns out he's an actual butcher. Just a regular guy.There's four of us –"

"Ahem," said Ravenus.

"Sorry, five of us, and only one of him. Between my Charisma, your Intelligence, Cooper's Strength, and… um…*Dave*…We can nab this guy."

Cooper scratched his head, like he was digging for something inside his giant half-orc skull. "If it's that easy, why would he pay *us*?"

"You see?" said Dave. "Even Cooper can see the problem here, and he's borderline retarded."

"Hey! Fuck you, Dave!"

"No offense."

Cooper poked out his big bottom lip and crossed his arms. "All right, then."

"Cooper's right," said Tim. "Dude looks like a prison rapist. Hard as fucking nails. Why would he need our help to chase down some butcher?"

Julian smiled and shook his head. "I can't believe you guys can't see what's going on here. *I'm* supposed to be the newbie...nooby? Am I saying that right?"

Dave narrowed his eyes at Julian. "What are you getting at?"

Julian cocked a thumb back at the bar. "That guy in there. He's a quest giver. The gold, the Experience Points, that's not coming out of his pocket. It's all just an arbitrary reward doled out by the game."

"Hmph," said Dave. "Game logic. It's like those old Nintendo RPGs where the guy at the weapon shop had the Sword of Ultimate Power that you needed to defeat the Demon Lord as part of his standard inventory, but the dude wouldn't sell it to you if you were short by one gold piece even though you were the only person standing in the way of a worldwide cataclysm."

"Exactly," Julian said, only peripherally aware of what Dave was talking about.

Tim laughed. "My favorites were the quests where some asshole would send you out to collect ten wolf teeth or some shit, and then you kill like six dozen wolves who haven't got ten fucking teeth between them, like they'd all been gumming you to death."

"That's right," said Julian, thinking he might have been better off spending less of his youth reading books and more of it playing video games. He was out of his element.

Cooper snorted. "Or when a big-ass frog the size of a fucking car jumps out onto the road, and assholes don't even slow down."

Julian pursed his lips. "Um... I guess that kinda works."

"But this isn't some 90s-era video game," said Tim. "Grab your big, goofy ears and you'll find that they're just as real as my tiny halfling dick."

"We could at least check it out," said Dave.

"Are you kidding me?" said Tim. "You were against this idea not two minutes ago. You're supposed to be wise."

"The game logic thing makes sense.We've been in enough situations in this world that wouldn't make a whole lot of sense in the real world."

Tim balled up his little fist. "Don't you see? We're in one right now!" He continued facing Dave, but pointed accusingly at Julian. "He's using his Diplomacy skill on you to undermine your Wisdom and make you think stupid things."

Julian would deny this if asked point blank, but thought it best to remain silent otherwise.

"I'm not saying we should go through with the whole thing," said Dave. "I'm just saying we could get the address and stake the place out. Make an informed decision whether or not to carry on from there."

Tim shook his head. "This is bullshit." He looked up at Cooper. "You've been awful quiet. What do you think?"

Cooper scratched his ass thoughtfully. "Are there dire frogs in the Monster Manual?"

Tim took a deep swig from his flask. "This is so fucking stupid."

Julian offered what he hoped was a reassuring smile. "I'll just pop back in and get the address then, shall I?"

*

Two hours later they were standing at the edge of a district of Cardinia known as Shallow Grave.

While the Collapsed Sewer District was a dismal, lawless shithole, the actual sewer collapse, and resulting shift in demographics, were relatively recent. Organized crime hadn't yet had a chance to take much of a foothold in the area. Frank had referred to it as Chaotic Neutral, which he said made it a good place for the likes of them.

Shallow Grave, on the other hand, was what Frank had described as Lawful Evil. He'd told them it was the one part of town they'd do well to avoid, a point that Tim had brought up several times during the long walk there.

It was usually difficult to tell exactly the point where one district ended and another began, but when dusk set in unexpectedly early, the buildings were all a uniform shade of grim, the air took on an abandoned hospital scent, and there was a noticeably higher concentration of orcs mulling around (as well as a complete absence of Kingsguard), Julian suspected they had reached their destination.

Aside from the occasional rat or stray cat digging through rancid garbage, the only sounds to be heard were their own hollow footsteps against the long neglected street.

"I guess we're here," said Julian. If he were in a car, he'd have locked his doors.

"How the fuck did we get to Detroit?" asked Cooper.

"The streets aren't marked," Tim observed. He hadn't yet drunk enough to steady the quiver in his voice. "How are we supposed to find the address?"

Julian had dreaded this moment. "There isn't, um… I wasn't actually given an address. He just told me to go to Shallow Grave and ask around."

Everyone stopped. Julian felt the pressure of his friends' stares on top of the yellow-eyed stares of the locals. He hadn't felt this uncomfortable since his high-school girlfriend's father, who had apparently not been informed of his being Jewish, asked him over a family dinner when he'd been 'saved'. It was a short-lived relationship.

Dave put his hands on his hips. "That isn't something you thought you should share with the rest of us before coming here?"

"I was curious!" said Julian. "I've never seen Shallow Grave, and I thought it would be okay in the daytime."

Cooper looked up at the overcast sky. "I don't think this place has daytime."

"That's just great," said Tim. "A butcher with no butcher shop. I guess he freelances." He tilted his head back, opened his mouth wide, and poured the last few remaining drops of stonepiss onto his tongue.

Julian frowned down at Tim. "Have you considered the thought that you might have a drinking problem?"

Tim jiggled his empty flask upside down. "Well I've sure as shit got one now, don't I?" He scanned the row of buildings up the right side of the street. "I'm going to see if I can get a refill. That looks like a general store next to the… Well fuck me. How did we miss *that*?"

Julian had been doing his best to avoid making eye contact with the locals, and had therefore missed out on most of the storefronts as well. He followed Tim's gaze to a sign above an open doorway. The once-white paint was cracked on the mildewed and rain-warped wood, and there were no words, but the pictures painted on it made clear the purpose of the shop. The heads of a cow, a pig, a goat, several types of fowl, and a few animals that Julian couldn't make out were painted in rusty brown, likely with the blood of each animal represented.

Julian started walking, but Tim grabbed him by the serape.

"Where the fuck do you think you're going?"

"It's a butcher shop," said Julian. "I'm going to ask if they know a guy named Barlow."

"When you go into a butcher shop, you order meat. You don't order butchers. They're not going to wrap the fucker up in brown paper and hand him to you over the counter."

"I wasn't going to *order* him," said Julian. "I was just going in to gather information."

"*You* don't Gather Information," said Tim. "*I* Gather Information."

"You're the one who declared me the 'face of the party', remember? I've got the highest Charisma score, so I've always got to be the one to do all the talking. Ring any bells?"

Tim slipped his empty flask into his inner vest pocket. "But you don't have any ranks in the Gather Information skill."

"It's just asking a question," Julian argued. "Excuse me, sir. Do you know where I might find a Mr. Barlow the Butcher?"

"Perfect," said Tim. "Sounds like a great way to get us all murdered while tipping off Barlow the Butcher that someone's put a price on his head."

"So what are you going to do differently?"

Tim folded his arms and looked smugly up at Julian. "I'm going to be coy, cunning. I'll make use of innuendo, double entendres, mixed signals, and the like until I know whether or not it's safe to pry further and ask more direct questions. Anyone can ask a simple question. It takes skill points, however, to Gather Information."

Julian shrugged. "Fine."

"Give me a couple of silver pieces, would you?"

"What for?"

"I may have to grease a few palms. It's all a delicate balance of knowing who, when, and how much."

"Yeah, yeah," said Julian. He reached under his serape into his belt pouch and fished out three silver pieces, which he slapped into Tim's waiting palm. "Be careful in there."

Tim nodded, then scampered giddily across the street and into the general store.

Julian shook his head. "That sneaky little shit."

A minute later, Tim reappeared in the doorway of the general store sipping from his freshly topped up flask, then walked into the butcher shop next door. It was probably for the best that he got his drink. He didn't have as high a Charisma score as Julian's, and he tended to get mouthy when he was cranky.

Somewhere in the alley on the other side of the general store, a cat moaned like it was calling out for the sweet release of death. Julian felt Ravenus getting fidgety on his shoulder.

"Sir," said Ravenus. "As long as we're all just standing around, would –"

"Go do your thing," said Julian, not wanting to hear the gory details. Ravenus launched off his shoulder like someone had fired the starting pistol. As much as he cared for Ravenus, he sometimes wished he could feed him normal bird snacks, like grapes or crackers or whatever.

"Don't fly off too far," Julian called out as Ravenus disappeared into the alley.

Julian, Dave, and even Cooper winced as the cat let out its final, disease-ridden, mortal feline cry.

Julian shrugged. "Bird's gotta eat."

Dave shivered. "I wish Tim would hurry the hell up. I don't like this neighborhood."

"Too many *orcs* for your liking?" asked Julian.

"I know where you're going with this," said Dave. "Don't even start on one of your lectures. Every big city has areas that are best avoided. If that happens to correlate with a predominant ethnic demographic, then…" It was fun to watch Dave squirm. "This isn't even the same thing as…" He tugged on his beard, then looked Julian in the eye. "You should know this better than any of us."

"Oh? And how's that?"

"You're the one who got mugged at gunpoint in New Orleans last New Year's Eve."

"Not by fucking orcs!" Julian paused to reflect on what he'd just said. If there was an analogy to be made, it was quickly slipping away from him.

"Would you stupid assholes keep your voices down?" said Tim.

Dave jumped. "Oh, hey Tim. I didn't hear you approach."

"I'm sneaky. That's kinda my thing."

"How'd it go in there?" asked Julian. "Did you *Gather* any *Information*?"

"I'm not exactly sure what happened in there," Tim admitted. "I either ordered six pounds of pork chops, or I put out a hit on a prominent family of gnomes."

"How does that even –"

"Keep your panties on. I got an address."

Cooper looked skyward, like something caught his eye. "Where the fuck is your bird going?"

Julian looked up just in time to catch a black mass flying eastward disappear behind a building. "Damn it, Ravenus." He shook his head. "The *one* thing I asked him not to do."

"Don't sweat it," said Tim. "We're headed that way anyway." He took a swig from his flask, turned around, and started walking, leading the group deeper into Shallow Grave.

"That's the one," said Tim after they'd walked a few blocks and turned a corner.

Contrary to Dave, Julian grew more and more uneasy the farther they went specifically because of the lack of people staring at them, orc or otherwise. This part of town looked utterly abandoned. Storefronts were boarded up. No windows were lit. The only sounds came from dark alleys, the scurrying of creatures that Julian hoped were only rats.

Cooper frowned. "That don't look like no butcher shop."

"It doesn't even look finished," said Dave.

The building Tim had indicated was not hard to pick out. It was easily the tallest structure in this part of town, at least five stories high with a sixth possibly in the works. It was difficult to tell for sure, because the entire exterior of the building was obscured by scaffolding.

Julian tried to imagine what this place might have looked like in rosier times, presumably before it became known as Shallow Grave. Clean streets, open shops, bustling crowds, an impressive new building in the works."I wonder what happened here."

"I think it's pretty obvious," said Dave. "It got overrun with –" In response to Julian's glare, he paused to consider how best to finish his sentence. "–crime."

In the past, the thick-beamed scaffolding must have been sturdy enough to hold teams of dwarven stonemasons, but closer inspection betrayed its age and neglect. The bamboo looked as porous as an old sponge, the rotted safety nets as fragile as fine lace. In its current state, Julian wouldn't trust it to support the weight of the termites which had no doubt eaten through most of the wooden platforms.

"There's a faint light coming from one of the third floor windows,"whispered Tim."I'll bet that's where Barlow's holed up."

Dave quietly cleared his throat. "I'd like to remind everyone that we don't actually have to go through with this. We can all turn around and walk away *right now*."

A caw and the cry of another dying cat rang out in the still air, causing all four of them to jump.

Julian laughed nervously. "Just Ravenus."

"How much cat can that fucking bird eat?" asked Cooper.

"He's got a high metabolism," said Julian. "Flying takes a lot out of you."

Tim scratched his head. "Not a whole cat's worth in the space of less than an hour, even if it *is* half starved. It sounds like he's just killing for sport now."

"He doesn't like his meat too fresh," said Julian, scrambling for some justification for his familiar's sudden bloodlust. "Stray cats are plentiful enough around here. Maybe he's just eating their eyes and moving on to the next one."

Tim gawked at Julian. "That doesn't sound...hmm, what's the word...*completely fucking psychotic* to you?"

Julian wanted to come to Ravenus's defense. He wanted to tell Tim to go screw himself. But what if Tim was right? Psychosis could explain why he hadn't felt any change in Ravenus's emotions. No sense of regret. Not even a rush of adrenaline during the kill. Could Ravenus have gone all Hannibal Lecter on him?

"I'm uh... I... I'm just gonna go see what he's up to," said Julian. He nodded up at the illuminated third floor window. "You guys decide what you want to do about that."

He jogged across the street, where the sound of cat murder had come from. He entered the narrow alley made narrower by garbage bins leaking pungent slime into the rivulets between uneven cobblestones.

Not wanting to draw too much unwanted attention, he whispered into the alley, "Ravenus?"

He was answered by the familiar sound of flapping wings, but Ravenus didn't come out to meet him. The sound was moving away. Julian ran into the alley, but he was too late. All he saw was the shredded, disemboweled remains of a dead cat.

Was this a side of Ravenus that Julian hadn't been privy to before? Did his familiar lead a double life as a serial cat murderer? Was he so ashamed that he couldn't bear the thought of Julian walking in on him in the act?

"It's okay, buddy," Julian said into the darkness. "We'll get through this together."

Julian stepped over and around debris as he made his way out of the dark alley and back toward the– Where the hell was everyone?

His heart beat a little faster as he scanned up and down the empty streets. A possible explanation occurred to him, and he quickly ducked back into the alley. They had to be hiding. That's the only thing that made sense. If they'd been in a fight, he would have heard. He hoped that whatever they were hiding from hadn't seen him.

A minute passed while Julian waited. He squinted and craned his neck, looking for anything unusual, but the streets were clear. Sadly, so were the sky and surrounding rooftops. He was alone, and starting to get more than a little scared.

Mustering up what little courage he could, he forced himself back into the street. If his friends were hiding, they'd surely be looking out for him and find some way to signal him. But the more he thought about it, the less likely his theory seemed. Tim could disappear in an empty room, but Dave and Cooper weren't exactly the stealthiest creatures in the world.

Julian cautiously crept further out into the street toward the exact spot where he had left his friends. About twenty feet from his destination, he suddenly lost his hearing. There's a fine line between the white noise of a quiet city street and complete deafness, and he had just crossed it.

"What the fuck?" he attempted to say, but no sound came out of his mouth. That did little to ease his nerves.

Still, he pressed on. There were dark spots on the old cobblestones that he was pretty sure hadn't been there before. He touched one spot, then looked at his finger. Red.Fresh blood. There *had* been a fight here. Why hadn't he heard it? Why couldn't he hear anything at all right now?

Frustrated, he kicked a stone toward the large, unfinished building. It bounced silently into the pile of debris and rubbish accumulated from the decaying scaffolding.

As suddenly and inexplicably as they had shut off, Julian's ears started working again. He heard voices coming from the third floor window.

"Good evening, gentlemen." The voice was nearly as high as Tim's, but colder. "That's a lovely tunic, Shitnose."

"Thank you, sir." The responding voice, presumably belonging to Shitnose, was gruffer than Cooper's, probably a full-blooded orc.

"Do they make them for men?"

A burst of deep, throaty laughter was cut short, as if the one laughing had been punched.

That's at least two orcs.

"Honestly, Shitnose," said the first voice. "You don't think that's a little fancy for work?"

"I, um…" said Shitnose. "I've got a thing afterwards."

The person with the high voice harrumphed. "So these are the conspirators you found? Why are there only three? Paulie said there's supposed to be a fourth one."

"These were the only ones we saw."

"Intriguing," said the first voice thoughtfully. "Did they put up much of a fight?"

One orc grunted out a laugh. "The short ones fell like little girls."

Tim! Dave!

"The half-orc took a few hits to bring down, but the human in him betrayed his weakness before long."

Cooper!

"Curiouser and curiouser," said the first voice.

"Shall I go and look for the fourth one?"

"No. I'll send Paulie. He's a far more efficient tracker than you. Did you bring back my stone?"

"I must have dropped it during the fight," said the orc.

"Shitnose! You incompetent fool!" snapped the first voice. "You know I can't sleep without it."

"Please accept my humble apology."

"Stop your blubbering. Just run down and fetch it once you've tied these three up."

"Very well, sir."

Julian exhaled. If they had to be tied up, they must still be alive.

"Grotch," said the one giving the orders. "Run down to Tommin's place and tell him I won't be able to make the meeting tonight, due to an unforeseen situation."

"He, um…" Even with Julian's keen ears, Grotch's voice was barely distinguishable from Shitnose's. "I don't think he'll be too happy about that."

"Have you lost your wits?" said the leader. "You don't *think*? You aren't supposed to *think*! I don't pay you to be a philosopher! You will walk out of that door and do what you're told right now, or you'll leave through the gods damned window!"

Large, booted footsteps sounded from around the side of the building.Grotch couldn't have gotten down there that fast.*Shit!*

191

Paulie!

Suddenly realizing that he was standing out in the open, Julian darted toward the rubbish pile. If the theory which had just popped into his head was correct – and it seemed to confirm itself a few steps in when he lost his hearing again – he should be able to dive right into the trash heap without making a sound.

Julian hit the rubbish pile with a force that should have reverberated along the empty streets for miles, but was as silent as a church mouse's grave. He sat completely still, hidden in garbage and debris that smelled like a highway rest stop: moldy wood, wet stone, and old piss. A minute passed with no sign of anyone. While he was grateful to be within the sound cover of the enchanted stone, it would have been nice to be able to hear footsteps coming or going.

A black blur flew past right in front of him.

"Ravenus!"Julian cried before he could think better of it. Fortunately, the sphere of Silence kept him from giving away his position. If he were to be discovered, Ravenus– loyal (and apparently violent) as he was – wasn't going to be very much help against the orcs who had so easily incapacitated the rest of his friends.

While his ears were currently compromised, Julian's eyes and nose were functional enough to notice the stream of urine meandering its way toward him. The footsteps he heard must have come from someone who had just stepped outside to take a leak. Julian pulled his feet back to let the stream pass without touching him. That must have been a hell of a leak. That big bastard had to have been pissing from at least twenty feet away.

With the immediate threat gone, Julian started planning. He had to find the enchanted stone. It would be his best bet for sneaking around unheard, and he needed every advantage this game would afford him.

There were dozens of rocks in the area. Julian wished he had kicked the damned thing anywhere but into a pile of rubble. He briefly considered just shoving every rock he could find into his bag, but any advantage perpetual silence might give him could easily be outweighed by the potential disadvantages of lugging around a sackful of rocks.

Replaying the kick in his mind, Julian remembered the rock in question to be smooth, oblong, and a little bit larger than a golf ball. He ended up narrowing down the most likely candidates to two, which he deemed an acceptable burden.

The window was Julian's best bet. He needed a visual assessment of exactly how deep in shit they were. Tattered remains of cloth safety nets would provide him with some cover from an observer at street level, and Julian was confident that this rickety bamboo scaffolding wouldn't support the weight of any pursuing orcs. If they tried to come after him, they'd just bring the whole thing crashing down on themselves.

Julian's first step snapped a length of bamboo in half, confirming his suspicions of how sturdy this structure was. But he found that if he kept his weight carefully distributed, and kept his feet near the joints where the beams were tied together, he could climb with relative ease.

As he climbed, he spotted an orc he guessed was Grotch heading for Timmon's place. He hoped Timmon's place was very far away. One less orc to deal with.

Finally, he arrived at the third floor window, but stayed off to the side. Unable to hear anything, he had a hard time judging whether or not it was safe to peek inside. Looking down, he saw another orc standing on the street just below him. That put at least two of at least three total orcs out of the room, which was probably the best odds Julian was going to get.

Chancing a peek inside, Julian spotted his friends, tied to chairs on the far side of a large room. Dave's head was slumped forward. Cooper's was lulled back and to the side, with a long strand of drool hanging down from it. Only Tim appeared to be awake, and his eyes went wide when they connected with Julian's. He jerked his head to the right and put a finger over his lips.

Julian nodded. Tim must have slipped out of his ropes already, and was biding his time before making a move. The Silence stone would be better off in his hands, especially if he was going to attempt an escape with Dave and Cooper in tow.

Julian leaned back out of view. He had to figure out which one of his two rocks was the Silence stone. If he tossed in the wrong one, he'd just be drawing attention to himself and Tim. It was time to gamble.

He scanned the surrounding area and settled for the alley in which he had spotted Ravenus's latest kill. If he threw the normal rock, the orc below him should look over that way. If he threw the magic rock, he should be able to hear again, for what little that was worth. But then at least he'd know.

He dug the two rocks out of his bag and *–Julian, you doofus! Detect Magic!* Why hadn't he done that in the first place? He whispered the incantation, but no words came out. *Oh, right. That's why.*

Back to the original plan. Julian based his decision on which rock was prettier, and threw the other one. It hit the wall of the far building and ricocheted into the alley. Still deaf, he supposed his judgement had been sound.

Not only did the orc below him look in the direction of the alley, the gullible bastard actually started jogging that way. *Score!*

Julian peeked in the window again. Tim looked to his right again and held up two fingers. There were two people in the room, and they obviously weren't looking at Tim. Now was as good a time as any. He held up the stone and made a tossing motion. Tim shook his head violently.

Julian laughed to himself. The notion of chucking a rock at them must seem preposterous to Tim, who didn't know of the stone's magical properties. Julian lobbed the rock into the room. Tim winced as it struck Cooper in the face, waking him up.

"Nothing to report, sir" said a shrill voice. It sounded like it was coming from a hallway outside the room, and it didn't sound anything like an orc."I couldn't find him."

Cooper was struggling in his ropes and trying to shout while Tim confusedly fingered himself in the ear. Julian shook his head and pointed at the rock.

Revelation shone on Tim's face. He nodded, picked up the rock, and gave Julian a thumbs up gesture.

"Never mind the fourth one," said the boss. He sounded like he was getting closer. Julian waved at Tim to find somewhere to hide. At least he hoped that was what he was communicating.

Julian craned his neck as far as he dared into the window. Hecouldn't see a doorway from where he was, but the boss's voice sounded like it was coming from just outside one now. "We'll beat what information we can out of the other thr— Where's the little one?"

The scaffolding creaked as Julian jerked back. He had to remind himself that he wasn't magically silent anymore. Tim's chair was empty, and he was nowhere to be seen.

"The craven little fool," sneered the boss. "Slipped out of his ropes and left his fr—"

That was a peculiar place to pause.

"—itnose! You idiot! What are you doing?"

"Boss!" said Shitnose. "What happened to you?"

"The sneaky little bastard got the jump on me. He's got my stone. Go after him!"

Julian felt vibrations as orc boots pounded out of the room.

"Hey asshole," said Cooper. "Let me out of these ropes."

"I don't think so, half-orc," said the boss."You and your companions have some explaining to do.Now I can use magic to compel you to tell me what I want to know, but I'd rather just beat it out of you. Who are you working for? Jimmy the Weasel? One-Eyed Pete? Who's trying to knock me out of my turf?"

"Come on, man," said Cooper. "My balls itch, and I've got a storm brewing."

"A storm brewing?"

"I was trying to be polite," said Cooper. "What I meant was– Aw shit. Too late." A slow, steady fart rumbled out from within the room. As it grew louder, it was interrupted by glurps and squelches. A fart that was much, much more than a fart.

"Gods have mercy!" said the boss. "What the... Have you no... I can't even... Ugh." His voice was getting farther away, close to where Julian estimated the door to be. "I need to think. And *breathe!*"

As far as Julian could make out, the room should now be

completely free of hostile forces, not counting Cooper's massive shart. He'd give it a few more seconds to let the boss get some distance, then –

"Aw, what's that smell?" said Dave. "Jesus Christ, Cooper!" He was awake now. That was good. "Would it kill you to find a bathroom?"

"Fuck you, Dave!" said Cooper. "In case you haven't noticed, I'm tied to a goddamn chair!"

"Use your Barbarian Rage to break through the ropes."

"Good idea," said Cooper. "I'm really angry!"

Julian looked in the window. Cooper's eyes turned red and his muscles started to bulge. The ropes binding him grew tense, but showed no signs of snapping. Instead, they dug deeper into his expanding body.

"Oh fuck!" said Cooper. "I'm cool! I'm cool! I'm cool!" He farted as his body deflated back to its normal size. "Damn. That hurt like a motherfucker."

Dave startedto panic, struggling against the ropes, his chair rocking forward and back. He made eye contact with Julian. "Ju—!" He said, just before his chair tipped forward. With his arms tied behind his back, he had nothing to brace himself when his face collided with the wooden floor. "Fuck."

Julian winced. That really looked painful.

Then Dave's panic kicked into overdrive. "Oh my God, no! Julian, help me!" Cooper had pissed himself as well, and the yellow-brown concoction of fluids beneath his chair was spreading slowly toward Dave's face. "No! No! NOOOOOOO!!!"

Julian's eyes stung as the wave of Cooper's stench reached the window. He couldn't even begin to imagine what Dave was going through so close to the source.

"Hang on, man!" Julian said, not knowing why he was even bothering to try to keep his voice down anymore. "I'm coming to –"

"CAAAAAWWWW!" cried an avian voice from just behind Julian.

"Ravenus!" said Julian, looking back just in time to see a black talon make a swipe at his face. He jerked his head back, lost his footing, and broke the bamboo shaft he had been standing on. Fearing the whole framework would collapse, he grasped for the only thing he could find that wasn't part of the scaffolding, a length of thick, sturdy rope which he hoped was attached to something at the top of the building.

The rope held his weight, but swung him away from the window.

"Ow!" said Cooper. "What the fuck, Ravenus? Julian! Call off your goddamn bird!"

Julian clung to the rope, devastated. Ravenus, his very own familiar, had just attacked him. That cat he'd killed in the alley near the butcher shop. It must have had rabies. That was the only possible explanation. He'd be okay. If clerics in this world could bring back the dead, they could surely cure a simple case of rabies.

"Goddammit!" said Cooper. His voice was more angry now than panicked. Dave was sobbing uncontrollably in the background.

"You okay, Coop?" Julian called out.

"Your stupid bird has lost his fucking mind!"

"It's not his fault," said Julian. "It's just the rabies."

"Rabies?" said Cooper. "What the fuck are you talk—"

"You there!" said the boss, poking his head out of the next window past the one Julian had been peering in. His face was small but plump, sporting a well-groomed and waxed black goatee. He looked down at the ground below Julian. "That's the fourth one! Get him!"

Julian felt a tug on his rope. He looked down. Just as he feared the rope reached all the way to the ground, and there was now an orc climbing up it. Grotch was still away on his mission, and this one wasn't wearing a fancy tunic, so that likely ruled out Shitnose. That only left...

"Paulie!" Julian cried.

The orc stopped climbing, looked at his boss, then back at Julian. "Is that supposed to be funny, elf?"

"Um... no."

"Good," said the orc. "'Cause it wasn't."

"Stop right where you are, Paulie," said Julian. "I don't want to have to hurt you."

"Ha!" said the orc, continuing to climb. "Now *that* was funny."

"Dammit, Paulie!" said Julian. He let go of the rope with one hand and pointed it down. "You've forced my hand. Magic Missile!" A golden beam of energy struck his pursuer in the chest.

"Ow!" said the orc. "You'll pay for that one, elf!" His ascent did not slow. He barely looked wounded.

Shit. Time to Bluff. "That was just a warning, Paulie. I've got more powerful spells than that!"

"Stop calling me that!" shouted the orc. Julian had apparently failed his Bluff check, as the orc continued to climb. "My name is Leo!"

Julian also started climbing, but it was clear that Leo would reach Julian before Julian could reach the top of the building. He tried to formulate a Plan C, but his mind kept wandering back to Leo. *Leo didn't sound anything like Paulie. Leo. Leo the lion. The Lion and the Mouse.* Julian had an idea.

The rope was thick, but it was old, and individual strands of it broke easily against Julian's incisors. It tasted like mildew and straw, but Julian gnawed it like it was made of chocolate and beef jerky.

When the first of three interwoven cords snapped, the rhythm of the orcs climbing changed. The rope was moving more violently now, knocking Julian's head against the wall.

"You stop that right now, elf!" said Leo, shaking the rope.

Julian's jaw was getting seriously fatigued, but he could see fear in the orc's yellow eyes. He opened and closed his mouth a couple of times to stretch his jaw muscles, then went back to chewing the rope even more vigorously, ignoring the pain in his head.

The pounding subsided as the orc went back to climbing. He was only about fifteen feet below Julian when the second cord broke. Strands of the third cord were already starting to split from the strain of Leo's weight.

"Stop!" said the boss, from much closer than Julian had expected. The rope lost its tension, and Julian hung still with the last cord in his mouth, ready to bite down.

Julian looked down. Leo was ten feet below him, arms and legs spread wide as he tried to distribute his considerable weight on the decaying scaffolding.

"There's nowhere to run, elf," said the boss.

Julian looked to his left. The little gnome with the slick, black goatee was perched confidently on the scaffolding not ten feet away from where Julian dangled.

"We don't want to hurt you," Julian tried to say through the rope in his mouth.

"Well that's where we differ," said the gnome. "Because I very much want to hurt you."

Julian's eyes moved left, then right, searching for options. He came up wanting.

"Do you know who I am?" asked the gnome.

Julian had a pretty good idea, but was still clinging on to the hope that he was wrong. He shook his head.

"My name is Barlow," said the gnome. "Do you know what my friends call me?"

It was a longshot, but Julian took one more crack at being wrong. "Barry?" he said, his mouth full of rope.

Barlow reached under the lapel of his jacket and pulled out a shiny steel blade. It looked like either a gnome-sized meat cleaver or a large straight razor. Neither of those possibilities was less frightening than the other."They call me Barlow the Butcher."

Julian's sense of hope had just reached a new depth when he saw a large mass of black feathers approaching from behind Barlow. After a brief, but steep incline, it reached an even newer depth when the bird landed gracefully on Barlow's shoulder.

The rope fell out of Julian's mouth. "Ravenus?"

"Over here, sir!" the familiar British voice rang out from across the street. "I've been looking everywhere for you, sir. Is everything okay?"

"Paulie," snapped Barlow. "Get rid of the bird."

"Right away, master."Paulie's voice matched the raspy voice Julian had earlier heard inside.

As precarious a situation as he was still in, Julian couldn't help but feel some small relief that his familiar was likely neither rabid nor psychotic.

"Oh dear!" said Ravenus, as Paulie flew over to engage him in combat.

"Listen, Mr. um… the Butcher," said Julian. "Let's talk about this."

"Your words bore me, elf," said Barlow. "Paulie is hungry."

"Bullshit," said Julian. "He just ate a cat like twenty minutes ago."

"I'm sure I don't have to tell you that Paulie prefers his meat to sit out for a while."

"Okay, you have me there," admitted Julian, trying to prolong the conversation while his mind raced for a Plan D. *Just keep talking.* "Look, I'm really sorry about all –"

"Apologies don't cut it in Shallow Grave," said Barlow, getting to his feet and brandishing his weapon. "Here there are penalties for trying to move in on another man's territory."

Julian narrowed his eyes. He knew what had to be done. "I wasn't apologizing to you."

"Who then?"

Julian maintained eye contact with Barlow while winding the rope securely around his wrist. "Primrose."

Barlow shook his head. "This may be the saddest appeal for mercy I've ever witnessed," he said. "And I've witnessed a few."

"Appeal for mercy?"

"This Primrose, is she your daughter? Your wife? Your special lady friend? You long to hold her in your arms just one last time? I get it, elf. I've got a special lady friend myself. In fact, I'm getting married tomorrow."

"Congratulations."

"Thank you."

"But Primrose is neither my daughter, my wife, nor my special lady friend."

"So who is she then?"

"My *Horse*!"

"Oh shit!" cried Leo as a large, brown draft horse materialized on the scaffolding behind Barlow.

Barlow's eyes went wide as the scaffolding shuddered, creaked, and snapped all around him.

With a terrified whinny, Primrose crashed through the first

platform. Barlow jumped at Julian, who caught him by his free hand. Julian felt the rope tug, then snap as Leo assisted the horse in tearing down the scaffolding.

"Let go of the blade, Barlow!" said Julian. The gnome wasn't too heavy, but both of their palms were slick with sweat, and Barlow's flailing threatened to pop Julian's arm out of its socket.

"Paulie!" cried Barlow, while failing to let go of his blade. "Help!"

"Leave the familiars out of this," said Julian. "The best he could hope to do is scratch and peck me until I let go, then we both die."

"Better the both of us than just me."

"I didn't come here to kill you!"

"What's that term you used before?" asked Barlow. "Bull's shit?"

"It's *bullshit*, and I'm not bullshitting you."

"Why should I trust you?"

"Because if I wanted to fucking kill you, I'd just let go of your hand right now!"

"You make a fair point, elf. Very well." Barlow let go of his knife.

A few seconds later, a horse screamed briefly, then fell silent.

"Primrose!" said Julian. He hadn't expected her to survive the fall. The layers of scaffolding must have cushioned the blow enough for her to survive… at least until she got stabbed in the back by a falling blade."Dammit!"

"Sorry about that," said Barlow. "So…Now what?"

"Good question."

"Julian?" Cooper called out from the window below them.

"Cooper!" cried Julian. "What took you so long?"

"Sorry, man. Tim only just got back and released us."

"This is Barlow."

"Uh… How's it going?"

"I'm going to throw him to you."

Barlow's hand gripped Julian's tighter. "You're going to *what*?"

"Don't worry," said Julian. "I've got a Dexterity bonus." He started swinging Barlow to the right.

"I don't know what that means!"

"Just let go on three." He swung back toward the window. "One!"

"I don't want to let go on three!"

Right, then left. "Two! If you don't let go when I do, you won't make it!"

"Wait!" cried Barlow. "Please consider –"

Right, then left. "Three!" Julian let go, as did Barlow.

It wasn't a great throw, but Cooper managed to reach out and catch him by the leg. "Gotcha, shitbag."

"I'll climb up to the top and come back down the stairs," said Julian. "Subdue Barlow, but remember we need him alive."

"Right," said Cooper. The next sounds Julian heard were a punch and a thud.

As Julian climbed the rope to the top of the building, he heard flapping wings and looked down to see a big black bird fly in through the window. Not knowing which one it was, he didn't bother calling out.

"Ow!" said Cooper. "Fucking hell, Ravenus! What's wrong with you?Dave! Stop crying and come help me!"

As Julian climbed over the unfinished wall at the top of the building, he looked down just in time to see a second bird fly in.

"Jesus Christ!" shouted Cooper. "What the fuck is going on?This is some Alfred Hitchcock shit!"

Julian hurried down the stairs until he reached the third floor. He sprinted down a corridor toward where all the noise was coming from, wanting to get there in time to make sure Cooper didn't accidentally kill Ravenus.

The scene he walked into at the end of the hall was a horrific one. Barlow lay face down, unconscious on the floor. Cooper was waving his arms around, trying to fend off two big ravens. Dave was huddled up in a corner, openly weeping. His beard was covered in liquid brown, like he'd been drinking from a chocolate fondue fountain. Tim was on the other side of the room, rolling on the floor with his hip flask and laughing his little ass off.

And the smell. It was like onions and napalm. Julian's stomach turned. He felt lightheaded and had to lean against the doorframe to keep himself upright.

When he felt confident enough that he wasn't going to throw up, he shouted over the chaos. "Ravenus!To me!"

As soon as one of the birds disengaged, Cooper swatted the other one out of the air with his open palm.

Paulie sailed across the room, smacked into the wall, and fell on the floor. He stood up on his wobbly bird feet. "I will defend my master to my dying breath!" From the sound of his voice, that breath might not be too far off.

"Holy shit!" said Cooper. "A talking bird!"

Julian shot Cooper an annoyed glare, then addressed Paulie. "Nobody has to die today. We were hired to deliver your master, *alive*, to a certain interested party. What his interests are and what he intends to do with your master, I know not. But I think your best chance at survival lies in cooperating with us rather than trying to fight us."

"Very well," said Paulie. He sounded as though Cooper had knocked most of the fight out of him anyway. "I shall accompany my master."

Cooper shoved Barlow into his sack, and Paulie allowed Julian to help him snuggle in next to his master. It said something about the bond between a wizard and his familiar that Paulie raised no objection to being carried in Cooper's sack. But in the room's current state, the sack probably didn't smell any worse.

Tim stopped laughing to knock back a swig of stonepiss and wipe the tears from his eyes. "We should get moving before Shitnose wakes up."

"What did you do to him?" asked Julian.

"I hid over a doorframe. When he passed underneath, I jumped down and beat him unconscious with that Silence Stone you threw at me. Then I tied him up, hid him in a closet, and…"

"And what?"

Tim smiled to himself. "Nothing. It's stupid."

"Where's the stone?"

"I left it with him, so that he wouldn't be able to make any noise when he wakes up."

*

Walking out of Shallow Grave was a lot more comfortable than walking in had been. The few locals out on the streets still followed the group with their eyes, but their stares didn't feel as hostile as before.

Everyone seemed to breathe a little easier once they had crossed the district line. Even Dave stopped crying when he found an unattended horse trough to dunk his face into.

Julian cradled Ravenus in his arms as they walked. "You really had me worried there for a while. You stay close by from now on, okay?"

"As I recall, sir, it was *you* who abandoned *me*."

"Sorry," said Julian. "I saw Paulie fly off, and I thought it was you."

Ravenus ruffled his feathers. "He doesn't look anything like me!"

Shit. "But it was dark, and he was far away, and he was moving so fast, and –"

"Big, black," said Dave. "You all kind of look the same to Julian."

Julian glared at Dave. "That's not... I didn't... You couldn't..." He exhaled. "You've still got shit in your beard."

*

It was pretty late when they arrived back at the Rock Bottom Pub, but judging from the noise inside, it was a lot livelier than it had been in the early afternoon.

Tim opened the door, and what seemed like every thug, ruffian, and ne'er-do-well in Cardinia ceased their merrymaking to stare at them. You'd have to combine at least two of any randomly selected occupants to get a full set of eyes, limbs, or teeth.

Across a long gauntlet of men, dwarves, half-orcs, and full-blooded orcs, any of whom looked like they'd slit their own grandmothers' throats for a flagon of ale, stood the greasy-haired bartender, smiling at them with yellow teeth. He'd changed into a less-stained wife beater. Must be a special occasion.

An orc stood next to the bartender. He hadn't been smiling when they entered, but he grinned when he caught Julian staring at him.

Walking across the pub floor felt like walking to the gallows. Even Cooper, who usually couldn't recognize danger until it was actually stabbing him in the face, was moving with slow, deliberate steps.

"Welcome back, gentlemen," said the bartender as they stepped up to the bar. "I believe you've met my friend here." He gestured to the orc standing next to him.

"Have we?" asked Tim.

"I don't think so," said Dave.

Cooper merely shrugged and set his sack down on the floor.

"Long time, no see," said the orc.

Julian recognized the voice at once. "Grotch!" Something was very wrong here. They'd been set up.

"Grotch?" said Tim.

Julian sighed. "One of your *captors*?"

"Oh shit," said Cooper. "That *is* embarrassing."

"I'm really sorry, sir," said Dave. "It was dark, and you were moving so fast, and –"

"Shut up, Dave," said Julian. "We've got more pressing matters to attend to." He snapped his fingers below the bar to get Dave's attention and pointed down at Cooper's sack.

Dave's eyes widened as all the pieces started falling into place. "Oh…"

Julian smiled up nervously, facing the bartender, then Grotch, then the bartender again. "It was nice catching up, but I think it's best we get going now."

"But we just got here," said Cooper. "This little fucker is heavier than he looks."

"Leave him!" said Tim, who had also seemed to catch on to the gravity of their situation. "Let's just go."

Julian was ready to set aside all pretenses and just bolt out of the door as fast as he could, but when he turned around, he found he was blocked at all sides. All of the pub's patrons had congregated around them. They were fucked.

Cooper's sack started moving, as evidence of their felony kidnapping chose the worst possible time to wake up.

"What's going on?" asked Barlow. He and Pauliepoked their heads out of the sack, looking at least as scared as Julian felt. "Where am I? What is –"

"SURPRISE!" the congregation around them shouted in unison.

A nearby half-orc grabbed Barlow and stood him up atop the bar.Paulie perched on the bewildered gnome's shoulder.

"Welcome to your last night as a free man!" said the bartender.

Barlow's shock melted into a wide grin as he realized what was going on. He turned around.

"Timmon, you son of a whore! Did you set this up?"

"I set up the surprise party a few weeks ago. The kidnapping thing didn't occur to me until these four idiots walked in here this afternoon asking if I had any quests."

"Quests?" asked Barlow. "What kind of question is that? Who asks something like that at a pub?"

"Like I said," said Timmon. "Idiots.So I cooked up this whole kidnapping thing on the fly. I honestly didn't expect them to live."

"Hey!" said Dave. "Not cool, man."

"They nearly killed me!" said Barlow.

"Relax," said Timmon. "I told them to bring you back here alive. Just think of it as payback for when you threw two dire rats into my cot while I was sleeping."

Barlow slapped his knees and laughed. "You should have seen your face!"

Timmon looked down at his feet. "Those furry little bastards have really grown on me." He spit on the floor and the sounds of scraping and licking came from behind the bar. Tim scampered up Cooper's side like a squirrel climbing a tree.

Barlow's face turned serious. He looked at Tim, who was eye level with him on account of being on Cooper's shoulders with his arms wrapped around his face. "Where are Shitnose and Leo?"

The quiet din of the congregation suddenly became completely silent. Everyone looked around at each other and confusedly put their fingers in their ears. Soon after, they spread out in a semicircle roughly the size of the Silence Stone's area of effect, revealing two pissed-off looking orcs.

Leo was bruised, bleeding, and covered in dust. Shitnose had a lump on his head, and his nice silk tunic was wrinkled and smeared with blood.

Shitnose tossed the Silence Stone to Barlow, who slipped it into a small, black pouch. Sound returned to the room.

"What happened to your tunic?" asked Barlow.

Shitnose lowered his head. "I bought it to wear to your surprise party. Now it's ruined."

"Are those words written on it?"

Shitnose flared his nostrils at Tim. "That sadistic little prick cut me with a piece of broken glass!"

"I barely scratched him," Tim objected.

"What does it say?" asked Barlow.

Shitnose stretched the bottom of his tunic down so that the letters were legible.Barlow read the words aloud.

NOW I HAVE
A CROSSBOW
HO – HO – HO

"I don't understand," said Barlow.

"I wasn't even carrying a crossbow!" said Shitnose.

"Explain yourself, halfling," demanded Barlow. "Was that meant to be a taunt?"

Tim sighed. "It was meant to be a joke. I thought it would be funny."

"What's *wrong* with you people?"

Timmon wore a perplexed frown. "What is *HO – HO – HO*?"

"Forget it," said Tim. "Can we just get our money and get the hell out of this shithole?"

The pub fell silent. The only way Julian knew the Silence Stone hadn't been reactivated was that he could still hear the dire rats behind the bar slurping up Timmon's spit.The crowd of thugs, ruffians, and ne'er-do-wells seemed somehow larger and denser than it had just a moment ago.

Barlow the Butcher shook his head, then looked at Timmon. The expression on his face was easy enough to read. *Do you believe the nerve of these assholes?*

Timmon addressed Julian. "I would like to renegotiate the terms of our agreement."

Tim choked on the last few drops of stonepiss in his flask. "No way, José!A deal's a deal." He tapped his empty flask on Cooper's head. "And who do I have to blow to get a drink around here?"

Julian glared at Tim, hoping his expression was as easy to read as Barlow's had been. *Shut. The. Fuck. UP!*

Tim ceased his antics and pursed his lips tightly.

Julian turned back to Timmon. He swallowed hard. "I'm listening."

Timmon grinned. If you and your friends can make it through that door alive, I won't feed you to my rats."

"Ahem," said Paulie.

Timmon looked at the bird. "Oh, right. The rats aren't too choosy. You get first pick, Paulie."

Julian turned toward the door. Shitnose and Leo were the two main obstacles between them and it. "Horse!"

As soon as the black and white speckled steed appeared, Julian slapped it on the ass. "Let's go!"

The startled crowd scattered as the horse barreled over Shitnose and Leo. They'd both been through a rough day, and Julian felt a little bad about trampling them with a magical horse, but Tim had blown any chance that they might have had at a diplomatic resolution.

Julian, Dave, and Cooper followed the horse out as fast as they could while mugs, axes, and even chairs crashed against the walls on either side of the doorway.

Tim, who was still riding on Cooper's back, flashed his middle finger at the crowd. "Yippee ki yay, motherfu—" His face slammed into the top of the doorframe as Cooper passed through, but otherwise they all made it out unharmed.

"Get them!" shouted Barlow the Butcher, apparently wanting to re-renegotiate the terms of their and Timmon's agreement.

Julian slammed the door shut. "Horse!"

A magnificent copper-colored stallion appeared in front of the door. Julian stroked its cheek and let out a sympathetic sigh. "Whatever happens, stay right here. Okay?"

The door only opened an inch before being blocked by the horse. Angry screams poured out from inside the Rock Bottom Pub. The horse didn't budge. He understood.

"That won't hold them for long," said Dave. "We've got to get out of here."

Cooper hoisted Dave up onto the black and white horse, then tucked Tim's unconscious body under his arm like a football. Tim, knocked out cold as he was, did an impressive job of still holding on to his hip flask.

They had only run three blocks when they nearly bowled right over a pair of patrolling Kingsguard. One was dwarven, and the other half-elven, but both were solidly built warriors, bringing honor to His Majesty's crest on their uniforms.

"Halt!" demanded the half-elf wielding a shiny-tipped spear. "What mischief do you make at this time of night?"

Julian shook his head nervously, his eyes constantly darting back toward the direction they had come from. "No mischief, sir. Just out for a stroll is all. I was having trouble sleeping."

"You're an elf," said the Kingsguard. "Elves don't sleep."

Julian rolled his eyes and flicked himself in the temple. "Well there you go, then. Thanks, officers!" He spotted a raven flying in a small, concentrated circle above their position. He wanted so badly to run, but felt like their conversation hadn't yet ended.

The half-elf eyed Cooper warily. "What's wrong with this halfling? Where are you taking him?"

"Um…Church?"

"Is that *shit* in your beard?" the dwarvenKingsguard asked Dave.

"I, um…" Dave stammered.

"I'm sorry, officer," said Cooper. "That's my shit."

The dwarf's eyes went wide. He looked back at Dave.

"Come down off that horse this instant," demanded the half-elf. "I want to know exactly what you gentlemen are –"

"There they are!" shouted Barlow.

"What in the heavens?" said the half-elf. He and the dwarf stepped away from Dave's horse, which had been obscuring them from the mob's view.

"Oh shit!" said Barlow. "Go back! Go back!"

The dwarf looked up at the half-elf. "Is that…?"

They both said in unison, "Barlow the Butcher!"

The half-elf turned quickly to Cooper. "See that this halfling drunkard makes it home safely."

"And you," the dwarf said to Dave. "Whatever kind of deviant acts you choose to partake in with this half-orc are your business."

"I wasn't –"

"But wash your beard. You bring shame on our people."

With that, they gave chase to the dispersing crowd of thugs, ruffians, and ne'er-do-wells.Kingsguard training evidently did little to improve the Movement Speed of a dwarf. Julian, Dave, and Cooper watched as the stout little soldier waddled off after his partner.

The End.

The Minotard

(Original Publication Date: April 8, 2015)

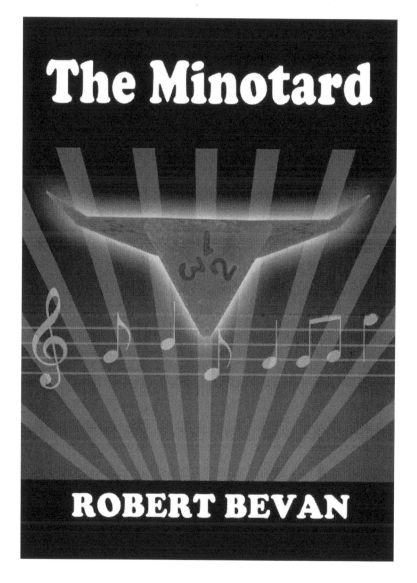

It had been a rough day, and Dave felt he could safely cross Armed Escort off his list of potential careers. Nevertheless, he was in fine spirits. The rain, cool and refreshing, had rinsed most of the goblin gore from his beard and armor. Now that he and his friends had returned to the relative safety behind the city walls, he used up his remaining zero-level Heal spells to clear up a few minor scratches and abrasions left over from the fight.

"What's that sound?" asked Julian.

"Shit, I'm sorry," said Cooper. "That chili from this morning is still doing a number on me. I thought the rain would drown out the noise, so I've just been letting them rip."

"I was talking about the music."

"Oh."

Dave was determined not to let Cooper's half-orcish gastrointestinal issues dominate the conversation. "I don't hear any music."

"It sounds like a violin," said Julian. "It's soft and sweet, and kind of sad." Julian's enormous elf ears could hear a mouse fart from across a meadow in a thunderstorm. "Let's go check it out."

"I've got a better idea," said Tim. "How about let's not?"

"A little culture wouldn't kill you guys. Cooper? *Dave?*" Julian said Dave's name like it was a challenge or a threat. He knew that none of them gave a shit about listening to some violinist. But not going along would give Julian more leverage to act all smug and superior.

Knowing that he, himself was being played like a violin, Dave sighed. "Let's go."

They had nearly reached the quad in front of the Great Library of Cardinia when Dave started to hear a melody through the rain.

By day, the public area between the Great Library and the Cardinian Multi-faith Grand Temple and Medical Center was a place of bustling commerce, but the rain and late hour kept all but a few wandering souls off the streets. Those who stood around to enjoy the music did so from at least a fifty foot radius of the musician.

The violinist stood tall and alone, pulling the bow back and forth against his instrument. A black leather hat sat upside-down at his hooved feet, presumably to collect coins which no one seemed in any great hurry to give. A matching leather cloak kept most of his body, as well as his violin, protected from the rain, but his massive, horned head was exposed. From the tone of the melody he played, Dave guessed the rain on his face might be mingling with tears.

"The poor guy," said Julian. "Look at everybody standing around enjoying his music, but not giving him any money."

"Look at the size of him," said Cooper. "You can't blame people for not wanting to get too close."

"Seriously," said Dave. "He'd probably just spend the money on booze anyway."

Julian's eyes went wide. His mouth dropped open. *Oh shit.* Dave had just given him an early Christmas present.

"Hold up," said Tim. "Weren't *we* going to spend the money on booze?"

Julian's attention was fixed solely on Dave. "It's people like you who exacerbate the problem, making up these fantasies so you don't have to feel guilty about being a selfish asshole while your fellow man has to beg on the street for enough loose change to pay for his next meal. I suppose you think he's driving around in a Porsche in his down time."

"He's a fucking minotaur," said Dave. "Of course I don't think he drives a Porsche."

Julian fumbled around a rebuttal. "Or, like... you know...A fancy... carriage or...something. You get my point."

"Stop masturbating the problem, Dave."

"Shut up, Cooper!" said both Julian and Dave.

Dave held out his hand, palm up, to Julian. "You know what? Give me a gold piece. I'll go put it in the hat myself just to shut you up."

Julian pulled a shiny gold coin out of their collective coin pouch and slapped it down on Dave's palm. "Go for it."

Dave looked at the minotaur, then back at his friends. "You guys come with me?"

"Fuck no," said Cooper.

"Anything to get this shit over with," said Tim.

Julian rolled his eyes. "Sure."

Dave led the way in spite of his short dwarven legs. It seemed none of his friends were in any particular hurry to approach a minotaur.

The beast had looked big from a distance, but he wasn't standing near anything that would give Dave a frame of reference. As they crept closer, it only seemed to get bigger. It was built like a Voltron made up of vikings. Its curved horns were as thick around as Dave's arms. The music stopped as one gigantic bovine eye opened and focused squarely on Dave.

"Is something amiss, sir?" asked Ravenus, poking his head out from beneath Julian's serape. "I couldn't help but notice a certain unease in – OH SHIT!"

Dave felt a little satisfaction at knowing Julian was just as afraid as he was. He held up the coin. "Th-th-thi-this is for you, sir." He tossed the coin into a hat big enough for Tim to bathe in.

The minotaur looked at the coin, then back at Dave. Its nostrils flared and its eyes were alive with wild, murderous rage.

"Thank you," said the minotaur, his voice like silk wrapped around gravel. "That's very generous of you."

Dave guessed that maybe he had confused wild, murderous rage with simple gratitude. He hadn't spent much time studying minotaur facial expressions. He relaxed a little. "Don't mention it. You're a talented artist. The way you play that..." Now that he got a closer look, it was not like any violin Dave had ever seen. It functioned the same as one, but it was made of metal, the body was curved in such a way that it looked like it would rest well on a log, and the neck was made up of two long spikes. They held the strings in place, but looked more stabby than musical. "...*instrument* is exquisite."

"You are too kind, dwarf."

Julian tossed another gold coin into the hat.

"Guys," said Tim. "Let's not overdo it, huh?"

"Such a melancholy tune," said Julian. "Does it have a name?"

"It's called *Lenore*," said the minotaur. "I wrote it for my long lost

214

love."

Tim clapped his hands together. "You know what cheers me up? Booze. You coming, Mr...."

"Call me Milo. Thank you, tiny halfling. It's been far too long since I've felt the warmth of drink and companionship." He frowned. "But I really shouldn't. I have a –"

"Nonsense," said Tim. "Come on. Grab your shit and let's get our drink on."

"Very well, halfling. Follow me. I know a place."

"I'll bet you do," Dave muttered so that only Julian could hear.

Milo glared down at Dave. "What was that, dwarf?"

Fuck!

"I... uh..." He had to spit out something. "I beg-a-boo!"

Milo furrowed his giant brow. "I am unfamiliar with that expression."

Julian folded his arms and grinned. "Yeah, Dave. I don't recall ever hearing that expression either. Tell us. What does *I beg-a-boo* mean?"

Dave was starting to sweat. "It means *Let's go!* It's like *Yoo-hoo!* and *Toodle-doo!* You know?"

"Dude," said Cooper. "Are you having a fucking stroke right now?"

Thirty minutes later they were standing outside the Piss Bucket Tavern.

"Hey," said Cooper. "I remember this place. We've been kicked out of here before."

Julian frowned. "Maybe we should find a different place."

"There is no other place," said Milo. "This is the only tavern that will serve me, on account of my –"

"Fucking racists," said Tim.

Dave thought back to their first night in Cardinia, and how they wound up at this very tavern because everywhere else they'd tried before that had turned them away. They'd refused to serve Cooper because he was a half-orc.

"I'm sorry," said Dave. "It's just that we've been specifically warned by the owner of this establishment to never set foot in there again."

Milo snorted. "Morty won't mind, so long as you're here with me." Before any further objections could be raised, he opened the door and stepped inside.

Julian tapped the bulge on his serape.

Ravenus peeked his head out. "Yes, sir?"

"We might be in here for a while," said Julian. "Why don't you go find a dead rat to eat?"

"I'm still rather full from all of those goblin eyes."

"Well then fly around and get some exercise."

Ravenus flew off, and Julian walked into the tavern unburdened by his fat, black familiar. Dave followed him in.

All conversation stopped when they stepped out of the small antechamber and into the tavern proper. That was no huge surprise; they were unwelcome guests here. But they'd been kicked out a long time ago, and Dave didn't expect them to be instantly recognized by every single customer in the place.

The Piss Bucket Tavern, contrary to what the name might suggest, was not the Mos Eisley of Cardinia. It was a clean, well-lit and well-maintained establishment in which patrons were expected to keep to certain standards of conduct. Violators of those standards were dealt with quickly and severely, as Dave and his friends had personally experienced. With the sudden hush of conversation, Dave expected they might be about to experience it again.

Milo stepped ahead of Dave and his friends, his hooves clopping on the wooden floor, and the collective gaze of the tavern's patrons moved with him. Dave, unaware that he had momentarily stopped breathing, exhaled.

The bartender placed a mug and washcloth down on the bar and wiped his hands on his apron. "Milo."

"Morty."

"I didn't expect to see you back so soon."

"My new friends invited me out for a drink."

Morty narrowed his eyes at Dave. "*Did* they?"

What the hell did minotaurs have against him? Why was he being singled out? Cooper was the one who'd wiped shit on the stool. Tim was the one who'd puked everywhere. Julian was the one who'd broken the *No Magic* rule. Dave was the only one of them who *hadn't* fucked up. And then it occurred to him, the unspoken message behind those mad cow eyes. Dave was going to be held personally responsible for any shenanigans his idiot friends got up to.

Julian should have stepped up to use his Diplomacy skill right about then, but the bartender was focused on Dave, so Dave did the talking. "I see you remember us, sir. I promise we're not here to cause trouble."

Morty's expression lightened to only mildly terrifying. He grinned with a mouthful of teeth that looked like they'd evolved to eat souls. "Relax, gentlemen. Come, Milo. Why don't you show your friends to your private room?"

Milo nodded solemnly, and the tavern grew noisy again as conversations picked up where they'd left off. Once again, Dave breathed a sigh of relief.

Making sure he was far enough back from Milo, Dave muttered to Julian, "The poor homeless minotaur has his own private room in a bar."

The tips of Julian's ears were red. For once, the bleeding heart elf was at a loss for words.

Milo led the group to the rear of the tavern where he slid open a seemingly inconspicuous section of wall, revealing a wooden staircase which led down into a basement. The huge minotaur trudged down the stairs, and the rest of them filed in behind him.

"Not a bad setup, my friend," said Tim, who was first in line behind Milo. "Smells like shit, but otherwise pretty sweet digs."

Upon reaching the bottom of the stairs, Dave had to guess that Tim was either blind, lying, or simply had very low standards for what he considered an acceptable place to get drunk. The cramped little dungeon of a room looked like the sort of place you'd interrogate suspected terrorists in, furnished only with rough wooden crates, the largest of which would serve as a table. A small, permanently enchanted Light stone hung on a thin chain from the ceiling, providing just enough light to remind a person of the poor life choices which led them to this time and place. The ancient brickwork was crumbling, leaving little piles of red dust and grit along the base of the walls. The wall opposite the stairwell had a giant hole in it, about the size of a doorway, but looked to have been punched through rather than crafted. Who knew where that led?

Milo knew. "Pardon me," he said, unbuttoning the top of his leather trench coat. "I must answer nature's call." He ducked under the hole in the far wall. Shortly after came a sound like water being poured from a height and the pungent stench of ammonia.

Dave sat on a crate, his head spinning with the smell of minotaur piss. He sharpened up when he heard another set of hooves stomping down the stairs.

Morty appeared in the entrance, his each of his hands gripping the handles of two massive tin pitchers. They were dripping on the outside, as if whatever was in them had been scooped out of a larger reservoir rather than poured in.

"Two gold. Paid up front."

"Of course, sir," said Julian, hurrying to produce the coins.

Morty grunted his satisfaction and set the pitchers down on the large crate, sloshing some of the brown liquid over the sides. Dave watched in disgust as a cockroach leg slid down the side of one. Hair, bug parts, and other miscellaneous unidentifiable bits were trapped in a greenish-brown foam floating on the surface of all four pitchers.

"What the fuck is this shit?" asked Tim. "Can't we get a beer?"

Morty held out his hand to Julian. "Milo prefers drinking from the well."

Julian's hand trembled as he hesitated to hand over the money. "I-I'm sorry," he said. "It's just that two gold pieces seems a little steep for…" He looked down at the pitchers. "…that."

"Well sludge only costs a silver piece per pitcher. You can think of the rest as a security deposit."

Julian swallowed. "That sounds fair." He dropped the coins into Morty's hand.

Morty put the coins in his apron pocket, from which he then produced four rusted tin cups and placed them next to the pitchers. Stepping into the stairwell, he faced them again, reached up over his head and pulled down a heavy iron portcullis. When it was all the way down, there was a spring and a clanking sound, and Dave knew he was trapped.

"Enjoy your drinks," said Morty. "If you behave yourselves, I may let you out later. Cause any trouble, and you get flushed."

"Hang on, man," said Dave. "What's this all about? You serve us well sludge and lock us in a dungeon? So we screwed up once. That doesn't mean you have to treat us like criminals. I told you we weren't here to cause trouble."

Morty snorted and furrowed his brow at Dave. "It's not *you* I'm worried about." He turned around and stomped up the stairs.

Everyone looked angrily at Cooper.

"The fuck did *I* do?"

"You spread your stool on his stool," said Tim.

"Well I didn't barf all over his floor and break his glasses like *some* little asshole I could mention."

The sound of running liquid stopped.

"Jesus," said Julian. "Did Milo only just finish taking a piss?"

"Big fucker must have been holding it in for a week," said Cooper.

"Some of us know how not to piss ourselves every five minutes," said Dave. He immediately regretted it. That was too low. Cooper's incontinence was a symptom of his low Charisma score. Dave shouldn't have said that. "I'm sorr—"

"Holy shit!" Cooper's attention was elsewhere. Specifically, focused on Milo. More specifically, on Milo's enormous dick.

Milo had returned from his piss, but hadn't bothered to re-button his coat. Whatever this minotaur's problems may be, physical endowment was not one of them. He looked like a wooly mammoth doing a handstand.

"Ah," said Milo, licking his lips and staring down at the pitchers. "Sweet sustenance!" He picked up one pitcher and greedily licked the outside of it, his purple tongue flapping around like a snake having a seizure. "Who's thirsty?"

"Uh...," said Tim.

Milo poured the well swill clumsily into four of the tin cups, not bothering to tip it back up between pours. He ignored the fifth cup, choosing instead to just use the pitcher as his own.

"Forgive me for not having asked your names yet," he said, raising the pitcher to his mouth. "I can be a bit *bullheaded* at times."

From the wide-eyed, helpless expressions on Tim and Julian's faces, Dave knew that they were suffering through the same conundrum as he was. Was that a joke? Should he laugh? Would laughing get him murdered? Would *not* laughing get him murdered?

"*Bull*headed?" Milo repeated, raising his eyebrows. He was clearly awaiting some kind of response.

"Heh... heh..." Julian started. A tentative start to a laugh that he still might be able to steer into a cough if he had to. Well played, Julian.

Milo grinned. "*Bull*headed. Huh?"

Julian nodded as his laugh/cough became louder and more committed to the former, a sign for the rest of them to follow suit.

"H-hee hee h-hee," said Tim, barely containing the nervous tremor in his voice.

"Ha ha har har," said Dave. It was as good a fake laugh as he could muster up.

Cooper frowned. "I don't get it."

Julian nodded for Dave and Tim to continue laughing while he himself stopped. "He's a minotaur," he explained to Cooper. "He's *bull* headed. He's got the head of a–"

"Yeah, I get that," said Cooper. "But what does forgetting to ask our names have to do with being – Ow!"

Julian's jaw was clenched as he glared at Cooper. Dave couldn't see their feet behind the large crate, but he was pretty sure Julian had just stomped on Cooper's.

"What the fuck was – Ow! How how haw haw ha haha." Cooper appeared to have finally caught on.

"You get it now?," asked Julian. "*Bull* headed?"

"Yeah. It's fucking hilarious."

Julian rejoined Tim and Dave in their terrible imitations of laughter, but soon Milo joined in with his own genuine laughter, drowning the rest of them out.

Eventually, Milo calmed down and took a swig from his pitcher. He wiped a tear from his eye. "Oh, that was too much!"

"I'll say," said Tim. "Jesus Christ I need a fucking drink." He grabbed one of the cups and necked back the contents, filth and all.

"It's only fitting," said Milo, "for a *pint*-sized lad like yourself." He didn't even wait for anyone else before he started his own roar of hearty belly laughs.

"What the fuck?" said Cooper. "Was that even a joke?"

Dave thought he might prefer to get punched in the face with Milo's fists than with his comedy routine. It was time to brave the well booze. He continued his fake laugh as he grabbed a cup, picked a dark hair off the top, closed his eyes, and choked it down. It was strong and sour, but the taste wasn't as bad as the texture. It was gritty, and though he may have imagined it, he thought he felt something in it move as he swallowed.

"Wow," Julian said when Milo stopped laughing long enough to suck back some more of the fermented sewage that passed for booze down here. "You're quite the jokester, aren't you?"

Milo's hairy face was wet with boozy foam, which didn't help him look any less crazy. "And you have quite an *ear* for comedy!"

"I don't...," Julian touched his ear. "Oh riiiight. Ear. Because I'm an elf. I have big ears. That's soooo funny."

"Oh my god," said Cooper. "Please stop. I'm begging you."

Julian doubled over in fake laughter and slapped his knee. "Yes, please stop! We need a moment to breathe."

"I'm an entertainer at heart," said Milo. "I tend to get carried away." His eyes were wet and puffy.

"You're a very talented musician," said Dave. "You could totally make it professionally."

Milo took a swig from his pitcher, and shoved a crate next to the one Dave was sitting on. He sat down, wrapped an arm around Dave, and pulled him in tight. Dave very much wished Milo's coat was buttoned, as their differences in height and the forcefulness of Milo's arm forced Dave to look directly at the giant, veiny moray eel between Milo's furry legs.

"I dream of one day playing for a real audience on the stage of Cardinia's Grand Concert Hall."

Dave took that as an opportunity to struggle out of Milo's

embrace without offending him. "I can see it now," he said, standing up. "Your name in lights on the marquee." He spread his hands wide in a gesture of grandeur. "MILO!"

Milo finished the contents of the first pitcher. "Your kindness knows no limits. But when I dare to dream such lofty dreams, it's my stage name which I see illuminated above the theater entrance."

"Oh?" said Julian. "What's that?"

Milo stood, gazing at the ceiling on the opposite side of the room, his eyes glinting with the seeds of fresh tears. He mimicked Dave's spread arm gesture. "The Minotard".

Dave, Tim, and Julian exchanged brief glances. The laughter which followed was hearty and genuine.

Cooper, having his first taste of well swill, sprayed a mouthful all over the three remaining pitchers, further contributing to their lack of appeal. "Now that's funny."

The only one not laughing was Milo. He stared severely at each one of them in turn as laughter unconvincingly turned into fits of fake coughing. There was no mistaking the rage in his eyes this time.

"WHY ARE YOU LAUGHING AT ME?" He hurled his empty pitcher at the wall leading out to the lavatory, widening the hole by half a brick.

The fake coughing subsided.

"It's nothing," Julian scrambled for something to say. "I… uh… We just… um… I had something in my eye."

Milo bent over, resting his hands on his knees, and started crying. As his body shook with sobs, his dick jiggled like a dead snake.

Dave looked questioningly at Julian and mouthed the words, *Something in your eye?*.

Julian shrugged helplessly. *What the hell was I supposed to say?*

"Why?" Milo said between sobs. "Why do they always laugh at me?"

"What… um…" Julian appeared to recognize his Diplomacy skill as the only way they might make it out of this dungeon alive. He was choosing his words carefully. "What made you decide upon that particular stage name?" *Move past the laughing. Get him talking. Attaboy, Julian.*

Milo sniffed back his sobs and sat down heavily on his crate. "I am a poet. Music and words are the tools of my art. I wanted a name which demonstrates how I can combine two words into one, thus creating something new. I combined the words *minotaur* and *bard*. Minotard."

Cooper choked on another throatful of well swill.

"Something wrong with your friend?" asked Milo, a hint of menace in his voice.

"Don't pay any attention to Cooper," said Julian. "He's retar— He's not right in the head."

Tim was holding his breath and bending his index finger back nearly to the point of breaking to keep his composure. Dave had to get him out of there before he cracked.

"I need to go to the bathroom," Dave announced. "Tim, can you help me?"

All eyes in the room turned to Dave as all of his blood rushed to his face. Unable to think of anything that could possibly further clarify such a request, he simply lowered his head and stomped toward the exit, grabbing Tim's arm on the way.

The cavern beyond the brickwork was carved out of bare earth. Dave didn't need any special dwarven mining knowledge to feel extremely claustrophobic in there. It was wide and high enough for a minotaur to move around in, but the slightest hint of a tectonic shift could see he and Tim buried alive in a second.

A saucer-sized hole at the rear had been bored into the stone floor, leading into some sort of chamber from which Dave could hear slowly running water. The three inch wide corona of wet stone surrounding the hole suggested that this was where Milo had relieved himself.

Tim fell to his knees laughing, and Dave pushed his face down into the piss hole to muffle the sound. Tim's laughter turned into hacking, then gagging, and finally vomiting.

"Are you good?" asked Dave as Tim ineffectually slapped at him. "You get that all out of your system?"

Tim ceased resisting and gave Dave a thumbs up.

Dave released him, and they both sat back against the wall, where

Tim swapped out the thumb for a middle finger.

"Don't give me that," said Dave. "I've got enough hoofprints in my armor as it is. That guy's unstable. If we push him the wrong way, he'll murder us all and go back to drinking."

"*He's* the one that called himself a minotard!" said Tim. "How does he expect people to react to that?"

"That's just it," said Dave. "I don't think he has any idea of how he comes off to people. He's big and scary-looking, not to mention a bipolar alcoholic, so people have always just reacted the way they think they're supposed to. He makes a terrible joke. People laugh. He calls himself a minotard. People say 'Oh, that's very clever' and laugh later behind his back."

"That's quite the diagnosis, Doc."

"Have you not been paying attention? When Morty locked us down here, he said 'It's not *you* I'm worried about'. I thought he was talking to me specifically, but he was talking about all of us. He doesn't give a shit about us. He can easily throw us out of his bar again. We're locked down here to protect his patrons and staff from his depressed, violent, booze-crazed minotaur friend."

Tim thought for a moment, then looked at Dave. "What do you think he meant when he said he'd flush us?"

"I don't know," said Dave. "And I don't want to find out. We've got to come up with a plan."

Tim nodded. "I know what we have to do."

Dave breathed a sigh of relief. "Good. What?"

"We have to outdrink him."

"Goddamnit, Tim. That's your solution to everything."

"Think about it," said Tim. "If we can get him to pass out, Morty might let us out of here before he wakes up."

"And how do you propose we outdrink him? Have you seen how big he is?"

"*You* can do it," said Tim. "You're a dwarf. You've got a Constitution bonus and all that shit."

"He's a fucking *minotaur*!" said Dave. "Compared to his Constitution, mine's just a preamble."

"Well then think. How can we–"

"THAT BITCH TOOK MY KIDS AND MY MONEY AND RAN OFF TO WILLOWHAVEN!"

"Shit," said Dave. "We'd better get back in there."

When they re-entered Milo's private drunk tank, Julian was wedged into a corner, both hands wrapped around his sloshing tin cup. Cooper was sprawled out face-down on the floor. Beside him lay the crushed remains of another pitcher. Milo was in the corner opposite the one Julian was cowering in, one hand bracing him against the wall, the other furiously choking his dire chicken.

"What the hell is going on?" Dave whispered to Julian.

"Do I really have to spell it out for you?"

"LENORE!" Milo groaned at the ceiling.

"What happened to Cooper?" asked Tim.

"Milo punched him in the face," said Julian. "Knocked him out cold."

"Jesus Christ," said Dave. "What did that idiot say?"

"Nothing bad. He just asked Milo if he wanted another drink. I guess Milo read something into it. He said 'You sound like Lenore' and decked him."

Tim looked at Milo. "Is that the same Lenore he's whacking off to in the corner right now?"

"One can only assume."

"WHY, LENORE? WHY?"

"So what do we do?" asked Dave. "I think his arm is moving faster. He might be close to finishing."

Julian thought for a moment. "Tim, do you think, if I put you on my shoulders, you could knock him out with a Sneak Attack? He's pretty distracted right now. You'd probably get a bonus to hit him."

Tim shook his head vigorously.

"Okay then. What if I summon a horse, and we –"

"What's all of this noise?" shouted Morty as his hooves pounded the stairs. "You're disturbing my customers! If I have to warn you again, I'll –" Rounding the bend in the stairwell, he saw Milo through the portcullis bars. "Gods have mercy! Milo! What's come over you? Milo! MILO!"

"Wha?" Milo's arm stopped. He turned his head. "Morty? You

distracted me. Now I'll have to start over."

Morty shook his head. "You were once a great minotaur, Milo. I was proud to call you my brother and my friend."

"Come on, Morty. Don't say –"

"You have gone too far this time."

"Please, Morty. Don't –"

"I'm sorry, Milo. I'm cutting you off."

Milo whirled around to face Dave, Julian, and Tim. His eyes were full of crazy, and his erect penis pointed at them like a cannon, complete with a furry sack of cannonballs. Dave now knew the face of fear.

Morty reached his hand up over the portcullis and looked at Dave. "I'm sorry, lads."

"What?" said Dave. "What does this have to do with –" He realized that Milo's crazy-eyes weren't focused on them, but rather the pitcher between Milo and them. "What's happening right now?"

The next couple of seconds seemed to pass in slow motion as Dave's brain processed sensations and stimuli he didn't understand, all happening at the same time.

Milo dove through the air, his arms stretched out in front of him, toward the last remaining full pitcher of well swill. "NOOOOOOOOO!"

Morty pulled some kind of lever which made a loud clicking sound.

Sudden weightlessness.

The bottom of the pitcher rose from the top of the crate while some of the liquid inside sloshed out of the top.

Tim screamed, "FUUUUCK!"

A single tear fled Milo's eye as his hands caught hold of the pitcher.

They were falling. The floor had disappeared from beneath their feet, and they were all being swallowed by a putrid, moist void.

It wasn't a long fall. He landed on his ass with a splash in foul-smelling water that came up to his shoulders.

The light began to fade quickly. Dave looked up just in time to see the floor rematerializing above their heads, like a fog condensing into solid stone, obscuring their only source of light, the enchanted stone suspended from the ceiling.

"Magical floor," said Julian. "That's so cool."

Only Julian would find anything *cool* about being dumped into the sewer.

"What the fubbblllggllbl," said Cooper, the sewer water having brought him out of his fist-induced slumber.

"Light," said Julian.

As a dwarf, Dave could see well enough to move around in complete darkness, but his Darkvision was in black-and-white, and limited in range. Julian's enchanted gold coin added rich textures of brown to the spectrum, allowing Dave's eyes to catch up to his nose in their appreciation of his surroundings. He was about to throw up when something shifted under his ass.

"Shit! I landed on Tim!" Dave got to his feet and plunged his hands into the murky water until he had a hold of a body.

"No you didn't." Tim's voice came from behind Dave. "I'm over here."

Whatever Dave had his hands on was definitely alive, and much too small to be Milo. "Then who is..." He pulled it out of the water. A muzzle full of sharp, bared teeth hissed sewer mist at him.

"Dire rat!" screamed Tim. "Kill it! Kill it!"

Dave trudged hurriedly through the water, intending to slam the huge rat against the wall, when its arms and legs started growing.

"What the fucking fuck!" said Dave. "What's happening?"

"I don't know!" said Tim. "Kill it more!"

The creature's fur retreated into its pale skin as it continued to expand. It was increasing in weight as well as size, and its limbs and face took on humanlike features. Dave hadn't gotten more than three steps when he found he was no longer carrying a giant rat, but instead hugging a naked man.

"Unhand me at once, you brute!" said the naked man who had just been a rat.

Dave removed his hands. "Who are you?"

"Why are you down here?" asked Julian.

"Why were you a rat?" asked Tim.

"What the fuck are we doing in the sewer?" asked Cooper.

The rat man put his hands on his hips. "I would ask you those very same questions!" He pursed his lips and thought for a moment. "Except for the rat one, as that doesn't really apply."

"We asked you first," said Julian.

The rat man wagged a finger back and forth between Dave and Julian. "Now you listen here, surface dwellers! This is *my* home you're invading and *my* body you're accosting! *I'll* be asking the questions!"

Dave looked at Julian.

Julian nodded. "Fine."

The rat man's eyes focused on the glowing gold coin in Julian's hand. "Who are you and what do you want?"

"My name is Julian, and all we want is to get out of here."

"How did you manage to get so far *in* here?"

"What do you mean?"

"The Cardinian sewer system is a veritable labyrinth of tunnels. Even if you knew the way out – and it's clear you don't – it would take you hours to get to an exit."

"Hours?"

"But judging by the way you screamed like little girls at the sight of a rat, it's a wonder how you've lasted more than ten minutes down here as it is. What you need is a guide. You're just lucky you ran into me first. Anyone, or anything, else down here might have just killed you outright. Now let's talk compensation. I'm a reasonable wererat. Let's just call it... say... whatever money you've got on you right now. For that I will grant you safe passage through – Rapha's mercy!"

Cooper frowned. "You kind of lost me at the end there."

"What is that?" asked the wererat, pointing his scrawny finger past the four of them.

Dave turned around. "Milo!" The minotaur's fur was slimy with shit water. He held the pitcher by the bottom in one hand as he rose to his full height, sucking in air so much air that Dave could feel the air around his own head rushing past in Milo's direction.

"Have you been underwater this whole time?" asked Julian.

Milo breathed in and out a few times. "I had to... uh... finish something."

Dave, Tim, Julian, and Cooper immediately backed up against the sewer walls, scanning the brown water between them for any curious streaks of white.

"It sounds like we've got a long walk ahead of us," said Julian. "Let's just pay the – Hey, where's the wererat?"

Dave turned around. Sure enough, the wererat was gone. Not even a ripple remained where he had been standing. "Looks like he fled."

"Good riddance," said Milo.

"No no no!" said Tim. "He was going to show us the way out of here!"

"Best not to put your faith in wererats. They are a shiftless bunch."

"Yeah," said Tim. "I feel much better putting my faith in Drinky the Minotard."

"Tim!" snapped Julian.

"Fuck this," said Tim. "I'm done being nice. We're lost in a sewer thanks to this moron. I am literally swimming in shit."

"Your words cut deep, little halfling," said Milo. "But your fears are unsubstantiated. Minotaurs are never lost."

"Of course!" said Julian, looking more optimistic than anyone stuck in a sewer with a violent, alcoholic minotaur had any right to look. "The Minotaur!"

"Very good, Julian," said Tim. "It's nice to see you've caught up."

"No, I mean the real Minotaur, from Greek mythology."

"Isn't that kind of a self-contradictory statement?"

"He lived in the Labyrinth."

Cooper scratched his head. "I thought that was David Bowie."

"I'll bet my shit-soaked hat that his description in the Monster Manual includes something about being able to find his way around a maze with no problem."

Milo nodded. "I know not of this *David Bowie* of *Greek mythology* of whom you speak, but otherwise, the elf's words are true. I am incapable of being lost in any labyrinth. Morty dumps me down here when I've had too much to drink, intending for me to clear my head during the time it takes to reach the surface."

"That's nice," said Julian. "I can tell he really cares about you."

"To be honest, the stench of raw sewage tends to clear my head right away. 'Tis fortunate I rescued this last pitcher."

Dave had met a lot of alcoholics in his day, but he wasn't sure he'd ever met one so dedicated that he could masturbate underwater, submerged in sewage, while holding his drink above the surface. The last thing they needed right now was Drunk Milo.

"Maybe you should take it easy?"

"There will be time enough for that when we reach the surface, dwarf. The sewer is not without its share of danger." Milo started walking.

Julian summoned a horse to carry Tim and Dave, whose already slow Movement Speeds were further hampered by having to move through water.

Milo walked briskly, turning left or right at each intersection. Dave felt more hopelessly lost than ever, but Milo seemed confident, never stopping to ponder or second-guess his choice of direction.

They traveled for about two hours before Milo stopped dead in his tracks at the intersection of two large tunnels. The elevation was slightly higher here, and the water was thicker, barely covering the top of Milo's hooves.

"Why did we stop?" asked Dave. "Are we near an exit?"

"Very nearly," said Milo. He sniffed the air. "But I sense we are not alone."

Squeaks echoed out from the darkness of the four tunnels surrounding them. Dave felt Tim's arms squeeze him just a little bit tighter.

Cooper started to unstrap his greataxe, but Milo placed a hand gently on his shoulder.

"Your weapons will not harm them. I'll handle this." He called out into the darkness. "What cowards are you who hide in the shadows? Come out and make yourselves known!"

"Dude!" whispered Julian. "I think you need a few more ranks in Diplomacy."

The darkness came alive with the sounds of squeaking, splashing, and feet squelching through shit on all sides. Two by two, eyes became visible, followed by forms. Some were dire rats. Some were humanoid. The vast majority were something in-between. A hybrid form with ratlike features, including whiskers and a long tail, but bipedal and human-sized. Some of the humanoids and hybrids were armed with daggers or small, rusted swords. They blocked every potential escape route, but did not advance.

Dave held tightly on the horse's reins and whispered to Milo. "If they meant to kill us, they would have attacked already, right?"

"They are choosing which of us they want to eat and which of us they want to turn into one of their own," said Milo. "Mind you don't let them bite you."

"Thanks for the tip, asshole," said Tim. "How the fuck are we supposed to stop them?"

"There's no need for that kind of language." Milo addressed the crowd of wererats. "I demand you stand aside and let us pass, or surely you will know my wrath!"

One dire rat in front of Milo grew and morphed into his human form. It was the same one Dave had landed on upon entering the sewer.

"Silence, man cow! The elf carries gold. He and the Halfling would make fine additions to our family. Leave them, and the horse and dwarf for us to feed on, and you and the half-orc may leave unmolested."

"And if we refuse?"

The wererat laughed, provoking his many, many companions to do the same. "Your bravery is commendable, minotaur. I'll give you that. But we outnumber you ten to one, and you have no weapons with which to fight us. Satisfy our demands, or we shall tear apart every last one of you."

"Your threats are as empty as your tiny, shriveled sack. Scurry back into the darkness, where your kind belongs."

The wererat looked livid. While it wasn't fair to compare his genitalia to Milo's, even for a gangly human he was not particularly gifted in that department. He held out a hand. "Sword!"

A nearby hybrid rat person handed over his shortsword.

Milo took a long swig from his pitcher, then handed it to Cooper.

"Hold this." He addressed the wererat. "Speak your name, rat. If you die with honor, I shall compose a ballad in which your memory may live on."

"My name is Roger," said the wererat. "Please, tell me yours, so that I may label the trophy I mount on my wall."

Milo snorted. "Very well. You may call me… *The Minotard!*"

The silence that followed was so complete that, had anyone blinked, Dave was sure he would have heard it. It didn't last long. The wererats erupted in raucous, howling laughter. Even those still in their rat forms squeaked and wheezed until they could scarcely breathe.

"What?" said Milo, the surprise on his face bubbling up into rage. "WHY ARE YOU LAUGHING? STOP LAUGHING AT ME!"

Dave cradled his head in his hands. This was the saddest thing he'd ever seen.

Milo heaved and trembled. The wererats only laughed louder.

"STOP! LAUGHING! AT! ME!" Milo ran forward and kicked Roger in the face. The laughter was cut short by the crunch of hoof against bone. Roger bounced off the ceiling, then hit the floor so hard that he bounced back up to a standing position, where two of his companions caught him.

His face was completely smashed in, a concave mess of blood, flesh, and bone.

Milo stomped back toward Cooper with tears in his eyes. "Why do they always laugh at me?"

Roger's face started to reform, like an inflating balloon made out of meat. When it was nearly back to its original shape, he shrugged off his friends' assistance. When his teeth had all straightened out and his nose was once again facing outward, he started to laugh. "The *Minotard?*"

The sewer came alive with a second deluge of laughter.

Milo balled up his fists, trembling violently. He turned around to face Roger.

"I can't take it anymore," cried Roger. He stopped laughing. "Kill them all."

A dozen humanoid and hybrid rat men lunged at Milo. He

punched the first two, and kicked a third, sending them flying in three different directions, but they quickly recovered from any damage he dealt, and there were more leaping onto his back than he could possibly fend off.

"Cooper!" screamed Tim. "Behind you!"

Cooper turned around and punched an approaching hybrid in the face, smashing Milo's pitcher and blinding the wererat with horrible booze.

Dave swatted another away with his mace, while Julian jabbed at one with his quarterstaff.

"There's an opening!" cried Tim. "Let's get out of here!"

"What about Milo?" asked Julian.

The suicidally brave minotaur had fallen to his knees, cowering inside the flimsy protection of his leather coat. Wererats piled on top of him, and while he was able to gouge one here and there with his horns, it was clear his time had finally come.

"Milo's done for," said Dave. "There's nothing we can do. This is our only chance. Let's –"

"SHIT!" cried Dave and Tim as they fell to the sludgy sewer floor.

"What happened to the horse?" asked Tim.

Julian smacked a dire rat golf-style with his quarterstaff. It squeaked as it flew out of the range of his light. "Spell timed out," he said. "I've gotten so used to them dying all the time, I forgot they had a spell duration."

The opening Tim had spotted wasn't completely free of wererats. It was merely less densely packed with them. Exploiting it would have required the mass and speed of a charging horse. With Milo secured, more of the wererats focused their attention on Dave and his friends, who were already having a hard enough time fending off the first wave with their ineffectual weapons.

Just as they looked about ready to charge en masse, one near Milo screamed.

"SILVER!"

The wererats scattered like shrapnel, running over each other to flee into the darkness.

Milo stood tall, his right fist raised. His violin-like instrument was strapped to his arm, the long, double-pointed neck sticking out of the top of Roger's head. The rest of the naked man hung as lifeless and limp as Milo's giant dick.

"Milo!" cried Dave. "You're alive!"

Milo lowered his arm, allowing Roger to slide off his instrument into a dead heap on the shit-covered floor. "It is unwise to traverse the sewers without silver or magical weapons." He frowned at the instrument strapped to his arm. "It will require tuning."

"That was amazing!" said Julian. "Did you see how fast they bolted? What a bunch of pansies!"

"I told you," said Milo. "Wererats are cowardly by nature. They will put up a façade of courage only if they know they have no chance of losing. Now please, give me my –" Milo gawked at the busted tin pitcher on the floor, then up at Cooper. He had the crazy-eyes again.

"What?" said Cooper.

Milo clenched his fists. "I asked you to hold that for me!"

"Are you fucking kidding me, man?" said Cooper. "I had, like, a hundred rat fuckers to deal with!"

"You could have set it down."

"Come on, man," said Julian. There was Diplomacy in his voice. "Cooper didn't mean anything by that. He got taken by surprise and that pitcher was all he had to defend himself with. We all saw it."

"Lies!" roared Milo. He pointed his instrument at Cooper, still dripping with Roger's blood and brains. "You judge me, half-orc. 'Do you want *another* drink?'"

"Hey guys," said Tim. "Let's take it down a notch, huh?"

"I didn't say it like that!" said Cooper. "I was offering you a fucking drink, and you punched me in the goddamn face!"

"You're just like Lenore!"

Cooper grabbed his greataxe with both hands. "You keep saying that. I'm starting to think Lenore must have been an ugly fucking bitch."

Tim shook his head. "Well I guess that's that."

"How dare you!" said Milo. His voice shook with rage. He brandished his weapon at Cooper even more threateningly. "Prepare to face the wrath of my vioLET!"

"Your *what*?" asked Dave, Julian, Tim, and Cooper simultaneously.

Milo lowered his arms and sighed. "My vioLET."

Dave stood between Cooper and Milo. "Are you saying *violet*?"

"VioLET," said Milo. "It's a combination of *violin* and *gauntlet*."

"That's the stupidest sounding name for a weapon I've ever heard of."

"That's because you're pronouncing it wrong," said Milo. "The emphasis goes on the last syllable. VioLET."

"No," said Dave. "I'm pronouncing it right. That combination of letters only has one pronunciation. Violet. As in a synonym for purple, or a fucking flower. Neither of those invoke the kind of fear you're going for."

Milo snorted through his flared nostrils. "I'm. A. Poet! I combine words to create –"

"You're a drunk asshole!"

"I'm warning you, dwarf!" Milo raised his gore-soaked arm. "I'll –"

"You'll what?" said Dave. "You'll stab me with your violet? Oh, I'm *so* scared!" He wiggled his fingers daintily at Milo.

"Dude," said Julian. "Take it easy, man. A rose by any other name, you know? Could still tear your face off? Is that how that goes?"

"He needs to hear this," said Dave. He addressed Milo. "You know what your problem is? Nobody's ever told you that you suck at certain things."

Milo's rage softened into confusion. He lowered his arm. "Suck?"

"You're a lousy poet. And your comedy is terrible."

Milo looked at Julian and Tim. "Is that true?"

Julian and Tim shook their heads.

"Dave's crazy," said Tim.

"I thought your jokes were hilarious," said Julian.

Milo turned back to Dave, eyebrows raised like he was expecting an apology.

"That's exactly what I mean! They only said that because it's what they think you want to hear and therefore you might not kill them. Cooper, what do you think of Milo's jokes?"

"They're fucking terrible."

"Who are you to lecture me on –"

"That's *precisely* the attitude I'm talking about!" said Dave. "You're so used to people feeding you false praise, you can't take criticism. You either drive away or murder anyone who criticizes you. That's not going to get you far in show business, especially when you go around insisting that people call you *The Minotard*, and then fly off the handle when they laugh."

"It's not funny," said Milo.

"It's literally the only funny thing you've said all night."

"I told you, it's a combination of the words *minotaur* and *bard*."

"I didn't interpret it that way."

"How can *I* be held responsible for how *you* interpret my words?"

"You listen to feedback!" said Dave. "You are absolutely one hundred percent responsible for making your words clear to your audience. You need to understand that when you call yourself *The Minotard*, not one single person ever is going to think *bard*. When you call your weapon a violet, no –"

"VioLET," Milo corrected him.

"NO NO NO!" said Dave. "You're still not listening! That's not what people hear. At best, it sounds confusing. At worst, stupid. Why couldn't you combine a violin and a lance? A violance? Sounds like violence. Not a flower. You see where I'm going with this?"

"Hmm…" said Julian. "I don't know. That one's kinda lame, too."

Milo frowned. "Not to mention impractical to carry around."

"It doesn't have to be that," said Dave. "You're missing the point. You have to stop blaming other people for how they react to your behavior."

"Are you suggesting I change who I am?"

"If by who you are, you mean a violent, psychopathic drunk, then maybe yes. Can you really blame Morty for locking you in a cellar and dumping you in the sewer? He's got a business to run. You're lucky he lets you drink there at all. Can you blame Lenore for leaving? You can't raise kids in that kind of environment. These are people who cared about you, and you pushed them away."

Milo sighed and sat down hard on the shit-caked floor. "I appreciate your candor, dwarf. Everyone I ever loved is gone. What is there for me now but to drink away the rest of my years, alone in this sewer?"

"So," said Tim. "Which way did you say the exit was?"

"Have you listened to a goddamn word I've said?" asked Dave. "You're still making excuses to live your life exactly as you have been. You can still turn things around, but you need to make an effort. You're an excellent musician. You have that much going for you."

Milo looked up at Dave with his big sad cow eyes. "You've seen the way people look at me. They think I'm a monster."

"That's not true."

"Julian?" Ravenus's voice echoed out from the tunnel Milo was facing. "Are you down here? I've been looking everywhere for – NO!"

Ravenus flew into the light and landed on Milo's head. "Run for it, Julian! I'll hold him back!" He pecked furiously on Milo's head, and Milo just sat there and let him.

"Stop it, Ravenus!" said Julian, collecting his familiar. "How did you get down here?"

Ravenus ruffled his feathers, keeping a wary eye on Milo. "The site of the sewer collapse is just a half a mile in the direction I came from, sir. I sensed you were in peril."

Tim was standing behind Milo, jerking his thumb in the direction Ravenus had indicated, mouthing the words "Let's go!" He followed that with a series of gestures including *Drink*, *Sleep*, *Milo*, *Crazy*, *Jerk-off*, *Me*, and *Drink* again.

"Even your bird sees me as a monster," said Milo.

Tim rolled his eyes and did the *Jerk-off* gesture one more time.

"You're a big guy," said Dave. "You can't change that, but you can change your image in other ways. Clean yourself up. Maybe get a more colorful coat."

"And some pants," Julian suggested.

"Perhaps you could invest in a violin that doesn't double as a murder weapon." Dave crouched down next to Milo and put his hand on the minotaur's shoulder. "Do you know what name I see lit up

237

above the entrance to the Grand Concert Hall?"

Milo lowered his head even further than it had been. "What?"

Dave waved up at the wall above the sewer tunnel. "THE VIOLINOTAUR".

Milo's head jerked up, his eyes wide and glistening.

Cooper snorted. "That's even –"

"... better than The Minotard!" said Milo.

Cooper shrugged. "I had a different adjective in mind, but whatever gets us out of here."

*

The sun was up when they reached the surface. Dave had hoped it would still be raining, but there wasn't a cloud in the sky. The only evidences of the previous night's downpour were large, muddy puddles in the poorly maintained streets of the Collapsed Sewer District.

Rolling around in the street earned them a few stares, but it got most of the shit off. When they stood up again, they evaluated themselves to be at acceptable levels of filth, so as not to be questioned upon returning to the Whore's Head Inn.

When the bathing was done, it was time to bid Milo farewell.

"Thank you, dwarf," said Milo. "You have touched a part of me which I feared would never again be aroused."

Dave could hear murmurs from the crowd which had gathered to watch the crazy people bathe in the street. He wished he was anywhere but standing eye-level to Milo's massive dong.

"You mean your *heart*?" said Dave, louder than was strictly necessary.

"Of course," said Milo. "What else would I have meant?"

Dave shook his head and laughed. "You can call me Dave. Take care of yourself, Milo."

Milo bowed. "Fare thee well, Dave." He turned toward the rising sun and skipped away, fiddling a happy tune.

Julian stood next to Dave, watching people scream and leap out of the way of the prancing minotaur. "How does it feel to make a difference in someone's life?"

"Hmph," said Dave. "He'll be back on the sauce in a week."

Julian nodded. "That's a distinct possibility. Only Milo can change Milo's life. All you can do is be there for him when he –"

"Oh my god," said Tim. "Can you two knock off this After School Special bullshit? I need to drink something that doesn't taste like fermented cow snot and pass out on the floor."

That sounded just fine to Dave. He clapped his hands together. "Let's go."

Julian frowned. "You guys don't think it's a bit early in the day to start drinking?"

"Fuck that," said Cooper. "It still counts as last night if you haven't gone to bed yet."

Julian wrung some of the shit water out of his serape. "You know what? Comparatively speaking, I'm liking Milo's odds."

The End

If this was your first time in the world of Caverns and Creatures, please do not be alarmed. You can get some answers to your questions by reading the novels…

Critical Failures

Critical Failures II: Fail Harder

Critical Failures III: A Storm of S-Words

If you enjoyed these stories, please leave a review. It would mean so much to me.

For updates on what I'm currently working on, reviews, or just to come by and say hello, you can find me here on Facebook, here on Twitter, and here at www.caverns-and-creatures.com.

Thank you.

You've been enjoying a DeadPixel Publications Book.

DeadPixel Publications is a group of people with day jobs, writing for the pure love of the craft and hoping for a little success along the way. By joining forces we help promote each other and create a community of sharing and collaboration with one goal in mind: Helping the public find some kick ass books to read (if we do say so ourselves).

Please visit our website.

www.deadpixelpublications.com

Made in the USA
San Bernardino, CA
17 April 2016